D0281017

A Christmas Wish
Chris Elliott

A Christmas Conspiracy
Kate Finnemore

The People's Friend
CHRISTMAS COLLECTION

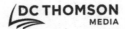

Published in Great Britain by DC Thomson & Co. Ltd,
Dundee, Glasgow and London.
© DC Thomson & Co. Ltd., 2020
www.dcthomson.co.uk

Both "A Christmas Wish" by Chris Elliott
and "A Christmas Conspiracy"
by Kate Finnemore were first published
in "The People's Friend"
Pocket Novel series.

4

A Christmas Wish

By Chris Elliott

New Beginnings

THE late October sun was shining bright through the window as the Green Line coach pulled out of the bus station. The trees were wearing their autumn finery. They looked like mystical fire birds, bowing in the wind.

Florence Fairchild waved goodbye, craning her neck until Aunt Beverly, who was waving back, faded in the distance.

Florrie's mouth trembled and she blinked back threatening tears. She leaned forward, staring at her reflection in the window. Not being a vain girl she didn't realise how lovely she looked in the reflected glass: shining hair, blue eyes, milky skin, a small straight nose beneath a generous mouth.

She swallowed the lump in her throat, pressing her cheek against the cool glass.

Florrie's Irish mother had been nursing the wounded soldiers on the front line in WWI. There she had met a doctor, John Fairchild, Florrie's father, and they'd married within weeks of meeting.

Florrie could still remember the weeks after her parents were killed. A doodlebug had hit their family home in London when she was nearly fifteen. She had been away at boarding school.

It had been her widowed aunt Beverly who had come to give her the terrible news. She had taken her home with her to Haslemere to live with her in her small bungalow with her cousin Phillip, who was ten years her senior.

It was Aunt Beverly who had comforted her, sitting up nights with her, when grief threatened to overwhelm her. She loved her aunt deeply, but there had been many months when she had wept for the special smile that had been her mother's and the gentle kiss of her father's.

Haslemere became her home until the age of seventeen when she'd left to start her three-year nurse's training before taking a post in St Mary's Paddington.

She had worked there as a fully qualified nurse

for four years, the last two as a theatre Sister, only taking three months leave of absence to nurse her niece Mary, who had contracted polio at the age of five. Now she was leaving again. She had been offered a new post as a theatre Sister at Lambeth Hospital.

She told herself firmly that it was a new start.

A few months after qualifying, she'd fallen in love with Edward, a junior surgeon at St Mary's hospital. A few months later they'd become secretly engaged. Florrie hadn't liked that, but Edward had persuaded her it was better to keep their engagement between them for now.

Because she loved him she had agreed. Then out of the blue he'd been posted to America for six months. He had promised when he returned that he would announce their engagement and she had to be satisfied with that.

Florrie wrote most days to Edward telling him about her days. At first she got a letter every couple of weeks, then as time passed she received one once a month. Then, the month before he was due home, she received none. She hadn't been too worried. After all, Edward would be back soon and he would arrive before the letter anyway.

Edward returned, but he wasn't alone. He brought his brand-new American fiancée.

Florrie had been heartbroken by Edward's betrayal, but time and hard work got her through. After that, she had decided to concentrate all her energies on her career and had applied for the position of a theatre Sister in Lambeth.

All her friends had been sorry to see her go, but thankfully they understood. It had taken all her willpower not to cry as they showered her with an armful of gifts on the day she was leaving. She had thanked them all, promising to keep in touch.

* * * *

On arrival at the coach station a couple of hours later, Florrie collected her case and went in search of a taxi cab. When she gave the driver the address of her destination, he looked at her sympathetically.

"You going in for an operation, ducks?" he asked. "Me missus had an operation there last year," he added, before she could reply. "Treated her like a queen, they did."

"No, I'm a nurse. I'm going there to work," she told him.

"Angels – that's what you lot are," the friendly man said. "You wait till I tell my Mary, she'll be that tickled that I picked up one of her angels today."

The cab drove through wide open gates towards the red brick buildings that were surrounded by a high stone wall. The driver stopped in front of stone steps leading up to a wide entrance.

The Victorian structures were similar in colour to her last hospital, even its stone mullions looked the same, but that's where the comparison ended. St Mary's had been only a fraction of the size of this hospital.

For a moment Florrie wondered if she had made the right decision. Here everything seemed magnified a hundredfold. Would she be happy, she wondered.

She told herself it had been her decision to come, though she hadn't expected it to be so big. It was five storeys high, with tall sash windows and a slate roof. Beyond was a maze of smaller buildings, one being the nursing home, she guessed.

The cab driver came around and opened her door, before fetching her case from the boot.

"Good luck, ducks." He smiled, handing Florrie her case.

"Thank you," she said, paying the fare, sure that the amount was much higher then he'd asked for, so she added a generous tip.

"Thanks, ducks," the cheerful man said, waving as he drove away.

She waved back and went through the great door.

The letter had said she was to report straight away to Matron on arrival on the third floor.

She crossed to the information desk and was

greeted by an efficient-looking grey-haired woman.

"Good afternoon. Can I help you?"

"Yes, please. I'm Sister Florence Fairchild. I was told to report to Matron on arrival."

"Take the lift along the corridor to the third floor," the receptionist explained. "It's the third door to your right. You can leave your case here."

"Thank you." Florrie gave the woman a grateful smile and left her case as instructed, before hurrying along to the lift. She closed the doors, before pressing the button for the right floor.

She was glad the lift was empty. She was feeling rather nervous and the few minutes alone gave her time to compose her thoughts.

Matron came forward across the room to meet her. She was tall, as well as being stylishly slender, her hair coal black with light touches of grey and she had twinkling violet eyes.

She shook hands with Florrie and indicated for her to sit down, before taking her own seat behind the desk.

After about half an hour and a warming cup of tea, Matron passed her on to Home Sister Greta Poole, who was a round little woman with a gentle smile and kind brown button eyes. She showed her to her flat, then took her down to the canteen where she introduced Florrie to some of the other sisters before leaving.

Poppy, a pretty, friendly girl, was the sister on men's surgical.

"Come and join our table when you've chosen your food," she told Florrie.

"Thank you," Florrie returned. "Please call me Florrie – everybody does."

Florrie chose warming beef stew, a filling rice pudding and a strong tea.

When she sat down she met Joan, a Sister on woman's medical – a plain girl, but when she smiled she looked beautiful. Then there was Annie, who was currently working on the children's ward.

Finally, there was Sarah, a Londoner, who was a theatre sister like herself. She was married to a junior surgeon, Tom Bailey. They lived near the hospital and Florrie found herself being invited around to the flat for dinner on the following Monday.

She accepted gratefully.

Within hours of arriving, Florrie found herself confiding to her new friends about her broken engagement.

Back at her own flat later, Florrie sat down to write a letter to her aunt, telling her about her new friends, before getting into bed and switching out the light. She thought about her day. It had been exciting. How kind everyone had been. She allowed her thoughts to dwell on her new friend, wistfully, but not enviously. It was obvious that Sarah was happily married.

Florrie plumped up her pillow.

"If only Edward hadn't gone to America," she mumbled into her pillow, "we would probably be married by now."

But her last thought before she fell asleep was that she didn't quite believe that.

* * * *

Over the next couple of months her emotions became more settled. Though she still looked back over the past few months with a sorrowful heart, she found to her surprise that she was settling down with more speed and making new friends more easily than she had anticipated.

Florrie was hurrying around a corner one day when she barrelled into a man. She blushed as firm hands steadied her. Catching her breath she looked up into olive green eyes. He had to be well over six feet tall, five or six inches taller than she was herself.

His strong mouth was curved into a mocking smile as he looked down at her. He looked like he belonged on the silver screen.

Florrie stiffened and stepped back, relieved to find he had a slight bump on the ridge of his nose. At one time that nose had been perfect, like the rest of him.

She swallowed a smile. Well, at least he was not all perfection. But near enough, she thought.

Destined To Meet?

DALE HARPER was heading along the hospital basement tunnels, the quickest way to get to the theatre. He sighed, as he thought back over the last five years since the war. He couldn't help wondering if he'd done the right thing in taking over his father's surgical post in the hospital.

It was a question he'd been asking himself for the past week. If his father hadn't broken his ankle in a car accident and if his own small son hadn't fallen ill days after they arrived back for a short visit, he wouldn't be here now.

The nurse seemed to have come out of nowhere. When she barrelled into him Dale automatically reached out to steady her. She was tall for a girl and he couldn't help noticing her startling blue eyes and the dusting of golden freckles scattered over creamy skin. Even her mouth was an artist's dream.

"Sorry, did I hurt you?"

Her voice was soft, rich and woven with an accent he couldn't quite define.

"No, but I'd refrain from dashing around blind corners, Sister," he cautioned. "You might hurt someone smaller in stature than you."

He didn't think nurses blushed nowadays, but

this one did. Even in the dim light of the basement the heat on her cheeks was vivid.

"I don't think you're going to win any prizes for tact," she batted back. "If my stature is on the tall side, yours is Herculean."

"Touché, Sister." He grinned. "I see you are not going to forgive me for my clumsy words."

"I suppose I must," she said, giving him a wary smile and before he could say anything to spoil their fragile truce she marched away.

There had been an openness about her manner that he'd liked. He liked that she had stuck up for herself.

Dale watched until she disappeared from view. He felt strangely empty now she was gone. From the moment she had first bumped into him, he had the feeling that they'd been destined to meet – which was utterly ridiculous because he didn't believe in destiny, or fate or happy ever after any more.

He scrubbed his hand through his hair, angry at his own musing. He guessed she was in her early twenties. She had the bluest eyes he'd ever seen, the colour matching the stone in his grandmother's ring. That dear lady had been also tall. She had left Dale the ring in her will.

He remembered the words she would often say when he was growing up.

"You will find the right girl to wear it one day, my boy."

His thoughts turned to Anna. Whenever she

walked into a room every head would turn. She was Helen of Troy, Diana and Aphrodite rolled into one woman. The only difference being that, unlike those goddesses, Anna's hair had been as white as snow, her silver grey eyes as bright as starlight, complementing her picture-perfect features and matchless curves.

They had met while working together at a military hospital and married near the end of the war. She died in a road accident not long after giving birth to Timmy. Now, nearly six years later, he was still a widower and Timmy motherless.

After Anna, he'd sworn never to get close to another woman. He had kept that promise to himself and would continue to keep it. Falling in love was for other men who had the right to happiness. He had lost the right and he couldn't see anyone or anything changing that fact – ever.

He hurried along suddenly, realising he didn't even know the name of the girl he had just encountered, or she his. It was better that way, he thought, as he took the stairs two steps at a time. It was a big hospital and the chances of them ever meeting again was almost nil.

So he wouldn't make enquiries about the pretty Sister, though he was very much tempted to. He would leave it to fate to decide if they would ever cross paths again.

Florrie was still bristling from the man's remarks about her height as she hurried along. All right, she wasn't short, but that didn't mean she was a giant, either. Hurt someone, indeed!

Once before, she had listened to a handsome man's advice and her world had splintered around her, leaving her heart crushed. She still wondered if she'd ever recover. Never again would she let herself be influenced by any man.

She looked at her watch. If she didn't hurry, she would be late, and that would never do. So, dismissing the rude man from her thoughts, she hurried her step.

Staff Nurse Mary Collins was already in theatre when Florrie arrived, as well as a couple of senior nurses, a junior and also an orderly. Florrie hurried to scrub up, before setting out the instruments and sterile cloths that would be needed for Mrs Thomas's appendix operation. Then with the junior nurse's help she donned her gown and mask.

The hospital grapevine had been buzzing for days. The surgeon filling in for Mr Harper was his own son, Dale. Still only in his mid-thirties, he had already made a name for himself in the medical world. Now they were all waiting for the surgeon to arrive.

All the trays were checked ready for usage. Everyone was a little nervous about working with the new man.

He came through from the scrub room,

followed by Tom Bailey, his registrar, who was married to Sarah.

"Good morning, Florrie," Tom said cheerfully, before turning to speak to his senior. "Sister Florence is worth her weight in gold, sir."

"I'm sure she is, Tom, worth every ounce."

Mocking green eyes met blue. Florrie ignored the thumping of her heart. It didn't help that the reference to weight had come up. Now the horrid man probably thought she was not only the height of a giant, but weighed as much. She was thankful that she was wearing a mask, because she was sure her face had turned the colour of beetroot.

Then he turned away to plunge his hands into a jar of alcohol. Staff helped him on with his gown. Another nurse held his gloves and an orderly tied on his mask.

"Patient all right?" he asked the anaesthetist.

Florrie, trying to gather her wits at meeting him again, was laying sterile towels over Mrs Thomas's abdomen, leaving a small area of iodine-painted skin. Mr Harper held his hand out for the small cutting knife. There was a sure movement of the gloved hand and a fine red line ran thread-like down the painted skin.

Florrie handed him the next instrument even before he asked. It was as if she could read his thoughts. Mr Harper began to explain what he was doing to the student doctors up in the gallery, his eyes intent on the movements of his hands. He was a good surgeon, one of the best she had ever seen.

His long fingers were surprising nimble and in no time he had skilfully removed the patient's appendix, after which he looked up and his eyes met Florrie's. It was as if he had read her thoughts, for his eyes were dancing with amusement.

He was laughing at her. She blushed and was thankful she was still wearing a mask. The appendectomy had been straightforward.

"Close her up, will you, Tom?" he said, removing his gloves.

He threw them in the bowl the junior nurse was holding then gave the girl an encouraging smile before heading for the scrub room.

Florrie told herself that she didn't mind that the horrid man hadn't wished her good morning or goodbye.

Determined to put him from her thoughts, she concentrated on threading the needles that would be needed for the sewing, though she was still fuming when she passed Tom the first needle.

"Sarah wondered if you'd like to come over to dinner tonight, Florrie?" Tom asked, as she passed him the last threaded needle.

"I can't tonight, thanks, I've got a date," she lied but told herself it was in a good cause. Sarah and Tom hardly had any time alone together as it was, with him being on call and

Sarah working nights.

"Anyone I know?" He quirked an eyebrow.

Florrie blushed. It was her day for blushing.

"An old friend." She lowered her gaze.

"Someone special, is he? Well, I won't pry." He laughed.

"It must be someone very special to have captured Sister's affections," an ironic voice she recognised said behind her.

She stiffened. She hadn't heard Mr Harper return. She nearly dropped the piece of strapping that she was about to place over the closed incision Tom had just finished stitching, but years of training saved her.

She stifled a biting remark as she placed the strapping on the neatly stitched wound. The man was annoying. She might be a giant in his eyes, but it didn't mean she was unattractive to all men, as his mocking tone implied.

She joined the two men in her office 10 minutes later, after helping to make sure the operating theatre was left as pristine as when she'd entered it.

Mr Dale Harper was standing at the window drinking tea. Florrie smiled. Annie was such a sweetheart whenever she returned from the theatre. The kind Cockney always made sure that there was a plate of warm buttered toast and a large pot of tea waiting for her return to the office. Tom was sitting in his usual place already raiding her toast.

"Mmm. Just how I like it, nice and buttery."
He grinned.

Florrie couldn't help smiling. Her mood lightening, she held the plate out to Mr Harper. After all, they were going to be working together.

"Sir?"

"No, thank you, Sister, I don't want to spoil my appetite. I'm lunching at the Savoy."

A spur of jealousy stung Florence, which was unlike her. She'd never envied her friends when they'd shared stories over supper in the canteen about the posh restaurants they visited with boyfriends.

So why should she be jealous of missing a slap-up lunch? She couldn't understand. Then it hit her. She'd only had a bowl of cornflakes earlier. She had been too late coming down for the cooked breakfast. That's it, she thought, just hunger on her part. Relieved, she bit into a slice of the hot buttery toast and sighed.

She poured herself a cup of tea and, feeling a little prickly, she wondered why Mr Harper had even bothered to stay for tea. It wasn't for the company, judging by his darkening frown. She wished he would go, so that she could enjoy her tea.

"More for me, then," Tom said, reaching for another slice of toast.

"Oh, no, you don't," Florrie said, grinning as she batted his hand gently away from the plate, "you'll never do justice to Sarah's home cooking if you gobble up all my toast."

"How's Mary?" Tom asked.

"The picture of health." Florrie beamed. Her cousin had brought Mary to the hospital on a flying visit a few weeks after she'd started and everyone had fallen in love with the little imp.

"You are a miracle worker. The limp is barely noticeable," Tom continued. "Polio can leave a terrible mark on children."

"It was the heat pads and the regular massages," Florrie said. "I just followed the rules."

"With added pinch of great nursing." Tom grinned.

"Thank you for the tea, Sister," Mr Harper said, placing his empty cup on the tray. The look he gave Florrie was piercing.

She raised her chin. He was looking at as if she'd just grown a second nose.

"You're welcome," she returned, deliberating not tagging "sir" on the end.

He can put that in his pipe and smoke it, she thought rebelliously.

Green eyes speared blue. To her annoyance, Florrie found herself blushing under his scrutiny.

Mr Harper gave Tom a friendly salute and left. After Tom drained his own cup before leaving, Florence drank the teapot dry and gobbled up the remainder of the toast.

She wondered who Mr Harper was lunching at

Savoy with. Some glamorous creature –
probably his wife. She felt dampened at the
thought – which was ridiculous, for both times
she'd been in his company, he'd offended her or
ignored her.

She comforted herself with the knowledge
that she wouldn't have to put up with her
antagonist for long. In a number of months his
father would return and Mr Dale Harper would
pass out of her life.

It was Annie's tea break so Florrie decided to
wash up the tea things herself. It was only when
she was drying the crockery, that Florrie realised
Mr Dale Harper could report her to Matron.
After all, he was a consultant and she knew she
should have addressed him in the proper
manner. She'd always prided herself on being
professional.

No, she would have to apologise to him, after
afternoon surgery, she thought. Not only
because it was the right thing to do, but
because it would be unprofessional not to.

A Date With A Difference

THE weeks passed into a regular routine. At the end of surgery, Tom would come to the office to drink tea as usual. Mr Harper, after he had given her his instructions for the patients' care, would leave, always declining her offer of a cup.

She had apologised to him that first day, when he'd returned in the afternoon, but, despite reassuring her that there was no need, relations between them hadn't really improved.

"Rude man," she'd often mumble to herself when she was alone.

It occurred to her that she would often find herself thinking more about Mr Dale Harper's behaviour than she did about Edward's desertion.

The following Monday they all worked extra hard, as a few emergency cases had been added to the already full list. The nurses went one at a time for their breaks.

Florrie waited until the surgeons had finished before going for her own break. She glanced down at her watch. It was nearly three and she was ravenous.

Thankfully they were still serving hot food. She had a tasty bowl of mushroom soup, quickly followed by stewed fruit and custard, all washed down with a cup of tea, before she hurried back to the operating room.

Luck was on her side. The doctors had not returned yet, which left her enough time to check everything before they arrived.

Mr Dale Harper hadn't looked in a good mood when he'd entered the theatre earlier, judging by the frown darkening his brow. Florence couldn't help speculating what had caused his mood.

Stop it, she told herself firmly. It's none of your business what or who caused Mr Harper to frown. As if he had just read her thoughts, he glanced up and she felt her cheeks heat below her mask.

What was it about this man that made her blush like a teenager?

Mind you, Florrie had to hand it to Mr Harper – bad mood or not, he did not snap at the nurses and his manner towards her was respectful.

They worked through the rest of the day's operations, thankfully with no complications. Each one was soon despatched up to the wards, until Casualty rang to say they were sending a young mother up for an emergency caesarean. It had taken a great deal of nerve, as well as great deal of skill, to save the child and mother.

After the men had gone, Florrie set about tidying up the theatre with her nurses. Soon everything was as shiny as a new pin. She sent them all off duty and went to write up her notes for the night Sister. She'd just finished when the door opened and Mr Dale Harper walked in.

"Hungry?" he asked.

She was so surprised, she blurted out her reply.

"Ravenous," she said, forgetting to call him "sir" again.

"Good – because so am I. I'll meet you in the entrance hall in thirty minutes. That should give you plenty of time to change out of your uniform," he said, his tone brooking no argument.

She was still sitting there, stunned, when the night Sister arrived five minutes later to take over.

"It would serve him right if I didn't meet him," she mumbled rebelliously as she hurried up to her flat in the Sisters' block, taking the steps two at a time, but she was in little doubt that if she didn't, the doctor would come to fetch her himself.

She pulled from her wardrobe the first dress she touched, a brown wool shift. It was old but still good enough to wear. She couldn't see him taking her to the Savoy.

After changing, she combed and pinned up her hair, before pushing her feet into black low-heeled shoes. Lastly, she pulled on her old tweed coat and blue silk scarf that her aunt had given her on her last birthday, before hurrying downstairs to meet her antagonist, with still a couple of minutes to spare.

He was waiting by the door, obviously sure that she would come.

"Punctual as usual, Sister," he said, his tone the same as when he was addressing her in the theatre. He steered her through the heavy door out to the car park.

Within moments she found herself sitting beside him in a black Wolseley. The car suited the man, she thought – handsome, but understated.

She resisted the temptation to sink back into the comfortable leather seat. She sat upright, still bristling at being forced to go out to dinner. She swallowed a smile. How many of her friends would envy her, being taken out to dinner by a top surgeon? Many, she suspected.

"You find me amusing, Miss Fairchild?" he said, pulling out into the busy traffic.

"No!" she said boldly.

"Then what was it that made you smile?"

Florrie couldn't exactly tell him that most of the nursing staff would have killed to be sitting where she was now. She didn't like lying, but she didn't have a choice.

"You can sit back and relax – I'm not kidnapping you."

"I never thought you were," she snapped back, wishing she had refused to come out with this annoying man.

Florrie decided to concentrate on the road.

They were driving past Buckingham Palace now. She was right about them not going to the Savoy; he was driving in the opposite direction.

She couldn't help wondering why he had asked her out. His manner had been formal and polite when he'd met her in the hall. She was tempted to ask him where they were dining, but thought better of it. He probably wouldn't tell her, anyway.

Finally he turned down Wimpole Street and drew to a stop in front of a house. He got out and came around to open her door.

"It doesn't look like a restaurant," Florence said.

"That's because it's not. It's my house."

"I thought we were going to have dinner."

"We are – here," he informed her, getting out and coming round to her side, to open the door. She got out hesitantly.

He caught her arm and his touch seemed to burn through her coat as he steered her into a narrow hallway, which widened out with a majestic carpeted staircase at the end, with a parquet floor running the full length of the hallway. The walls were full of very expensive-looking paintings. It was all very grand. She suddenly felt out of her depth.

"If you still feel in need of a chaperone I could ask my housekeeper to join us."

He was laughing at her again.

"There you are, sir. Timmy's been waiting for

you to say goodnight – all excited, he is," a rosy-cheeked, grey-haired woman said as she came along the hallway to meet them."

"Mrs Dobbs, meet Sister Fairchild," Mr Dale Harper said, introducing them before removing his own coat and handing both coats to Mrs Dobbs. "We'll go straight up."

Florence knew what Alice felt like when she found herself in Wonderland.

Who was Timmy? And why had Mr Harper invited her to dinner at his house?

As the doctor led the way upstairs, Florence resisted the temptation to run back down and out of the door.

On the landing, he turned to look at her.

"I brought you to meet my son, Miss Fairchild."

Before she could say anything he opened the nearest door and ushered her inside.

The room was painted pale blue with a frieze of trains running around the walls, as well as on the wooden boards of a truckle bed. They were even on the curtains. In the middle of the room was a low table and two chairs. A large white cupboard was set beside the chimney breast, its large doors wide open. It was filled top to bottom with trains, cars and games.

Sitting beside the bed was a young slim girl reading to a little boy of about five or six propped up against pillows. He had snowy white hair. As he saw Florrie he gave her a cherubic smile and her heart was captured.

The girl looked round, saw them and closed her book, before standing up.

"Nanny, this is Miss Fairchild, who has come to meet Timmy."

"Please call me Jenny." The girl held out her hand and smiled.

"Pleased to meet you," Florrie returned, smiling, shaking the girl's hand.

"Will you leave us for a few minutes, Jenny, please?"

"Of course, sir."

"She's a pretty lady, Daddy," the little boy cried.

"Where are your manners, Timmy?" the doctor said, his voice gentle. "Say hello to Florence. She has come especially to see you."

Florrie's heart bumped. That was the first time he had called her by her Christian name. She was surprised he knew it. At the hospital it was "Sister this" and "Sister that".

Maybe she had misjudged him. But common sense told her this new informal way of addressing her was not for her benefit.

Not waiting for the child to speak, she moved over to the bed.

"Hello, Timmy . . . "

"You are as pretty as my mummy," Timmy announced, his voice full with pride. "There's a painting of her downstairs in the drawing-room."

Florrie smiled and held out her hand.

"Well, thank you, kind sir," she replied, shaking his small hand. "My friends call me Florrie and I hope you will, too."

That's when she noticed the small calliper in the corner of the room.

"What do you say, scamp?" his father said.

"Yes, please," Timmy beamed. "I like you lots and the little dots on your face."

"He means freckles." Mr Harper laughed.

"Can Charlie call you Florrie, too?" Timmy added, lifting the small teddy bear, sitting beside him on the bed.

"Of course. How do you do," she said, shaking the golden bear's paw.

Timmy giggled.

"Now, young man, it's time you went to sleep," Mr Harper said, planting a kiss on his small son's forehead.

"Florrie must kiss me, too," Timmy demanded.

Florrie bent down and kissed the small cheek and for good measure she kissed Charlie on the nose, as well.

Her reward was a hug from the child.

"Would you like Florence to come and see you again, Timmy?" Mr Harper asked, bending down and giving his son a hug.

"Yes, please!" Timmy cried.

"Well, if you are very good, I'm sure she will soon come back again," he said, pressing a kiss to the small forehead.

Before Florrie had time to digest this new turn of events, Jenny returned and Florrie followed the doctor downstairs.

He showed her into the drawing-room, a pretty room with chintz sofas positioned either side of the Georgian fireplace, whilst the large oval mirror presided over the room.

On the right of the fireplace was a painting of a young woman. Florrie didn't need to be told who the sitter was. The likeness to her son was startling. She wanted to ask where the child's mother was now, but she knew if the doctor wanted to tell her, he would.

So instead she glanced out of the window at the garden. A high brick wall enclosed the space, with a good-sized lawn set in the middle. Further along was a small summer house. It was a pretty garden with an abundance of colourful flower borders.

"Sit down, please, Sister," Mr Harper said. "What would you like to drink?" She couldn't help being annoyed that he had gone back to addressing her as if they were at the hospital instead of his drawing-room.

"Sherry, thank you," she returned, more sharply that intended.

The doctor gave her a questioning look.

She took a seat. Why had he told the child that she would come again? Well, whatever Mr Harper's reason for bringing her here, she was sure she would find out soon enough.

Shock Proposal

IT was obvious he hadn't brought her here because he enjoyed her company. Florrie found the thought more disappointing than she liked. She watched him move to a Chinese cabinet. He opened the doors and inside was a mirrored interior, reflecting back a range of bottles. He looked even more handsome, if that was possible, in a Harris tweed suit and a white polo shirt.

As he passed her the glass, his hand brushed against hers. Florrie felt an electric shock shoot up her arm. She tensed, nearly spilling her drink. Whoa, girl! He's a married man, she reminded herself. Even if he was free, he wouldn't be interested in someone like her. She told herself her overreaction to his touch was the result of nerves on her part.

Then she smiled inwardly at her own contrary nature. Florrie was certain of one thing – neither of them liked the other. She wasn't going get upset about that . . .

Mr Dale Harper's frown deepened, as if he'd read her thoughts. He took his seat across from her.

"You are of course wondering why I brought you here tonight," he said. He sounded serious.

Whatever he was going to say was interrupted by the arrival of Mrs Dobbs, coming to announce that dinner was ready.

The dining-room was just as enchanting as the drawing-room, with its pretty oval table and cushioned chairs. Everything was perfect from the floral china, crystal glasses, to the beautiful silver cutlery, all the way up to the grand chandelier.

A walnut sideboard was set on one wall, with a large silver bowl bulging with fruit. Across the other side of the room was an ornate glass cabinet filled with pieces of china and silver that wouldn't have looked out of place in a museum.

He pulled out a seat for her. She sat down, silent questions still on her lips.

"I hope you don't mind that we have to serve ourselves," he said. "Only it's Mrs Dobbs's night off."

"Of course I don't mind. I'm used to serving myself," she said, not wanting him to think she was used to being waited on.

The minutes flew by, yet her host did not return to the topic of conversation that he had started in the drawing-room.

Florrie ate the roast beef, which was heavenly. Perhaps Mr Harper had changed his mind about telling her why he had brought her here tonight. She was beginning to think he had forgotten when suddenly he spoke.

"I'm sure you are still wondering why I

brought you here, Sister."

"Yes," she told him honestly.

"Timmy contracted polio. With luck, it will only leave him with a weakness in the left leg. I'm sure you noticed the calliper."

She nodded. Her heart went out to the little boy up in bed, for all that he had gone through already and for what he still had to suffer on the way to recovery over the coming months.

"His nurse is leaving to go back home to Dorset to nurse her father who had a stroke. So you see I need to find a replacement quickly. And, as you have experience in nursing your own niece, you are the perfect person to take over from Sister Brown."

Florrie took a few minutes to respond. The man was unsettling enough in the theatre. The thought of working under his roof was daunting.

"What makes you sure that I am the right person to do the job?" she asked.

"From what I saw upstairs earlier, my son likes you. Timmy is very shy and does not take to strangers easily. I have spoken to Matron and she has agreed that your post at the hospital will be yours again, once you have finished your work here."

"So it has been all arranged between you."

"Only with your consent," he returned. "If you decide to take the position, you will of course live in."

Oddly, Florrie believed him about accepting her refusal, if she decided not to take the job.

She didn't know what to say, as a range of emotions washed over her – shock, confusion, anger that he should speak to Matron before speaking to her first. She was tempted to refuse. Then the image of the little boy upstairs overwhelmed her.

"Is Mrs Harper in agreement with me living in, sir?"

"I am a widower," he informed her, shuttering his gaze. Her heart went out to him.

"When do you want me to start, sir?" she found herself saying, to her surprise.

"Tomorrow, if that is suitable."

"Of course."

"There is one more thing, Miss Fairchild. I do not require you to wear your uniform while you are working here."

"If you say so, sir."

"Good. Now that's settled, after dessert, we'll have our coffee in the drawing-room."

His smile caught Florence off guard and she felt compelled to return it. He held her gaze and for a moment she found herself unable to look away.

They had just taken their seats in the drawing-room when Mrs Dobbs arrived with the coffee.

"Thank you, Mrs Dobbs, but you shouldn't be working now – it's your evening off," the doctor said.

"Oh, go on with you, Mr Dale, it's no trouble," the housekeeper said, setting the tray down on the table between the sofas.

"It was a wonderful dinner, Mrs Dobbs." Florence smiled warmly and was rewarded with a beaming smile from the friendly woman.

"Shall I be mother and pour?" Florrie asked, feeling suddenly shy as the housekeeper left them alone again.

What was it about this man that unsettled her? She had already established that they didn't like each other. She decided maybe dislike was the wrong word. She hadn't been completely sure about anything since Edward had jilted her.

They had planned a future that was never to be. Now again she was being backed into a corner by another man.

Her one consolation was that Dale Harper would be working at the hospital for most of the time while she was here, if she was lucky. Maybe their paths wouldn't cross much if he went out to dine, or to see a show, probably with the woman he'd lunched with at the Savoy. But even that thought didn't lighten her mood.

"Thank you, if you would. Black with one sugar, please."

As she passed the doctor his coffee, her hand brushed his once more and like before, sparks ran up her arm. She sank back against the seat, thankful that she was sitting down. Whatever was happening to her she didn't like it. It was as if he'd turned on a switch in her with his touch and she couldn't turn it off.

"A penny for your thoughts, Miss Fairchild. You looked a thousand miles away a moment ago."

"You have a beautiful home," she said, changing the subject. If the doctor noticed that she had diverted the conversation, his next words gave no indication.

"Yes, I was lucky. A friend of mine was moving to America and wanted a quick sale, and luckily I managed to persuade Mr and Mrs Dobbs to stay on. So . . . tell me about yourself. All I know is that you have a niece."

"More a cousin, really, I suppose. My cousin Philip's daughter. I went to live with him and his mother, my aunt Beverly, when my parents were killed in a bombing raid in forty-three when I was nearly fifteen."

"It must have been tough losing them so young. We lost Timmy's mother when he was still a baby," he said, putting down his coffee cup and moving to the window. He must still love his wife very much, she thought.

"You are very pretty and bright, Miss Fairchild, I should have thought there is some young man in the background."

Florrie felt the colour drain from her cheeks.

It was funny how a combination of words

reminded her of the pain. Edward always called her sweet and pretty, only he'd forgotten to add naïve as well. She swallowed hard as a picture of Edward was suddenly there in her mind. She saw his handsome face in every detail, so serious, until he broke into that broad smile of his that had always made her heart jump.

Only he hadn't smiled at her when he returned with Carol Summers on his arm. Her father was the chairman on the hospital board where Edward was working in America. She was an heiress.

"No young man," she managed to say lightly. "Nursing is important to me. I don't suppose I'll marry for many years yet."

Mr Dale Harper gave her a questioning look. She ignored it and turned the conversation back around to her duties and Timmy.

By the time they had finished coffee, the surprises of the day were beginning to take their toll and it was a relief when Mr Harper said he would drive her home.

* * * *

Dale waited until she had entered the nurses' home before he drove away. He felt strangely alone now she was gone. From the moment he had bumped into her he'd felt restless.

He hadn't expected her to accept his offer to work for him so easily. He frowned. He had gone over the girl's head to Matron. He hadn't liked doing that but Timmy's needs came first.

She didn't like him. He'd be a fool not to have realised it but he didn't like that thought.

She was pretty enough, he acknowledged. Not the painted kind of pretty that you got out of a make-up box. The natural kind that shines from within. She was young but he had seen for himself that she was an exceptional nurse.

He wasn't surprised she'd risen to the height of theatre sister so young.

He was sure there had been some man in her life. Maybe there still was. Strangely, he felt very protective towards the girl, for reasons he couldn't explain to himself. Underneath all that efficiency, there was a fragility that he was sure Sister Fairchild wished to keep hidden. Probably the man had hurt her.

He told himself it was none of his business. So why couldn't forget about it? He didn't like to think of some man hurting her. Then he reminded himself for the second time that Sister Fairchild's private life was her own business. But he couldn't seem to shake off the memory of the way she'd paled, when he'd called her pretty and bright.

Florence Fairchild had disturbed him more than he would admit, even to himself.

Hope Fades

IT was only when Florrie was back in her flat, standing in her bedroom and deciding what to pack to take with her, that the full realisation of what she decided to do hit home.

She sighed. She had given her word and she couldn't break it now.

She consoled herself with the fact that she'd be helping a little boy recover. Also it would give her a break from her usual theatre work and all the memories she associated with Edward.

She stood there mulling over her thoughts for some time until the telephone ringing broke through her reverie and she went to answer it.

"What's this I hear about you being driven off in Dale Harper's car last night?" Sarah said.

"How do you know?"

"Well, if you wanted to keep it a secret, pet," Sarah teased, "you shouldn't have met in the hall. It went around the hospital like wildfire."

Florrie groaned silently. So much for avoiding being gossiped about.

"It wasn't a date. He wanted me to meet his son."

"Why?"

"He wants me to nurse him for a few months. He's not long come out of hospital. The poor little love caught polio."

There was a short silence, while Sarah digested this information.

"So you're leaving the hospital to work for him now?"

"Only temporarily."

"So what is the little boy like?"

"Timmy is as cute as a teddy bear."

"So what's the big chief like away from the hospital?"

"Superior, bumptious, controlling," Florrie replied.

"And handsome," Sarah teased.

"Handsome," Florrie repeated. "I guess so, if you like over-confident men who arrange your life to suit them."

"Don't you like him?"

"He's all right," she hedged.

How could she tell her friend that she didn't like Dale Harper, when she wasn't even sure herself? Not forgetting that when they touched, sparks flew through her body. Whatever she felt about the man, it went far deeper than like or dislike.

* * * *

Florrie slept badly. She rose early, dressed in a pleated skirt and a matching cream twinset, before setting her feet in sensible shoes. Next she gave her flat a clean before going along to see Matron, who assured Florrie that her job would be waiting for her when she returned.

Next she went along to her office, where she spent an hour with the temporary Sister who was to take her place. After which she went along to the nearest bookshop and brought Timmy "The Lion, The Witch And The Wardrobe". She asked the assistant to wrap it in the brightest paper that they had.

Finally, she returned to the flat and packed her case. Her wardrobe was not extensive, but she had a few good items of clothing, like the wool dress she had worn last night. She wasn't expecting to be eating dinner with Mr Harper while she was working there. She probably would eat in the kitchen with Mrs Dobbs, but she had one suitable evening gown, in dove grey with a modest scalloped front, if she was asked occasionally to make up the numbers at dinner.

An hour later she caught a bus. It was threatening to rain as she alighted at her stop. She decided to make a dash for the house, which was only a short distance away. Thankfully she was only a few steps from the house door, when the heavens opened. She ran up the steps sheltering under the porch. When she rang the bell the door was opened by Mrs Dobbs.

"Come in, dear, out of that rain." The kindly housekeeper bustled her inside. "Now put that case down and get out of that wet coat. I'll put it in front of the kitchen fire to dry.

Dale Harper was coming downstairs looking relaxed in slacks and an open-necked shirt.

Top surgeons are not interested in ordinary girls, she reminded herself. Hadn't Edward proved that to her?

Not that she was interested in her new employer. She was here to help Timmy.

"Just in time for lunch, Sister," the doctor said. "I'll take care of Miss Fairchild," he informed the housekeeper, "if you can ask your husband to take the case upstairs when he gets back from the garage, please."

Florrie had hardly taken her coat off and handed it to Mrs Dobbs, when the doctor was steering her towards the dining-room.

They ate a delicious lunch, and as she glanced up she found his eyes upon her. As she was going to be living in his house for some time, it would be better for them both if she at least tried to get on with him.

After they had moved back to the drawing-room and were in front of the blazing fire, Florrie poured the coffee that the housekeeper had left ready for them.

She handed Mr Harper his cup.

"Now I think with we should discuss Timmy's treatment – with your permission, of course."

Florrie was taken by surprise.

"Very well, sir," she said, dumbfounded by this

new considerate man sitting across from her.

They went over Timmy's routine and treatment. She'd apply the heat pads three times a day, following this with gentle massage.

As well as discussing all of Timmy's medical needs they went over a general outline of her other duties concerning the little boy upstairs. Also she would be expected to take her time off between treatments, as the heat pads, massage and exercise for the first months were continuous throughout the day.

"You can start the treatments tomorrow, Sister. I thought today you could spend the time getting to know each other a little more."

Florrie wasn't sure if she was to answer him, so she stayed quiet.

"You approve of this plan, Miss Fairchild?"

"Yes, sir."

"Good. I have to go to the hospital now. Wait here and I will send Mrs Dobbs along to show you to your room. After that, you can go along to my son's room and get reacquainted.

"I'll just fetch my coat from the kitchen," Florrie said when he was nearly at the door.

"No need, Sister. Mr Dobbs will bring it up later."

"Thank you," she said, surprised at his consideration.

It was the second time Dale Harper had astonished her like that. She swallowed a smile. Maybe they could be friends after all.

The bedroom Mrs Dobbs showed her into was bigger than she'd expected.

"Well, I'll leave you now, Sister, if you don't mind. I've got a pot roast in the oven and I don't want it to spoil."

"Thank you for taking the time to bring me up and showing my room."

When the friendly housekeeper had gone, Florrie took in her new surroundings.

It had pretty white furniture and over the head of the bed hung a white canopy. A little writing table was set in front of the window. The colourful rugs were in pastel blues which matched the floor to ceiling curtains in the same colour wave.

The tables either side of the bed matched the rest of the light furniture. On each sat white lamps with pink shades. An inner door led into a bathroom. The tub was big enough to fit a family in. On white painted shelves there were enough towels to dry a whole ward, beside which sat bottles of bath salts, bottles of shampoo as well as bars of expensive-looking soaps.

When she entered Timmy's room later he was sitting up in bed. Sitting beside him was Jenny reading to him.

"Florrie!" Timmy cried as she crossed the room.

"I'm sorry . . . I didn't mean to interrupt your reading time," Florrie apologised, turning to leave and return later.

"Please don't go, Sister, come and listen to the story." The young girl smiled. "I'm sure Timmy would like it if you stayed.

"Call me Florrie and may I call you Jenny?"

"OK, Florrie it is." Jenny grinned.

"'Winnie-the-Pooh'," Florrie said, noticing the title as she sat down on the edge of the bed. "My favourite was Rabbit because he pretended to be grumpy, when really he was as soft as mashed potato."

"You are funny." Timmy giggled.

She grinned back.

"Now who's your favourite character then, young man?" Florrie asked.

"Winnie-the-Pooh."

"Mine's Tigger," Jenny volunteered.

A couple of chapters later they were all giggling over Pooh's antics with the honey pot.

It was only when the book was closed that Florrie remembered the gift she had brought for her young patient.

"Oh I nearly forgot! I have a gift for you, Timmy," Florence said. "It's in my case." She hurried along to her room. Within in a few minutes she was back.

"I hope you like it," she said, handing him his gift.

"Thank you," the boy cried, tearing off the wrapping paper. "'The Lion, The Witch And The Wardrobe'! Whoopee!"

"I could read you a chapter now if you like? If Jenny doesn't mind," Florrie offered. Her reward was a beaming smile.

"Off course I don't," Jenny announced. "Well, I'll leave you for a while, I've a stack of ironing to get through, if that's OK?"

"Of course," Florrie reassured the young girl, sure that they were already friends.

Timmy Harper was certainly a good-looking boy, Florence thought as she plumped up his pillows before settling down to read.

His snowy white hair was a mass of curls. His eyes were grey, like his mother's, and his skin tone was much lighter than his father's and his features more fine. She reminded herself it was not uncommon for a child to take after one parent and pushed the subject from her thoughts, as she sat down and opened the book to read.

She had read the whole of the first chapter and was a few pages into the second when Jenny returned.

Florrie closed the book with a promise to read again tomorrow.

"I like Peter," Timmy told Jenny, his face flushed with excitement. "Tumnus is a faun and he lives in a secret world. Lucy stumbled through at the back of the wardrobe."

Florrie left when Mrs Dobbs came in with Timmy's tea tray. She left him to eat his boiled eggs and bread and butter soldiers, washed down with a tall glass of milk.

The housekeeper caught up with her on the landing.

"I don't know what you did," the woman beamed, "but I haven't seen the lad tuck into tea so readily in a long time."

"It was the book I got him," Florrie said, and explained to the mystified Mrs Dobbs.

"Magical worlds at the back of a wardrobe." She shook her head. "Well, I've never heard the like, but if it helps the boy, all to the good, I say. I've hung your coat up in your wardrobe for you, miss."

"Thank you. I hope I'm not causing you too much work, Mrs Dobbs."

"Not a bit, my dear, it's no trouble at all."

They'd only arrived in Florrie's bedroom a moment, when a short grey-haired man with a cheery smile knocked on the open door.

"Your case, miss," he said, setting her case down by the bed.

"Thank you, Mr Dobbs," Florrie said.

"You're welcome, miss," he replied, giving her a another cheery smile.

"We'll leave you to unpack, Sister. Tea's in the drawing-room at four," Mrs Dobbs said.

It didn't take long for Florrie to unpack her clothes and put them away. An hour later she was enjoying a delicious tea. Afterwards she took her tray to the kitchen.

"You shouldn't be doing that, Sister," the

friendly housekeeper scolded.

The kitchen was homely and welcoming, just like its occupants. Two rockers sat either side of the fireplace, where a welcoming fire was crackling away. The cream Aga was the only thing in the bright cosy kitchen that had a hint of the more modern era.

"The doctor's such a good employer," Mrs Dobbs said, putting her cup down on her saucer. "Such a shame he hasn't a wife to come home to in the evenings. He works long hours and what that little boy upstairs needs is a few brothers and sisters to play with."

"I should think he will marry one day; he's still young," Florrie said.

"Yes, I dare say you're right, Sister, but I hope he chooses someone who understands he has to work long hours and who will love that dear child upstairs as much as he does."

Then Mrs Dobbs was smiling at her, and Florrie had the distinct feeling that her new friend had just decided that Florence was the perfect person to fill the job.

Mr Harper was the last man she would want to marry. She was sure he'd say the same about her.

* * * *

The next morning Florrie was heading for the dining-room when she met the housekeeper in the hallway.

"Morning, Sister. Did you sleep well?" Mrs Dobbs asked cheerfully.

"Very well thank you," Florrie said, smiling back before turning towards the dining-room.

"Not that way, Sister, breakfast is served in the small morning room." The housekeeper smiled, pointing to the door opposite the stairs which led down to the kitchen.

The room was at the back of the house. When Florrie entered, her heart lifted. It reminded of her aunt's dining-room in the country. The morning room was smaller than the dining-room. The table was a warm golden pine with matching chairs and the china was simpler in style and the cutlery plainer.

The curtains were chintzy, giving the room a homely feel. A long matching sideboard was set against the back wall, on top of which stood two long china dishes with covers to keep the food warm.

"Good morning, Sister," Mr Harper said behind her.

"Good morning, Mr Harper," she said, surprised, nearly dropping the scrambled egg she was setting on her plate, wishing that she hadn't piled her plate so high with all the breakfast goodies on display.

Now he would think her not only a giant, as well as being overweight, but a glutton as well.

"The fried bread is delicious," he said, the

edge of his perfect mouth twitching. He was laughing at her again. Well, let him, she thought defiantly. She wasn't a girl that liked small portions.

The faint hope of yesterday that they might be friends, faded. So much for being more polite, she thought.

* * * *

The days fell into a pattern, with the doctor reading his post at breakfast, and when he was home for dinner, he would excuse himself straight after and go to his study.

She was beginning to think, as far as Dale Harper was concerned, she was invisible.

Florrie told herself she didn't care if the doctor did not want her company. So why did she feel so despondent?

No, she told herself, she wasn't even going to think about that.

Not ever.

Beautiful Stranger

THE following Monday, Florrie nipped down to the post office to buy a new writing pad, envelopes and stamps for the letter she was planning to write to her aunt that evening.

It started to rain on her way back to the house. She sheltered in a bookshop doorway waiting for the rain to ease. In the window display was a book, "Thomas The Tank Engine". She couldn't help smiling at the brightly coloured trains. She went inside and brought it.

The rain had stopped by the time she left the shop. She had just reached the traffic lights at the end of Wimpole Street when she noticed a familiar car driving past heading for Oxford Street. Sitting beside Mr Harper was the most beautiful woman that Florence had ever seen, wearing a sable coat.

Florrie's heart plummeted. She scolded herself for her reaction. The lights changed and they drove on. She was thankful that the doctor hadn't noticed her. It had begun to pour down again as she'd waited for the lights to change. Her wet hair was hanging limply. Her old tweed coat wasn't looking its best. She didn't know why it should matter to her that Mr Harper should see her looking so dishevelled, but it did.

After she'd finished applying the heat pads later that afternoon, Florrie presented her little charge with the new train book. Her reward was squeals of delight.

"I want to be able to walk across the room to Daddy on Christmas Day," her young patient confided, while she was removing his heat pads. "It's my special Christmas wish," he added, his lip wobbling now.

"So you will, poppet," Florrie said, blinking back tears as she sat beside him on the bed, putting her arms around him. "But not if you don't eat all your greens," she teased, playfully.

Timmy gave her a wide grin now.

"I think you are the best nurse in the world."

"I think you are not so bad yourself, young man." She grinned back.

A few evenings later Florrie was crossing the drawing-room on her way upstairs to bed, when the strap of her bag broke. Before she could move, Mr Harper began picking up the items, giving each amused glance. A rabbit's foot that her aunt had given to Florrie when she'd started her nursing training. A silver charm that had belonged to her mother and a small photo of her and Edward in happier times, which must have been buried at the bottom of her bag.

"Are you superstitious, Miss Fairchild?" he asked, his green eyes glinting with amusement.

"I suppose so," she replied, letting him believe what he wanted.

He stood up and handed her the charms, but hung on to the picture, studying it. Then he glanced at her.

"Your brother? A cousin?"

"No."

"Ah, I see . . . someone special," he said, his amusement faded now, as he handed back the photo.

The annoying man! His moods were as changeable as the weather.

"Well, goodnight," she said, in the coolest voice she could manage, forcing herself to walk slowly upstairs to her room.

The weeks that followed flew by. Before she realised it, it was the middle of November. She spent long days working with Timmy. The child was an angel, never complaining when he was tired. When she wasn't with him, she would take long walks in the park or look around the local shops.

Each day brought a small improvement in the boy's movement.

One afternoon Florrie was reading Timmy another chapter of "The Lion, The Witch And The Wardrobe", while Jenny was ironing the boy's clothes, when Dale Harper arrived unexpectedly.

Florence's heart thumped at the sight of him. He was looking particularly handsome in a grey wool suit and he must have shaved before coming into the room, for she could smell his fresh aftershave.

"Daddy, are you going to stay and listen to the story?" his small son asked, hugging his father who bent to kiss him. His father's reward was a beaming smile.

"Sorry, old chap, not today, I'm already late for a very important meeting," he said, ruffling the boy's hair gently. "I'm afraid to say I won't be back in time to read you your bedtime story, either."

Timmy's smile vanished, which his father hadn't missed.

"But I'll read you two stories tomorrow and if you're really good an extra one as well."

Timmy's smile returned.

"I'm sure Jenny won't mind reading an extra story tonight as well," he said, giving the young girl an apologetic smile. "I'd like a word with you in my study before I go, Florence."

She didn't even register for a moment that he'd called her Florence.

Hundreds of possibilities raced through Florrie's mind. Did he disapprove of the way she was nursing Timmy? Was he going to dismiss her? Well whatever it was, she would learn about it soon enough.

She took a deep breath and followed Mr Harper downstairs.

The study looked just as she expected it to look. A large oak desk sat in the middle of the room, overflowing with papers and files. Three of the walls were lined with floor-to-ceiling bookcases filled with leather-bound books. Set on the last wall were more family portraits, she thought, judging by the likeness to the doctor.

She was a little surprised not to see more paintings of his wife around. Maybe the memory of her loss was too still too painful.

"Please take a seat," Mr Harper said, indicating for her to take the leather armchair nearest the fireplace, where a roaring fire was blazing, before he moved to the seat opposite.

"I just wanted to talk to you about Timmy's progress," he began, then changed his mind.

"Would you like some tea, Sister?"

It always surprised Florrie how Mr Harper managed to switch so easily from his usual formal address, to the informal whenever they were in Timmy's company. She found the situation confusing.

"No, thank you."

Whatever he had to say, positive or negative, she just wanted this interview over and done with.

Thankfully since her arrival, their contact had been minimal. The doctor was often called to the hospital, or he dined out with friends. Florrie had found herself often speculating about those times he was away, as well as who he was with – which wasn't safe on her part.

She told herself that she would be curious about anyone who she saw on a daily basis but even then, she wasn't sure if that was the true reason.

"I wanted to say that my son is progressing well," he said, pausing for a moment. "His muscle strength is getting stronger. For that you have my gratitude," he said, giving her one of those smiles that he usually saved for Timmy.

Florrie watched him turn and glance at the photograph on his desk of his small son.

Impulsively, she leaned forward and touched the doctor's hand. She could feel his fingers stiffen, as he moved his hand away from hers.

She sat back as if stung. She should never have been so forward.

Mr Harper stared at the fire and it was a full minute before he spoke.

"Of course there is still no guarantee that the massages will make much difference as yet."

There it was. She had been fooled for a moment, but only a moment. The bottom line was he didn't want her friendship or compassion. All he wanted was results from her. Never mind that she had feelings, just like him. Tears prickled her eyes. She had been foolish to try to comfort him. She drew herself up.

"There is no guarantee the treatment will work, sir, but that doesn't mean I'll stop using every skill that I have to make sure that little boy upstairs gets the best outcome possible," she said firmly.

Anger replaced her normal caution, when

dealing with anxious parents. That's when it hit her. The truth of the matter was that Dale Harper might be a renowned surgeon, but right now he was an anxious parent and she should have remembered that. She was just about to apologise for her outburst, when the telephone on the desk rang.

"Thank you, Miss Fairchild, I think we have said all that needs to said, don't you?"

So she was being dismissed. Florrie marched past him without giving him a backward glance. Outside in the hallway, she took a deep breath.

She had burned her bridges now. The doctor would certainly ask her to leave after the way she had spoken to him. She had never spoken to a senior surgeon the way she'd spoken to Timmy's father.

Only when she reached her bedroom did she realise she wanted to stay – and not only for the child's sake. Confused, she moved to the window, then pushed it up, and breathed in the cold crisp air. Her pulse slowed and her sense of humour reasserted itself.

She was attracted to the doctor. The thought seemed so ridiculous that she nearly burst out laughing at the very idea. The Dale Harpers of this world did not fall for their employees, her sensible self reminded her. She was not Jane Eyre, though the arrogant man downstairs would be a good stand-in for Mr Rochester.

Florrie moved to the dressing table, sitting

down on the stool, her cheeks still flushed.

The idea of herself even remotely attracted to Dale Harper made her stifle another laugh. I'm just lonely, she thought.

"You silly girl," she told her reflection. "Now pull yourself together and forget all this nonsense. You'll most likely be sent packing tomorrow."

Down in the study Dale sat staring at the door. He hoped that he had not given Miss Fairchild the impression that he did not appreciate her sympathy.

She was so gentle and kind with Timmy. If she decided to leave, his son would be heartbroken. Her gentle spirit had touched everyone in the household in one way or other.

The phone rang again. It was the hospital, there had been an explosion in a factory and they needed every available surgeon. He picked up his keys and hurried out to the car, for now all other problems forgotten.

Dangerous Emotions

FLORRIE woke, tears streaming down her face. She had been dreaming about the day Edward had proposed. Only it hadn't been her ex-fiancé's face she'd seen in her dream, but Dale Harper's.

She sat up, shocked, and fumbled for the lamp switch, trying to banish the memory away. The clock read quarter to five. She groaned and rubbed her face free of sleep. She decided what she needed to dispel her troubled dream was a cup of cocoa.

She had just poured boiling milk into the chocolate pot when Mr Harper walked in. Her heart jumped.

"Just what I need – a cup of cocoa, after the night I've had," he said, taking a seat at the pine scrubbed table.

He laughed and she thought how pleasant the sound was.

"Just how I like it, milky and sweet," he said, spooning three sugars into his cup, "after hours in surgery."

"Surgery?" Florrie repeated.

She had thought he'd gone on straight to dinner from the hospital.

"Yes, there was an explosion at a paint

factory., I was called back to the hospital," he said, holding out his cup to be filled again.

"Thankfully nobody was killed," he added, "but quite a few burn cases and broken legs and fractures.

"So what brought you downstairs so early?" he asked. "I hope it wasn't our earlier discussion, because I'm afraid what I wanted to say came out all wrong," he said, his face suddenly serious.

"You are doing a great job with Timmy and whatever the outcome, I know it will be better because of your nursing."

"I woke early and couldn't get back to sleep." She stared deep into her cup. She didn't want to talk about her dream, but something of what she was feeling must have shown on her face because the doctor's words startled her.

"Love is a curious emotion, isn't it, Florence?" he said quietly. "We are so certain once we fall in love that afterwards our lives will be all happiness. I take it you once believed this to be true?"

"I once believed that," she admitted.

"Now you no longer believe in happy ever afters?"

"No," she said truthfully.

"In that we are the same."

Clearly, he had nothing more he wanted to say about the subject and she found that disappointing, as she poured the remainder of the cocoa into the cups.

"Do you think Mrs Dobbs will mind us raiding her biscuit tin?" he said, grinning, moving to the cupboard and taking out the tin of homemade biscuits.

"I don't think she will mind just this once," Florrie said, grinning conspiratorially.

"Well, I think we should both try to get a little sleep," he said, after they'd polished off half the tin.

"You go, I'll wash up. Can't have Mrs Dobbs coming down to dirty dishes as well as a half empty tin of biscuits."

He came across and leaning over, put his crockery in the warm water next to hers, before picking up the tea towel.

"You wash, Sister, and I'll dry."

She was tempted to lean back into his arms. She shut her eyes. Good heavens, this would never do, she thought. She washed the cups, saucers and rinsed the cocoa jug out vigorously, before setting them on the draining board.

Then she abruptly muttered an excuse, before hurrying up to her room.

She stood for a long time against the door, a blush heating her cheeks. She should leave, that would be the sensible thing to do.

This – whatever it was that was happening to her – had to be nipped in the bud if she wanted to stay in this house, she scolded herself sternly.

The temptation to pack her case and leave

right now was strong. But Timmy needed her. She had come here to do a job. Only when it was finished would she leave. Perhaps it would be better if she avoided the doctor.

But somewhere in her confused mind, she knew she didn't want to do that either.

On Sunday Florrie caught a bus to Sarah's flat. She hwas looking forward to spending some time with her friend.

"I can't stay long – a couple of hours at most," Florence said, taking off her rain coat.

"Tea?" Sarah asked.

"Perfect," Florrie said, following her friend into the small kitchenette. It was a bright kitchen with its painted yellow cupboards and black and white chequered lino. It was a cheery room, just like it owner.

"Something smells nice," Florrie said, sitting down at the small table.

"It's only leftovers from last night's beef stew, with a few added extras." Sarah giggled.

"I could eat a horse," Florrie declared, which was true, because she had hardly touched her breakfast.

The doctor had been more distant than usual. He had never even glanced up from his post, when he'd returned her good morning and the rest of the meal had passed in a cool silence, on both sides.

Disappointed, Florrie had thought at least they had moved on to more communicative terms, since their meeting in the kitchen early this morning. But obviously she'd been mistaken. Being a fair girl, she admitted she hadn't helped by panicking and running away from him last night.

Sarah brought the freshly brewed tea to the table, where two places had been set.

"You don't mind eating in the kitchen, do you, Florrie? Only I have to be go back on duty in a couple of hours myself."

"Of course not," Florrie reassured her friend.

"So how it going over at Mr Harper's house?"

"I don't really see him a lot," Florrie hedged, "but Timmy's adorable," she added, changing the subject, which worked because Sarah filled her in on what was going on at the hospital and who was dating who.

"You know Staff Nurse Poppy on men's surgical?" Sarah said. "Well, the other day she was leaving the hospital when a man asked if she knew a Florence Fairchild.

"Anyway, the long and short of it is, she told him you were on temporary leave and wouldn't be back for a while. She says he was quite a heart-throb with blond hair and the bluest eyes she'd ever seen.

"It seems she was about to tell him that you were working for Mr Harper, but he was talking to the porter in the doorway. She wasn't sure if he had heard the stranger ask where he could find you, but when Mr Harper passed her he didn't look too pleased."

There was no doubt in Florrie's mind that it was Edward who had come looking for her. She didn't understand why he'd want to see her now.

She realised than she felt nothing at the thought of seeing him, not even a flicker of interest. Something had changed. The spell that he'd woven over her had broken and she saw him now for what she suspected he always was – ambitious, selfish and self-serving.

An hour later she was riding on the bus back to Wimpole Street. Though she couldn't help worrying why Edward was looking for her. She told herself she was making a mountain out of a molehill and the chance of them ever meeting again was unlikely.

By the time she got off at her stop, Edward was pushed from her thoughts.

* * * *

The following afternoon was taken up working with Timmy. He had surprised her by walking a few steps without his calliper for support.

When she came down to tea in the drawing-room later, it was to find a visitor had arrived.

She recognised the lady at once. Mrs Harper senior was a stunning woman. Her silver hair looked chic in a neat bun, and her blue suit suited her still trim figure.

"I've asked Mrs Dobbs to bring an extra cup and saucer. I hope you don't mind me joining you for tea," she said, as Florrie came forward.

The few times Florrie had met Mrs Harper at hospital functions she had liked her.

"Of course not," she assured the doctor's mother and meant it.

"I hope my son is not working you too hard, Florence," Mrs Harper said, after Florrie had handed that lady her tea.

"No, and I have lots of help from Mrs Dobbs as well as Jenny."

"I know that Dale works himself too hard," she confided, giving Florrie a smile that so much reminded Florrie of her son. "He has a tendency to forget that others need to relax."

She paused for a moment, then lowered her voice.

"I was beginning to think he'd never think about marrying again after Anna, though there is a chink of hope. His father was telling me that Dale has become quite fond of a certain young lady. Though he said Dale hasn't given him the young lady's name, as yet."

The piece of seed cake that Florrie was biting into seemed suddenly too dry. She took a large sip of her tea to help it down.

Thankfully the conversation turned to Timmy after that, and Mrs Harper went back upstairs with Florrie and spent an hour with her grandson, before leaving.

As the days passed, Florrie tried not to think about what Mrs Harper had told her, yet the more she tried, the more she thought about it. She told herself that she was worried about Timmy's reaction to a new mother.

Her opinion of the doctor had altered dramatically since her arrival at the house. Since she had seen the way he was with his son, her respect for him had grown in leaps and bounds, though for some reason she didn't understand, the thought of meeting Mr Harper's intended unsettled her more than she wanted to admit.

* * * *

Florrie had very little time to wonder about the doctor as the weeks passed. Timmy was growing stronger and she stepped up his exercise routine to four times a day. She decided to ask the doctor in a few more weeks about carrying the boy downstairs to the drawing-room in the mornings where he would be comfortable enough on the sofa.

Even if he couldn't go out to the garden yet, at least he could look out at it.

"Can we play games again, Florrie?" Timmy asked, breaking into her thoughts.

"Of course, but you must give me a chance to win at least once, young man," she said.

"You're funny," Timmy said, grinning. "I never want you to go away ever."

"Well, I'm not going anywhere at the moment," she soothed, gathering him close in her arms and hugging him gently. "So just remember you promised to let me win some games."

Later she left him in his nanny's care and went to change for dinner. For some reason she wanted to look her best. Which was ridiculous, she reminded herself. Dale Harper wouldn't notice what she was wearing.

She chose the dress with the scalloped neckline. She had brought the outfit for her first dinner date with Edward. It had been far too expensive, but she had wanted to look her best.

Now she was fascinated by another man, only this time, although he was even more handsome, his smile was mocking.

She ordered herself to stop thinking about her employer, a man who would only ever see someone like her as the nurse who was caring for his son. She was in no doubt that she would be easily forgotten when she returned to the hospital.

But Mr Dale Harper would not be that easy to forget, however hard she tried.

An Irresistible Kiss

FLORRIE was wrong about that, however. The doctor was thinking about her as he drank his coffee in the consultants' lounge. He was remembering how pretty she looked at breakfast in a pale pink jumper and a plaid skirt that suited her neat figure. He still hadn't told her about the man who was looking for her.

He had been talking to the porter when he heard a man ask one of the staff nurses if she knew Miss Fairchild. He hadn't liked the look of the stranger – or the fact that he was inquiring about Florence.

A spur of something he didn't want to acknowledge struck him. He wondered if this man was the one who had made her skittish of men. Dale watched the man, only half listening to the porter. The stranger was using his charm on the nurse, obviously trying to wheedle information out of her. Dale was tempted to call her over, but stopped himself.

He wished the porter goodbye, passing the pair on the steps. The girl seemed flustered; obviously she'd seen him standing in the doorway. That was weeks ago and he hadn't seen the man since.

Florence was in the drawing-room reading a

letter when he arrived back at the house.

"Letter from home?" he asked, sitting down on the opposite sofa.

"Yes, it's from my aunt."

A surprising feeling of relief lightened his mood. At first he had thought it might be a letter from the young man.

"Would you like a sherry, Miss Fairchild?"

"Thank you," she said, folding up her letter and putting it back in the envelope.

At first when he entered the room he'd thought for a horrible moment that the man he had seen outside the hospital had found out the address. He sighed with relief as he poured out the drinks.

"You've had a good day?" he asked, handing her the sherry before taking his own seat, whisky in hand.

"Very, thank you." She nodded. "I was hoping you would be in this evening. There is something I want to talk to you about."

For a moment the wind was knocked out of his sails. Had the man been to the house after all? Was she about to tell him she was leaving?

"It's about Timmy . . . I think with your agreement he should come downstairs for a couple of hours each day now. It will help bring back a sense of normality into his life."

Of all the things he had expected her to say, it wasn't that.

"I think that's a very good idea."

"So how was your day, Mr Harper?"

"Busy. We had few appendectomies and two caesareans in the morning, both mothers and babies are doing fine. In the afternoon a young boy with a shattered leg. It took a few hours, but I think we managed to save the it. I'm going back later to keep a check on his progress."

He liked the fact that she asked about his work. Despite his decision not to let anyone past his defences, he smiled at that thought. He knew that he would miss her company when she left.

She was a good listener and because she was a theatre sister, she understood about his work, without him having to explain.

Yes, he would miss her, far too much.

* * * *

The next morning Florrie spent a couple of hours with Timmy applying the heat packs and giving him his massage, after which Mr Dobbs carried him downstairs and settled him on the sofa. They played Snakes and Ladders, followed by two games of Ludo, which Florrie had gladly let him win. Soon he was sleeping peacefully after the excitement of the games.

Florrie had just put the boards and counters back into the boxes, when Mrs Dobbs popped her head around the door.

"There's a phone call for the doctor, miss, in

the study," the housekeeper said, her expression worried. "I told the lady that the doctor wasn't here but she wants to talk to someone else. Could you speak to her?"

"Of course, Mrs Dobbs."

So, leaving Timmy in the housekeeper's care, she went to speak to the caller.

"Hello. Can I help you?"

"Who are you?" the woman on the other end of the phone asked.

"Sister Fairchild."

"Dale's housekeeper tells me he is out," the caller, a young woman, said in a panicky voice. "I've rung the hospital and he's not there. Do you know where he is?"

Florrie was just about to do answer when the doctor walked in the room.

"The doctor's just come in," she told the woman, sure that the woman on the other end of the line was his intended bride.

"A call for you, sir," she said, handing the doctor the receiver.

The look he gave her was questioning.

"Thank you," he said, his tone dismissive.

"Don't worry," Florrie heard him say into the receiver. "I've made all the arrangements for the big day. I'll be there in ten minutes."

Florrie quietly closed the study door. It had sounded as if Mr Harper had already booked his wedding day arrangements, but he hadn't even informed his son. She clenched her fists, disappointed by the doctor's unnecessary secrecy, for more reasons than she wanted to admit. She returned to the drawing-room, her mood flat.

As if right on cue, the doctor entered the room.

"I won't be in for lunch, Mrs Dobbs," he said, looking down at his sleeping son. He smiled then and Florence wished that he would smile at her like that.

He bent down and picked up the child.

"I'll just take him back upstairs before I go," he told them, but at the door he turned. "You have a couple hours off now, don't you, Sister? If you like I can drop you off by the shops. I'm going that way."

So they were back to addressing each other formally. All right she had called him "sir" first, but that was only because she didn't want to overstep the boundaries of convention in hearing of his intended.

"I don't need to go out," she said briefly.

It was only after she'd heard the doctor's car pull away that she remembered she needed to post her latest letter to her aunt. She wrote home once a week, knowing that her aunt would be disappointed on not receiving her news.

She went to fetch her coat, slipping it on and putting her letter in the pocket. She'd nearly an hour before lunch – plenty of time for her to get to the post office and back.

She'd just reached the corner at the end of the road when she saw Edward crossing further down. She ducked into the teashop, hoping he hadn't seen her. He was the last person in the world that she wanted to meet. Her thoughts were confused enough.

She sat down and ordered a pot of tea from the waitress. She couldn't risk leaving until she was sure the coast was clear. Unluckily, Edward must have seen her, for five minutes later, he walked into the tearoom.

"I was sure it was you on the other side of the road," he said, sitting down at her table.

"What do you want, Edward?"

"You."

"Florrie swallowed her surprise.

"I don't think your wife-to-be would like that," she snapped.

"I broke off my engagement."

"You have a habit of doing that," she returned. "I do hope you at least told her. Something you never thought to tell me."

"I made a mistake, Florrie," he said, reaching across the table and taking hold of her hands. "Say the word and we could get a special licence and be married in days.

Florrie had no idea that Mr Harper who was driving past at that moment had glimpsed her holding hands with the man he'd seen at the hospital.

Florrie pulled her hands away from Edward's. "I'm sorry, Edward. It's too late."

The waitress returned with the tea, ending all conversation.

Florrie poured the tea, thankful that her hand didn't shake. She was feeling decidedly uncomfortable.

"You don't mean that, you know you don't."

"I do," she insisted, hoping he would get the message.

"Is there someone else? Is that it? You've fallen for someone else."

"No!" she said. An image of Dale Harper came in to her mind and she felt her cheeks heat.

"Then I'm not giving up," Edward stated. "I was a fool to let you go."

"I won't change my mind." It was her turn to be insistent.

He tried to take hold of her hands again, but this time, she was too quick for him and placed them in her lap.

"You don't mean that, Florrie. What we had was special."

She was tempted to tell him that he hadn't thought so, but they were drawing too many looks from the other customers and the waitress, who had been practically hovering around their table since Edward arrived.

"I have to go," she said, indicating for the waitress to bring the bill, "I'm already late." Which wasn't strictly true, she still had a half an hour, but she wasn't going to tell him that.

"You go. I'll pay the bill – my treat," he said. She stood up to leave. "I'm not going to give up, Florrie," he added.

She hurried out.

The winter air was refreshing after the heat of the shop. She hurried back to the house, her mind a whirl of confusion, all thought of posting her letter forgotten.

If Edward had asked her to marry him straight away, before he came back from America, she would have had no hesitation, but now the thought left her only feeling empty.

She was surprised to see the doctor's parked car outside the house. He was back. Her heart beat faster.

She rang the bell, expecting Mrs Dobbs to open the door. Only it wasn't that lady who answered the door.

"Just in time for lunch, Miss Fairchild," the doctor said, scowling down at her.

"I had to go out after all," she replied. It was obvious he thought she'd deliberately refused his lift to the shops. She didn't know why it mattered, that he had thought she'd lied but it did . . .

Her thoughts still a jumble of confusion, she followed him in, closing the door behind her.

"As you see I came back earlier than expected," he said. "You still have time to freshen up," he added, striding away towards the dining-room.

She hurried upstairs, combed her hair and washed her face and hands before coming back down.

"So where did you go to when you went out?" the doctor asked, putting down his knife and fork on his cleaned plate.

Florrie put her own cutlery down.

"I went to post a letter," she said, consoling herself that it wasn't a lie. That had been her original intention.

"The lady who called – is she all right?" she plunged in, anxious to change the subject. Then she wished she hadn't. The look on Mr Harper's face was thunderous.

"I think, Miss Fairchild, you overstep your position."

Unreasonable man, she thought, attacking her food with more force than necessary. So it was all right for him to ask about her comings and goings, but she wasn't allowed the same luxury.

"Well, I won't overstep my position again," she snapped.

The rest of the meal passed in an awkward silence, after which Florrie rose from the table.

"With your permission, sir, I will return to my work."

She had almost reached the door, when he was across the room barring her way. She was left with only one way out, which was to edge past him.

"Excuse me, sir," she said in her best theatre sister voice.

Then before she realised what he was going to do, his mouth covered hers. Florrie melted against him, then as the kiss deepened, a sigh escaped. She never wanted him to stop.

Suddenly he sprang away as if burned, his breathing uneven.

"I do apologise, Miss Fairchild, my behaviour was unforgivable." His words shot her back to reality.

"Yes, it was," she retorted, her smile brittle. "After telling me I have overstepped the mark! I thank you to remember I am here to nurse your son. Not a distraction for your amusement."

Not waiting for his answer, she pushed past him and fled upstairs.

Dale groaned. He should never have kissed her. She had obviously made it up with the man who had hurt her.

She hadn't done anything wrong. She was a grown woman. It wasn't for him to decide who she met in her own time. So why wouldn't the memory of them together fade?

This madness had to stop. If she wasn't progressing so well with Timmy, he would ask her to leave, but he didn't want to let her go; not until he worked out what about Miss Florence Fairchild made him behave so irrationally.

Late Night Request

BEFORE going to Timmy's room, Florrie went to her own room. Hurrying into the bathroom she splashed cold water on her burning cheeks, cooling her face. She traced a finger over the lips he had kissed.

She had never felt so responsive to Edwards's kisses as she had to the doctor's downstairs just now. Even when Edward had asked her to be his wife, she had never felt such a tide of emotion.

The doctor was right, his behaviour was unforgivable, but so was hers. She knew he was practically engaged, yet she hadn't wanted him to stop. Shame at her own response overwhelmed her and she sank down of the edge of the bath.

Eventually she calmed herself before combing her hair and powdering her nose, as well as applying a touch of lipstick.

She couldn't help wondering what would happen now. Would he dismiss her? The thought of being sent away disturbed her more than she wanted to admit even to herself.

By the time she headed along the hall to Timmy's room, she had resolved to treat the matter as if it had never happened. It was not as difficult as she had imagined. When she went downstairs later, she was told by Mr Dobbs that the doctor had left for hospital and he would be dining out this evening.

* * * *

In the days that followed, Florrie often caught glimpses of him going to his study or occasionally passed him on the landing. Florrie was sure it wasn't only work and friends that kept the doctor away.

She had noticed when she came down for breakfast, he was always going out of the door. She told herself that she was glad he was avoiding her, it gave her time to overcome her own embarrassment of responding to his kiss. She was just thankful that nothing had been said about replacing her with another nurse.

It seemed that the situation would have continued but fate decided to meddle. Florrie was passing Jenny's room, when the young girl called her in. A suitcase was on the bed and she was packing clothes.

"My mother's had a fall at home, so I have to leave," her friend explained, looking flustered. "I'm sorry to leave you in sole charge of Timmy, but I must go. Mum's sprained her ankle and she's on her own. I've told the agency and I'm sure they'll send a replacement. Can you explain to Mr Harper for me?"

"Yes, of course." Florrie nodded. "Timmy and I will be fine," she reassured the agitated girl. "I'm sure Mrs Dobbs will help if needed. So don't you worry. Shall I call you a taxi?"

"That's OK. I'll walk down to Oxford Street. I can catch a bus that goes straight to Clapham Junction from there."

Later Florrie was wrapping Timmy in a large fluffy towel, before getting him changed for bed, when the doctor walked into the bathroom.

"Daddy," her young charge cried, his face flushed with excitement.

Florrie felt her cheeks heat, as she remembered the last time they had been together. Thankfully she could put her warm cheeks down to the heat in the bathroom.

"Where's Nanny?" he asked, lifting up his young son and pressing a kiss on his snowy head, before carrying him through to the bedroom and setting him down on the bed. He then proceeded to towel dry him gently, before putting on his pyjamas.

"She had to leave. Her mother twisted her ankle," Florrie stated, grateful that she didn't stumble over her words. What was it about this man which made her feel so unsettled in his presence?

Needing a minute to gather her composure, she moved to bank up the fire, before turning back.

"Jenny informed the agency," Florrie added, raising her eyes no higher than the middle of her employer's tie.

"I see, well thank you, Florence, for taking over," he said, before turning his attention back to Timmy.

Florrie's heart skipped a beat, though she knew she was being silly. After all, he only ever called her by her Christian name in Timmy's presence.

"You are free to go now, Florence," Mr Harper said, picking up one of the boy's books and opening it.

She was being dismissed. Anger replaced hurt.

"Thank you, sir. I promised to meet a friend," she lied but he didn't need to know that. "So if you'll excuse me, Mr Harper, I am already late," she added moving to plant a kiss on her young charge's forehead.

She was almost at the door when the doctor spun round, his expression unreadable.

"I hope you have a good evening," was all he said.

It would have to be window-shopping, then a film with a fish and chip supper after the film, she supposed. She was sorry to miss one of Mrs Dobbs's good dinners. She smiled at her folly, as she put on her coat and velvet berry hat.

"That will teach you, my girl, to tell lies," she told herself sternly, as she collected her handbag before hurrying downstairs to the kitchen to tell

Mrs Dobbs she wouldn't be in for dinner.

The housekeeper was standing in front of the stove stirring something in a pot, but turned to face Florrie when she entered. The smells emanating from the contents made Florrie's mouth water.

"Going out?" Mrs Dobbs asked.

"Yes, I'm sorry it's a last-minute arrangement," Florrie said.

"Nothing that won't keep, Sister." Mrs Dobbs gave her a reassuring smile. "You'd better take my key to get back in," she added, moving to take a key from the hook on the wall by the door, and placing it in Florrie's hand.

"Thanks," Florrie said, giving the housekeeper a grateful smile, before popping it in her bag. She was tempted to tell the housekeeper the truth, but it would be unfair to involve Mrs Dobbs in her deception.

* * * *

Florrie was a little envious of the couple sitting along the aisle from her in the cinema, holding hands. It was obvious that they were in love. All of a sudden the image of the doctor holding hands with the woman he loved made her heart sink.

She told herself she was overreacting, and pushed the image away.

The film was a western: "Bend In The River",

starring James Stewart. Throughout the film she found she couldn't really concentrate on the story. Afterwards she ate her fish supper at a café a few doors down from the picture house.

She had lingered over her tea, not wanting to get back till she was sure everyone was asleep. She was sure the doctor was angry with her, but she couldn't understand why.

By the time she got back to Wimpole Street, it was nearly half past 11. She was fishing in her bag for the key Mrs Dobbs had given her, when the door opened and the doctor was standing there.

"Good evening, Sister, I hadn't expected you to be back so late."

He opened the door wider for her to pass. She skirted past him.

"There was no need for you to wait up for me, sir. Mrs Dobbs gave me her key," she said.

She heard the door close and moved towards the stairs.

"I wish to speak to you, Miss Fairchild," Mr Harper said. "I will meet you in the drawing-room in ten minutes."

Florrie couldn't help wondering if the doctor was going to dismiss her after all.

Her employer was standing by the garden doors when she entered the room. Her heart bumped again at the sight of him. He looked even more handsome, if that was possible, in a white shirt and brown cords.

Mustering all her courage for the news to come, she moved on leaden feet to sit on the sofa.

The doctor moved to sit beside her. As he sat down, his arm brushed against hers. She felt an electric spark shoot though her once more. She stiffened and sat straighter.

Mr Harper frowned.

"I know it is late, Miss Fairchild, but this is the only time I have to talk to you alone, as I have back-to-back surgery for the next few days, something I'm sure you understand."

He smiled then.

"I wanted to ask you if you would take on Jenny's duties until she returns. I know it will be more work, but I feel that bringing a stranger into the house at this time, might slow my son's progress."

Florrie sat stunned. She had been expecting her marching orders and so it took a few moments for her to recover.

"I shall be glad to take on Jenny's duties as well as my own," she assured him.

"Are you sure it won't be too much?" he asked, giving her one of those special smiles he usually saved for Timmy.

"Of course not!" she assured him. "Anyway, Jenny shouldn't be gone too long."

"You are an unusual young woman."

"Not in the least." She laughed.

"I disagree," he declared, looking into her

eyes. "Coffee?" he asked. "Mrs Dobbs has gone to bed, so you'll have to accept my poor effort, I'm afraid."

Florrie nearly giggled. She couldn't imagine Mr Dale Harper doing anything as ordinary as making coffee.

"Come along to the kitchen with me and you can make sure I don't burn it," he said, a smile curling his mouth now.

She followed him down to the kitchen and sat in one of the rockers by the banked fire, watching him move around the cosy room collecting what he needed. Florrie was surprised to find he knew where everything was. As if he had read her thoughts, he turned and looked at her pointedly.

"I get in late from the hospital so I have learned to find my way around the cupboards," he said, another smile quirking his lips.

Florrie poured the coffee and handed him his cup. She couldn't help envying the girl he was going to marry. She didn't have any doubt that he would make a wonderful husband. Just for a moment, she wished that she was the one he loved.

Startled by her thoughts, she sprang to her feet.

"It's getting late, I'd better go to bed."

He stood up and moved closer and she felt herself caught by the green lights of his eyes. She knew he was going to kiss her. So it was a relief when the telephone trilled down the hall.

Mr Harper gave her an apologetic smile and gestured for her to wait, before heading to his study. Florrie knew if they hadn't been interrupted, she would have allowed him to kiss her.

She must have stood there for a full minute, before common sense kicked in. Did she want him to come back and kiss her? Her sensible self said no, but she realised that was a lie. He had asked her to wait, but she told herself that he was only being polite, as she headed out into the hall.

She could hear the doctor talking as she tiptoed past the partly open door. It sounded as though he was making arrangements to visit the caller tomorrow.

She quickened her step, then heard a voice behind her.

"Not trying to avoid me, are you?"

She swung round to face him.

"I'm not trying to avoid you," she said.

He smiled at her.

"I don't believe you, but I won't push you for the real reason tonight.

* * * *

Florrie woke up with a start. She had been dreaming about the doctor. He had been standing at the altar beside his bride. Florrie couldn't see the face of the girl standing beside him, as her face was covered by a veil.

The vicar was asking if there was any reason why this man should not marry this woman.

Florrie was shouting, "Yes" but no-one seemed to hear her.

She groaned and rubbed her face. Somehow she had got Dale Harper mixed up with Edward in her dream. She wished she could take all the painful memories of Edward's rejection away.

Wide awake now, she slipped out of bed and pulled on her dressing gown, before moving to sit on the cushioned window seat. The fire was banked low, and she shivered. Tying the belt of her gown tight around her, she looked out at the full moon that looked so bright above the chimney pots.

But it wasn't Edward's image that loomed large in her mind. She had been lucky only to escape with her heart a little bruised with Edward, but she couldn't shake off the feeling that she was in danger of a much bigger threat from Dale Harper, if she wasn't careful.

Definitely Not Love

JENNY returned a fortnight later, a couple of days after Mr Harper announced that he would be away for five days at a medical conference in Paris.

Florrie missed the doctor more than she wished to admit. It didn't help that she had visions of him chaperoning his bride-to-be around the wonderful sights, when he wasn't in meetings.

She reminded herself Mr Harper was taking too much of her thoughts, which wasn't safe.

Timmy was missing him, too. He was quieter than usual, and when he snuggled down in his bed, he would still be clinging on to Florrie's hand long after he went to sleep.

The morning before the doctor was due back, Jenny left them to spend the day with her mum. Florrie and Timmy spent a productive few hours working on the boy's strengthening exercises, after which they played board games down in the drawing-room until lunchtime.

The afternoon followed a similar pattern.

After her charge had been bathed and dressed for bed, Florrie read the yawning boy another chapter of "The Lion, The Witch And The Wardrobe".

"I never want you to go away," Timmy whispered, as she was tucking him in.

"I'm not going anywhere yet awhile," she promised.

An hour after Jenny arrived back, Florrie went down to take a walk in the garden before dinner. She had always loved the weeks running up to Christmas, despite the cold. There was always something magical in the air around this time.

She could still remember dressing the tree with her parents, then with Aunt Beverly and her cousin in the country. Those times with her new adopted family had become special, too.

The grass was crisp, with frost under her shoes. She pulled her cardigan around her tightly, as she walked across the lawn towards the little summerhouse set in the corner of the walled garden.

She couldn't help wondering what time the doctor would arrive home tomorrow. Then she reminded herself again, it was none of her business . . . though it didn't stop her wondering.

She didn't know how long she sat out there pondering. Suddenly, a familiar voice broke through her thoughts.

"Good evening, Miss Fairchild."

Florrie whirled around on the seat in shock. He wasn't due back until tomorrow. She blushed hotly because he'd been so much in her thoughts. If Mr Harper noticed he didn't comment.

"Shall we go in? It's freezing out here," was all he said, his tone scolding, as if she was a child who needed chastising.

"Good evening, Mr Harper," she returned, swallowing her annoyance. "I think I'll stay a few more minutes," she added defiantly, raising her chin.

"Well, if you are determined to stay, Sister, I shall, too." There was laughter in his voice now. Then he removed his jacket and placed it around her shoulders and sat down beside her on the bench.

* * * *

The temptation to put his arms around her as well as his jacket was so strong, Dale clasped his hands together. He had missed her more than was safe. He had taken an earlier flight than intended. He had rushed upstairs to see her and his son, only to be told by Jenny that Florence was downstairs.

He had stayed long enough to kiss his sleeping son then hurried down, in search of Florence.

His attraction to her was growing stronger. She was trying not to, but even with his coat on, she was still shivering. He liked that stubborn streak in her that she stood up to him.

He was used to women agreeing readily to his

suggestions and plans. No, Florence was not the sort of girl who would blindly follow. His mouth curled into a smile. He wondered what she would say now, if she could read his mind. He had a sudden impulse to lean in and kiss her.

As she pulled his coat tighter around her body, her hand brushed against his shirt sleeve and he felt the heat of her touch. The dining-room light came on, showering the lawn with light.

"We'd better go in now, I think Mrs Dobbs is about to serve dinner," Dale said, swallowing a smile as he listened to her teeth chattering. .

Florrie looked down despairingly at her old wool cardigan and wished she'd changed into a smarter outfit. He must think her a frump, after the glamorous fur his companion had been wearing in the car that day she'd seen them.

Then her common sense reasserted itself. There was nothing wrong with her clothes; they were functional. Anyway, it wouldn't matter what she wore – he wouldn't notice anyway. She told herself she was glad of that. So why didn't the thought make her feel any better?

* * * *

The following afternoon, Florrie was having tea in the drawing-room when the doctor's mother walked in, wearing a smart cream cashmere suit.

Florrie stood up as the elegant woman crossed

the room to meet her.

"Sit down, my dear, I'm afraid this is becoming a habit, me interrupting your tea." She took a seat beside Florrie on the sofa. "I can't stay long, it's my day for reading to the children at the hospital. But I wanted ask you if it would be all right if we had the family dinner here at Christmas."

Florrie was grateful that she wasn't holding her tea cup at that moment, because she would have dropped it in her lap.

Her confusion must have shown on her face because Mrs Harper continued.

"Men don't know how to organise these things. And as there has been no further talk of this mystery woman, I thought if we put our heads together we could arrange everything together – with Mrs Dobbs's help, of course."

The image of the beautiful girl returned. Was she the same woman he had spoken to his own father about? Mr Harper was a good father, so why hadn't he invited the girl home to meet his son?

Florrie reminded herself, for the umpteenth time, it was none of her business what Mr Harper did or did not do. Maybe they were going to announce their engagement at Christmas.

"So, will you help with the arrangements, Florence?"

"Yes, of course," she agreed readily.

"Now I'll just pop my head around my grandson's door before I go," Mrs Harper said.

So together they went up to see Timmy. By the time the doctor's mother had left, Florrie felt she had made a firm friend.

The doctor didn't return home for dinner and it was Jenny's night off, so Florrie ate dinner in the kitchen with Mr and Mrs Dobbs.

Afterwards Mr Dobbs went off down to the local pub to play darts with friends. Florrie offered to help the kindly housekeeper with clearing up. After they had finished they settled down at the table with a well-earned pot of tea.

"I know Jenny does her best, and the lad loves her, but it's not the same as having a mother figure. Though he's real sweet on you, he is, Sister."

Florrie couldn't help wondering if Jenny and Mrs Dobbs had put their heads together and come up with the idea that Timmy's nurse was the perfect match for the position of wife and mother. If only they knew that there was already a wife-to-be waiting in the wings, but it wasn't her secret to tell.

"I am sweet on Timmy, too," she confessed.

An hour later upstairs in her room, with a last look at the stars, Florrie drew the curtains and prepared for bed.

"Jane Eyre" awaited her on the night table and she hoped it would relax her. She opened her well-thumbed copy, which she had returned to often over the years.

It had been her mother's, given to her when she was a girl, which she had passed down to Florrie on her fourteenth birthday, and Florrie wouldn't have exchanged her well-read copy for all the world.

Tonight for some reason she needed the comfort of the past. She'd just finished the first chapter when there was a knock at the door. Sometimes Jenny came in for a chat before going to bed.

"Come in," she called automatically.

She stared, stunned, for the doctor opened the door. His hair was ruffled, as if he had been pushing his hand through it and his face was starting to darken with stubble. He leaned against the door frame, his hand still holding the handle, looking weary.

She was sure his surgical list had been extensive today. He had that look of strain in his eyes, which surgeons had after operating for hours. She found herself longing to smooth his hair aside, to kiss the weariness from his eyes.

She was shocked at her wayward thoughts. She reminded herself that the doctor wasn't free and even if he were, he wouldn't want her kissing him.

"Ah, I didn't realise you were in bed, Miss Fairchild."

"I thought you were Jenny," she said, thankfully finding her voice. A blush heated her cheeks, she worried that he would think her forward for inviting him in.

Mr Harper crossed to her bed, towering over her.

She pulled her sheet up, which was ridiculous. She was wearing a heavy cotton nightdress, buttoned up to the neck, that any Victorian miss would be proud of. His green eyes swept over her hair, set in two plaits.

She didn't miss a hint of a smile curl his perfect mouth. She wanted to groan. He must think her so unsophisticated, with her hair braided and her plain gown. Then sudden panic filtered through her embarrassment.

"Is it Timmy? Has something happened?" she asked, dropping her open book down on the bed and quickly scrambling out of bed, all thought of embarrassment forgotten now.

"No, Timmy was fast asleep when I checked on him a few minutes ago," he reassured her.

She sighed with relief and sat down on the bed.

"Mrs Dobbs told me that my mother called today," he said. "I wondered if she left a message for me with you?"

"No, Mr Harper," she returned, surprised at his reason for asking her now. Surely his question could have waited until the morning or he could have phoned his mother.

"In that case, I shall leave you to your book," he said, glancing down at the novel that was lying open on top of the bed quilt.

She blushed again as he looked up and their eyes met.

"It was my mother's," she said.

"A gift to be treasured." His voice was unexpectedly tender.

"Yes," she said, feeling suddenly shy. He had surprised her. She wouldn't have expected him to understand what the book meant to her, but he did. It showed in the warmth of his tone.

"Goodnight, then, Florence," he said, leaning over and kissing her forehead so lightly, so briefly, that before she could catch her breath, it was over.

He left then, closing the door after him, leaving her shaken. She sank against her pillows, wondering if she had imagined him calling her by her Christian name.

Her sensible self told her that she had.

* * * *

Down in his study, Dale sat in the darkened room behind his desk, telling himself that he was seven times a fool. Why had he given into the impulse to kiss her? Being an honest man, he knew he'd wanted to kiss her since he first entered the room. She'd look so prim, so innocent, so sweet.

He had come home, seeking Florence's calming presence, after hours operating in the theatre. He had managed to save the baby, but not the mother, victims of a hit and run. The loss of life still affected him, as it always did when he lost a patient on the table.

When Mrs Dobbs told him that his mother had called today and that Miss Fairchild had gone upstairs early tonight he had battled for nearly a quarter of an hour, trying to come up with an excuse to go up and see Florence.

He knew that his mother had fallen under Miss Fairchild's spell on her first visit. According to his mother, the girl was an angel. Dale wasn't surprised. Florence had a quietness about her that was soothing, calming and restful, more than any woman he had ever known.

He had been racking his brain trying to think of an excuse. That's when it came to him. Of course, that was it. He could ask if his mother had left a message for him, with her. As excuses went it was a bit flimsy, but it would have to do.

The need to see her had overridden his normal common sense. Her bedroom light was showing under the door, and before he had had time to think, he knocked.

When he entered the room and saw her sitting up in bed, looking so young in her Victorian nightdress, the compulsion to cross the room, take her in his arms and soundly kiss her was so strong he'd slumped against the door frame, gripping the handle tightly to stop himself from crossing the room and doing just that.

He knew he should send her away, but he knew he wasn't going to do that, not only for his son's sake but for his, too. Since she had been installed in his home, he enjoyed her presence too much. She soothed his soul as well as his mind.

He slumped back in his leather chair. Seeing this woman every day, he knew he would have to manage these new budding feelings. She was his employee and he had to respect that.

He switched on the light on his desk. A mountain of letters were waiting for his attention. He picked up the first one on top of the pile. He had always found peace in his work, but not tonight. He put it back on the top of the pile and headed upstairs to his room, his feet dragging on the stairs.

This isn't good, he told himself, then smiled. You've behaving like a young man in the first throes of love – which was ridiculous! Hadn't he turned his back on love and all it entailed?

* * * *

Timmy was taking a well-earned nap after a morning of exercises. Florence had sent Jenny down for her lunch and was tidying up when Mr Harper strolled into the room.

Yesterday Timmy had managed to walk halfway across the bedroom with his calliper without help. The child had been insistent that his father should not be told. He still wanted to keep it as a surprise for Christmas.

"He's sleeping," she whispered, ignoring the jump of her heart.

Dale moved to the bed and softly brushed back his son's curly hair. Again Florrie was struck by the difference in their colour, as well as the shape of their features.

She was sure, if his wife had lived, that they would have had a household of children by now and more than one would have inherited the doctor's features, as well as his colouring.

Maybe his new wife would produce such a child. The thought sent such a shaft of pain through her heart that she nearly dropped the towel she was folding. Why hadn't she seen it coming, recognised the signs?

Then the truth of her feelings hit her and the world tilted.

"Sister Fairchild, are you all right?" he asked, his warm rich voice laced with concern.

"Of course," she said, too quickly.

"I asked you twice if you'd had your lunch but you didn't seem to hear me," he added.

"I'm afraid I must have been wool gathering," she said, shuttering her gaze, so he wouldn't see the truth of discovery in her eyes.

She had to get away. She loved him so much. She was terrified.

"If you will excuse me, Mr Harper," she said, dropping the towel in the wash basket, "I've a pile of letters to write."

That wasn't strictly true; she only had one to write to her aunt.

She didn't give him time to answer as she made her escape. She didn't realise she was holding her breath until she reached the safety of her bedroom.

"This won't do, my girl," she whispered to the room. "So you love him, but he is never going to love you back."

Even her own sensible advice didn't stop the tears falling unchecked, as she sat at the writing table to write her letter. Her first attempt had been discarded to the waste paper basket. The tears had made the ink run.

Her second attempt finished, she glanced at her watch. If she were quick, she could catch the second collection in the postbox at the end of the street.

She washed her face, put on her coat and hat, slipped the letter in her pocket and hurried downstairs.

She'd almost reached the hallway, when her heel caught on the last step, causing her to fall forward. Just before she hit the floor, strong arms caught her around the waist.

She didn't need to look up to know who had saved her. His touch sent waves of sensation streaming through her body.

He was holding her so close, she could smell the scent of his skin. She never wanted him to let her go. She felt like she'd been catapulted to heaven.

But his words sent her falling back to earth, with a jolt.

"Not falling for me are you, Sister?" he said, his smile mocking.

"Certainly not," she snapped. The last thing she wanted was for him to guess the truth.

"You dropped your letter," he said.

Leaning down he picked up the envelope. Then as he handed it back and their hands touched, an explosion of sparks shot through her. It took all her willpower not to slump to the floor.

"Thank you," she managed to say, lowering her gaze as she slipped the letter into her pocket again.

She moved to pass him on wobbly legs. She had only taken a couple of steps, when he twirled her close, covering his mouth over hers, but as the kiss deepened she pulled out of his embrace.

"This has to stop!" she cried, gasping for air.

It had taken all her strength to pull away. If he kissed her again, she knew she wouldn't have the willpower to resist a second time.

"That was a mistake on both our parts." She forced the words out. "We both got carried away," she defended.

"Of course you are right," he returned.

She had known the kiss had meant nothing to

him, but hearing him say it still hurt.

She felt ashamed at her own behaviour. After all, she had kissed him back.

"Well, if I don't hurry I'll be too late to catch the post . . ."

"Yes, it is late; too late, I think," he said. "It must be a very important letter for such a hurry. A young man?"

"Yes," she lied, thankful that he hadn't read her aunt's name on the envelope.

"I see. Well, you'd better hurry," he said, his tone mocking, as he stepped forward.

She fled, heart pounding, not stopping until she reached the street outside.

She knew that he was laughing at her. That hurt more than all the mocking words he could have said. She wasn't sophisticated, like the woman he'd known.

She had kissed him, knowing that he wasn't free and she was thoroughly ashamed. Florrie told herself she was a fool to love him, but one couldn't choose who one loved. She cheered up at the thought that in a few weeks, she would return to her hospital work.

Still, Florrie knew she couldn't stay there. She would have to find a post in another hospital, far away from London, maybe even somewhere abroad.

What she needed was to forget about that kiss. She had no doubt that the doctor had forgotten it already.

Moon Madness

THE next day started badly. On her way to Timmy's room Florrie caught her favourite cardigan on a door jamb. Then later in the afternoon, she slipped on the stairs and laddered her stocking.

Thankfully her little patient had been as good as gold and never complained once, even though she knew he was tired after his morning exercise and massage. He was quieter than usual, but she put this down to tiredness.

She had taken her usual walk in the garden after lunch and was returning to her room when she met Jenny coming out of Timmy's room looking worried.

"I know it's your free time, Sister, but I'm a bit worried about Timmy. He refused to eat his lunch and he said his tummy hurt, then he was sick."

"Don't worry, it's probably something he ate that disagreed with him," Florrie reassured the girl.

It was obvious Jenny would be more than concerned, after his polio attack. Florrie was sure it was nothing more than a seasonal bug, or something he had eaten that hadn't agreed with his weakened system, but she couldn't take that for granted. She hurried along to the boy's room.

Timmy was sitting up in bed, looking paler than when she last saw him. The bilious attack had obviously left him weakened, though his eyes were alert and focused.

She sighed silently with relief.

"Is your tummy hurting, poppet?" she asked, stroking his curly hair away from his eyes.

She lifted his arm and checked his pulse. It was a little fast, but not dangerously so. Next she examined his tummy, after which she checked his throat, then his blood pressure, and finally she took his temperature.

"My tummy hurts," Timmy whispered.

"Well, I'll soon stop that," she promised, giving him a reassuring smile, before turning her attention back to the child's nanny.

"Jenny will you nip downstairs and ask Mrs Dobbs to make a cup of chamomile tea? It will ease Timmy's cramping."

"Of course, Sister," the nanny said, her troubled expression already starting to brighten.

Within five minutes Jenny returned, followed by Mrs Dobbs with the tea, which she set on the table beside the bed.

"If you need me to make any more tea, just send Jenny down," the friendly housekeeper said, giving Timmy a reassuring wink before leaving.

"It smells funny," Timmy said.

"Well, this is a special tea. It will ease the pain in your tummy," Florrie promised.

"Is it a magic tea?" he asked, as Florrie pulled him forward gently before plumping his pillows and settling him back against them again.

"Yes, sort of," she answered, swallowing a smile.

"I've never had magic tea before," he whispered.

"It's only given to brave boys to help them get well," she said, bending and kissing his cheek. "If you drink it all down, I'll give you an extra kiss."

"What's only for brave little boys?" the doctor asked, coming to stand by the bed.

Florrie's heart raced at his nearness, as it always did. She hadn't heard him come in.

"Magic tea," Timmy told him.

"Chamomile," Florrie interpreted. "Timmy has a pain in his tummy, but it will soon pass once he's drunk his magic tea."

The doctor studied her for a full minute, then without a word he sat down on the end of the bed.

"Can Daddy have some?" Timmy asked. "He likes extra kisses, too."

There were times when everyone wished that the floor would open and swallow them up. Florence thought it was one of those times.

She could feel herself flush all the way down to her toes.

"I'll fetch more tea," Jenny volunteered, and hurried away, but not before Florrie had seen the smile curling the young girl's lips.

Florence felt her face burn now.Unexpectedly, the doctor came to her rescue . . .

"Only little boys are allowed magic kisses."

"It tastes like flowers," Timmy stated, swallowing all of his tea, which made them laugh.

Florrie bent and kissed his cheeks as promised.

"Now, young man, I want you to close your eyes and try to sleep, so that the magic can begin its work."

Within five minutes the child was fast asleep.

Florrie felt suddenly awkward. Thankfully, Jenny returned at that moment carrying the promised tea. After Jenny had set the tray down on the side table she excused herself, saying she had promised to help Mrs Dobbs with something in the kitchen.

Florrie didn't believe for one moment her friend's excuse for leaving them alone. Obviously Jenny must have picked up the atmosphere on her return and being a romantic had come up with the wrong conclusion.

The door had closed behind the girl.

"Will you be mother?" the doctor asked.

Heart thumping, Florence poured the hot golden liquid into the delicate china cups.

She kept her gaze centred on his tie.

"Do you like the ballet, Miss Fairchild?"

"Why, yes, sir," she said, her eyes widening in surprise.

"Only I've got a spare ticket for 'Swan Lake' tomorrow night. I wondered if you'd like to come, as my companion is unable to join me," he said.

Florrie's heart slumped. For a moment she was tempted to say no, but she loved the ballet. Her parents had taken her often and her favourite had been "Swan Lake".

She swallowed her disappointment at being his second choice and gave him the brightest smile she could manage.

"I'd love to come, thank you, sir," she answered him truthfully.

"That's settled then, we'll leave at seven and after the show we'll go on to dinner at the Savoy."

* * * *

An hour later, after trying on her small collection of dresses, she decided none of them would do. Even her grey evening dress with the scalloped neck wasn't smart enough.

The next morning she took the bus to Selfridges to find a suitable dress. She'd almost given up hope of finding one in her modest price range when she spotted a darling blue velvet dress. It was a third of the original price. She also splashed out on a small matching jacket, as well as black suede shoes.

She descended the stairs in her blue velvet that evening to find the doctor waiting at the bottom of the stairs.

He looked at his watch.

"Right on time, Miss Fairchild," he said, giving her a smile that melted her bones.

"I never like to be late," she replied, matching his smile.

Florrie wished this was a real date, that she wasn't simply going because his intended couldn't make it.

She told herself she wasn't hurting anyone if she pretended just for tonight that she was going out on a real date.

On the drive to Covent Garden, her companion had hardly spoken a word, but as he helped her out of the car, he turned to face her, giving her one of those startling smiles.

"Thank you for stepping in at such short notice. I'm really very grateful," he said, before linking his arm through hers.

Sparks ran along her arm, as they always did at his touch.

"I'm looking forward to seeing 'Swan Lake' again," she told him truthfully. "I haven't seen it since I was a girl," she added, grateful that he couldn't hear her heart hammering.

"Will you allow me to say you look enchanting in your own fine feathers?"

"You are also looking very dashing tonight,"

Florrie returned.

"Ha!" The doctor laughed. "I can translate. That's female speak for, it's a great improvement on my usual surgical gown."

"The Christmas lights are so pretty, they make the streets look so magical," Florrie enthused.

"Speaking of lights, we'd better hurry. We want to be in our seat before the theatre lights go down," he said, clasping her hand now as he hurried her along the street.

Florrie felt a thousand more sparks shoot through her. It felt like she'd touched a live wire. She was tempted to pull away but, not wanting to draw attention to her reaction, she willed herself not to.

But when they arrived at the theatre he released her hand as he handed the attendant their tickets. She let out a breath she hadn't known she was holding.

"We have time for a drink in the bar before it starts," he said.

He put his hand under her elbow and led her up the sweeping staircase. Florrie felt the sparks fly again. She felt like Cinderella going to the ball, except the doctor wasn't her handsome prince and she didn't have a glass slipper.

Mr Harper guided her to a table near the bar.

"What would you like to drink?" he asked, pulling out her chair.

His hand brushed her shoulder, as he pulled away and the sparks flared again.

"Stop it," she told herself silently.

"Sherry, please," she said.

The next 20 minutes flew by as they talked about everything and nothing. They were so absorbed they didn't notice they were the only ones still sitting in the bar.

It was only when an attendant pointed out that the ballet was about to start, that they hurried up the stairs to the circle, muffling laughter and out of breath. They managed to take their seats a couple of minutes before the curtain rose.

Florrie got the idea that the doctor was not a regular theatregoer. His eyes glazed over and he shifted in his seat several times. When he dozed off she didn't have the heart to wake him.

In the interval he looked worried.

"Are you enjoying the ballet?" he asked Florrie. "I seem to have lost the sense of it, I'm afraid."

Florrie stifled a giggle and proceeded to explain the plot.

"The swan queen is under the spell of an evil magician and reveals to the prince that by day, she and her friends are turned into swans."

He gave a rueful grin.

"Nicely explained. I assume at the end the prince and the queen fall madly in love and live happily ever after, like all fairy tales."

"Not exactly," she whispered. "I won't tell you the ending – you'll have to wait."

She thought silently that all fairy tales didn't have happy endings and nor did real life. Being in love didn't always mean you got a happy ending.

Florrie was soon lost in the story unfolding in front of her eyes, recognising the irony of the heroine destined to be denied her love. She stole a glance at the doctor, who now seemed fully absorbed in the story.

He turned and gave a smile that made her heart leap in her throat. After the last curtain call they made their way towards the Savoy for dinner. The streets were full with people leaving the theatres. Mr Harper held her arm again as they made their way through the bustling throng.

"I don't want to lose you!" he shouted above the noise.

Florrie ignored the sparks again, but she couldn't help wishing that he would never lose her, ever. Then she reminded herself that she wasn't a heroine in a fairy tale, but an ordinary woman.

The waiter escorted them to a seat near the piano. Florrie stared at her glass. How could his intended have let him down at the last moment? Didn't she know how lucky she was?

Not many men would be so considerate to take their newly intended out to the ballet and to dinner, after a long day in the operating room.

"I hope you like the food."

"I'm sure I will," she said. "Thank you," she added shyly.

"No, it is me who should be thanking you.

"Let's hope I don't fall asleep during dinner," he said, grinning. "It was very kind of you to let me sleep."

"You're welcome," she replied, matching his grin.

Surprisingly, throughout the meal Florrie found herself relaxing, so much so that she found herself wishing that all their meal times together could be so comfortable.

Later, as the Wolseley drew up outside the house in Wimpole Street, a full moon shone like a golden globe in the navy blue sky.

The doctor followed her up the steps to the front door.

"Thank you, sir, I had a nice evening."

"Only nice? I had hoped for 'exciting' or even 'wonderful' but I'll settle for nice." He gently brushed her hair from her cheek.

"You're shivering," he said, removing his jacket and putting it around her evening jacket.

She was glad that the shadows hid her reaction to his touch. He was so close she could barely breathe. Then he bent his head towards her. Her lips parted waiting for his kiss, but he brushed his lips lightly over her cheek, before turning to push the key in the lock.

Once inside she made straight for the stairs. At

the bottom she whirled around.

"Goodnight again," she mumbled, then not waiting for his reply flew up to her room.

She kicked off her shoes and sat down on the bed. She knew he wasn't free, yet she had wanted his kiss.

She fell into a troubled sleep: she was walking along the street, the sun was shining brightly. She stopped to look in the window of a flower shop, at the dozen red roses displayed in a giant silver bucket.

She went in and brought all the roses including the silver bucket. Before she reached the door, the flowers began to bleach away all their colour, until they were as white as Christmas snow.

The bucket slipped out of her hands and she widened her arms trying to catch it, but it hit the stone floor with a crash. She jolted awake, only to discover she had knocked the bedside clock down on to the wooden boards.

"Are you all right, Miss Fairchild?"

Mr Harper was standing in the doorway. She pulled the bedspread around her and stood up.

"I was dreaming. I knocked the clock on to the floor."

"It's nearly one o'clock. I was going to my room when I heard the crash."

In the light from the hallway she could see his hair was ruffled.

"I'm sorry I disturbed you," she said gently.

"Should you be working so late?"

The doctor moved to where she stood. He leaned over and kissed her, so hard, so briefly, that before she could blink, it was over.

Then he was gone.

Florence sank down on the bed, her heart racing. She sat there staring at the door. It was a long time before she got into bed.

* * * *

In his room Dale Harper stood before the window and gazed up at the full moon. Moon madness, he thought.

"I wish I could ask your advice," he muttered. "There's this girl . . . No," he corrected, " . . . woman. I find her spellbinding, refreshing, fascinating. I know I should avoid her but instead I find myself making up excuses to see her, such as pretending that I had been let down at the last minute, when I'd especially got the tickets to take her to the theatre tonight."

He slumped down. He would have to find a way to manage his feelings. It had taken all of his willpower not to kiss her longer. Thankfully common sense had taken hold.

The problem still not resolved in his mind, he headed for the bathroom. He was operating early in the morning on a difficult fracture. He would need all his wits about him, if he was going to save his patient's leg.

Christmas Is Coming

THE Christmas tree is arriving tomorrow, Sister," Mrs Dobbs said, setting the tea tray down on the coffee table. "Mrs Harper asked me to tell you that she's sending over Christmas decorations with her driver today."

"Oh, goody!" Timmy said, clapping his hands in delight. "Can I help decorate it, please?"

"Yes, of course you can, dear, if Sister says it's OK," the housekeeper said, ruffling his hair gently.

"Can I, Florrie?" the child asked, his face expectant.

"Of course you can, poppet," she told him, her love for him shining in her eyes.

"Of course he can what?" the doctor asked, putting down his Sunday newspaper, before crossing the room to sit beside her on the sofa.

"Help dress the tree," she returned.

"Can I, Daddy, please?"

"If Florence thinks it's a good idea, then I must agree," Mr Harper returned.

Florrie's heart leaped at the sound of her name on his lips, then dropped just as quickly. Of course, he'd only addressed her by her Christian name for Timmy's benefit, though she took some heart in the fact he respected her medical judgement. She told herself she was happy to settle for his respect, but she knew that was another lie. She wanted so much more.

* * * *

Mr Dobbs set the Christmas tree up in the drawing-room the following day. There were still two weeks to go but Florrie thought that its pine smell somehow intensified the magical day to come.

It was the biggest tree that Florence had ever seen. The promised decorations were in expensive-looking boxes set beside the tree.

Florrie opened the boxes, the ornaments were delicate, especially the coloured bells, but they would look sparse amongst the long branches.

She decided that she would dress the tree with holly from the garden and when she did her Christmas present shopping she would nip into Woolworths on the high street to get some extra things to hang.

So, after her first session with Timmy, she left him in Jenny's care once more and headed for the high street.

She bought a small crystal vase for Sarah and Tom, a silk scarf for the housekeeper, and a wallet for Mr Dobbs. She purchased a bottle of lavender water for Jenny and lace handkerchiefs for her aunt, which she had wrapped, before taking them along to the post office to be sent to Haslemere, along with her cousin's and his wife's gift of silver teaspoons and puzzles for the children.

Next, on impulse, she went into the stationer's and bought a leather-bound note book for the doctor. Then she walked along to the bookshop, where she purchased another "Thomas The Tank Engine" book.

Afterwards she hurried along to Woolworths where she bought some chocolate soldiers to hang on the Christmas tree and two boxes of coloured bells. Finally she brought five packets of paper chains.

Only when she was nearly back to the house did she wonder if the doctor would approve of the paper chains, but she was sure the little boy would enjoy the bright colours. He would be so proud to have a part in making them.

After lunch Florence and Jenny decorated the tree while Timmy happily helped by unpacking the coloured bells on the sofa. Later, after his nap, they began assembling the paper chains.

Florrie couldn't help smiling at her young patient's comical expressions, as he licked the gum on the coloured strips, before joining them together. They had nearly finished two long chains between them, when Mr Harper entered the room.

Florrie's heart jumped, as it always did at the sight of him.

"Watch out, Daddy, you nearly stepped on the

paper chains!" the excited child cried.

"You all look very industrious," he said. He was manoeuvring his way around the chains, when Mrs Dobbs came in.

"Sorry to disturb you, Sister, you have a visitor," she announced. "I asked him to wait in the hallway. I hope that was all right, sir?" She directed her question at her employer now.

"Perfectly all right, Mrs Dobbs," he told the housekeeper, but Florrie hadn't missed the frown that vanished as fast as it had appeared. "Ask him to come through."

Mrs Dobbs hurried away to give the message.

"It's time you had your nap, son," he said, gathering up Timmy. At the door he turned back. "Come along, Jenny, I am sure Miss Fairchild wishes to see her visitor alone."

Florrie stared at her unexpected visitor. She blinked a few times, hoping that her imagination was playing tricks on her, that Edward wasn't crossing the room, crushing the paper chains beneath his feet without thought.

"Stop!" she ordered, pointing to the carpet. "The paper chains! You're stepping on them."

"Sorry," he said, just managing to side-step another stream.

"How did you know I was here?" she asked.

"Surely you realised I would come, darling?"

"You haven't answered my question."

He smiled and began moving towards her again. So sure of himself, she thought.

119

"I followed you back here after you left the café."

Florrie was speechless.

"You had no right to come here. Now will you please leave," she stated, brushing his hand away.

"If you agree to meet me again?"

He obviously thought he could change her mind.

"No."

"At least give me a chance to apologise."

"I can't. It wouldn't be fair to either of us."

"I see whatever I say won't change your mind," he said, "Well, let us at least shake hands, part as friends."

Relieved, she stretched out her hand. Edward grasped it, pulling her close and planted a kiss on her lips.

"I hope I'm not interrupting."

The voice sent a spear of shock through Florrie. The doctor had come back down.

Mr Harper's eyes were as cold as the weather outside. Florence could tell at once that her employer had thought she had encouraged Edward to kiss her. A hot colour burned her face.

"I came down to collect some more paper chains," was all he said, picking up a new packet from the coffee table, before turning on his heel.

She waited until the doctor had left the room,

before turning back to face Edward.

"You should leave, Edward. I've said all I have to say."

"You don't mean that."

"I do. I never want to see you ever again."

"Is there someone else?"

"There is no-one else." She told herself it wasn't a complete lie. The doctor would never love her the way she loved him.

Florence watched Edward walk out of the front door. She felt no regrets, only relief.

* * * *

Dale's whole body had tensed as he'd watched Edward kissing Florence. He groaned silently, raking his hand through his hair.

The temptation to go back downstairs was so strong, he sat down on the window seat, only half listening to his son's chatter, as he and Jenny looped the paper chains together. He watched Edward walk down the street. Only then did he relax.

He wanted her to come to upstairs, tell him that Edward had forced that kiss upon her, that he was someone whom she no longer had any affection for, but the minutes dragged by and she still didn't come. How could she still want him, after he'd hurt her?

Edward was a handsome man, young to boot. No doubt she found her boss stuffy and boring in comparison.

The thought stirred up a whirlwind of emotions in him that he thought long buried. Why had he thought that she was different? She had seemed a sensible young woman. It was obvious she was still in love with the young man. He gripped the arms of his chair and stood up. He deserved an explanation and if she wouldn't come to him, he would go to find her.

* * * *

The sight of the doctor walking down the path towards her made Florrie catch her breath. How could she explain? She hadn't asked Edward to come to the house, let alone kiss her without her consent. She was tempted to tell him the truth of why she would never have kissed Edward willingly.

But she collected her wits. She couldn't tell the doctor. He would never understand. How could he, when she didn't herself? She knew she owed him an explanation. She decided now was a good moment.

"I want to apologise about the scene in the drawing-room, sir. It won't happen again."

She was close to tears, failing to the note the glint of anger in the doctor's eyes.

The space between them seemed to shrink. She was tempted to run to the safety of her bedroom.

"You can't be thinking of going back to that man?" His expression was thunderous.

"I can do whatever I choose."

She moved to stand in the shadow of the oak and he followed.

"You're a fool if you take him back."

"You don't know how I feel," she shot back, anger replacing despair.

He tilted her face up to his.

"But I do," he whispered as his mouth claimed hers.

Florence wanted time to stop so that she could stay in his embrace for ever. As the kiss deepened, he groaned and the sound shot her back to reality.

She freed herself and stepped back against the tree, shaken.

He was out of line, but she should never have responded to his kiss. He was due to announce his engagement.

"I think that you should respect my feelings to marry who I wish," she said, her voice breathy.

"So you are going to marry him?"

"Who I marry, or don't marry, is none of your concern," she scolded.

"Then you have my congratulations," he returned.

"And I don't need your approval," she added.

She knew she was being unspeakably rude. Let him think what he liked. It was better than him knowing the truth – that she was in love with him. She didn't want his pity, for she was under no illusion – that was all he could ever offer her.

* * * *

When Florrie came downstairs later that afternoon, Mrs Dobbs told her the doctor would be dining out. Florrie told herself that she was glad. The less she saw of Mr Dale Harper, the better for her peace of mind.

Later, before going up to bed, Florrie phoned Sarah.

"How is our lord and master treating you?" was the first thing her friend asked, when she picked up the receiver.

"The same as usual," Florence said, crossing her fingers. She couldn't let slip that the man had kissed her. What if it got back to his bride-to-be?

"When are you coming back to work at the hospital?"

"Early in the new year, I guess, maybe sooner. Timmy's coming on in leaps and bounds."

Before their call ended, Florrie had given a firm promise to get over to the flat for a visit on Wednesday week.

Unable to sleep, she picked up her well-thumbed book.

"Why can't there always be a happy ending in real life?" she whispered to the empty room.

Impossible Man!

FLORRIE woke early, despite hardly having had any sleep. Last night she had been feeling sorry for herself, but she decided that was going to stop now.

When she entered the dining-room the next morning she found the doctor seated at breakfast reading his post.

She helped herself to scrambled eggs, bacon, sausage and tomatoes and took her seat at the table. Her employer's only acknowledgment of her presence was a slight nod, before returning his attention to his letters. It was as if he'd already forgotten the kiss in the garden yesterday.

She told herself that she didn't mind but she couldn't help being a little hurt – after all, he had kissed her first.

One thing was certain – she didn't understand her employer one little bit. One minute he was kissing her, the next he was ignoring her.

She sighed, putting her knife and fork down beside her still full plate. Heartache was definitely playing havoc with her appetite. At this rate she'd soon be slim enough to slide through the floorboards.

"Are you feeling all right, Miss Fairchild?

You've hardly touched the food on your plate," the doctor said, his voice laced with concern.

His sudden concern was too much, after practically ignoring her since she'd sat down.

"I'm fine, thank you, sir," she responded.

To prove this, she picked up her cutlery and began to eat.

"So I see, Sister," he said, his mouth curving with amusement.

He was laughing at her.

"Impossible man," she mumbled under her breath as she returned to tackling her breakfast, determined to eat every morsel on her plate.

"Did you say something, Miss Fairchild?"

"No, sir," she said, spearing a sausage with her fork. Finally, she cleared her plate.

She was about to excuse herself when the housekeeper bustled in carrying a fresh pot of tea on a tray.

"I've made you both a nice fresh pot of tea," she said, setting the pot on the table, "Shall I pour for you, sir?"

"Thank you, Mrs Dobbs, but I think you'd better pour Miss Fairchild one first, her need is greater than mine."

He was laughing at her again. She resisted the urge to stamp on his foot under the table.

To her relief, ten minutes later the doctor left for the hospital. Florrie told herself that she was glad that he had gone. So why didn't she feel glad? It seemed whatever the mocking man did or said, her feelings for him were as strong as ever.

* * * *

As Christmas approached, Florrie found she was grateful for the extra work in helping arrange the Christmas dinner with Mrs Dobbs. If Florrie was being honest with herself, the more she worked, the less time she had to think about the doctor. But at night there was no escape from her thoughts. Even her dreams were filled with him.

The evening before she was to due to visit Sarah and Tom, Jenny had a headache so Florrie had stepped into her shoes. Her young patient had been a little teary, because his father hadn't arrived home to read him a story. But after Florrie explained that he must have been held up at the hospital and she had read the little boy two extra chapters of "The Lion, The Witch And The Wardrobe", Timmy went to sleep with a smile on his angelic face.

After dinner she went back upstairs and sat on the chair beside Timmy's bed. She didn't want to be alone with her thoughts. She must have dozed off, for when she woke, the bedside clock read a quarter to 11. She was about to go to her room when the door opened.

"Did he ask for me?" Mr Harper said.

"Yes, sir, but he soon calmed down after a

couple of chapters of 'The Lion, The Witch And The Wardrobe'," she reassured him, standing up to leave.

"Ever the efficient sister."

To him she would never be anything more than a nurse. The thought was painful.

"I've been in the theatre since three – nasty road crash," he explained. "We've been so busy, I couldn't get to the telephone to let you know I'd be late home," the doctor explained, meeting her gaze.

Florrie noticed the tiredness in the doctor's face. She had thought him out on the town when all the time he'd been operating for hours.

"Goodnight, sir," Florrie whispered, avoiding his gaze, ashamed of her unfair thoughts.

"Did you think I was out on the town?" he asked.

She blushed guiltily.

"I think you should have had more faith in me," he whispered close to her ear.

Then without saying a word, he left her standing there staring after him, as he left the room.

* * * *

The following day Florence went to visit Tom and Sarah and they exchanged Christmas presents. Over coffee they gave her some exciting news. They were expecting! After the meal Tom left for the hospital, leaving the two girls alone.

Florrie was happy for them. They would make wonderful parents. Though she couldn't help wishing that fate had been a little kinder. She could see her own children now, handsome little boys and girls with olive green eyes . . .

Then her friend's next words shattered the wistful image.

"You're not really going to marry Edward, are you? Only Mr Harper was telling Tom after surgery yesterday that when you leave to marry Edward it would be a loss of a good theatre sister. So spill, am I going to have to buy a new hat for the big day?"

Florence groaned.

"No," she said. "He's got it into his head that I'm going to marry Edward. At the moment it suits me that he thinks that."

"My lips are sealed," Sarah promised.

"Could you come to the Christmas morning service with me, Florrie?" Sarah asked as they were carrying the plates to the kitchen. "Only Tom's working and I don't want to go alone."

"I'd love to go with you," Florence said, smiling.

She couldn't see the doctor objecting to her going to church. Christmas dinner wasn't until two thirty so she would have plenty of time to get to the church and back.

Magic Moment

CHRISTMAS DAY dawned. Florrie pulled the curtains and looked down at the garden now covered with a blanket of snow. She still felt there was something magical about the starry white flakes fluttering down.

Florrie had discovered from Timmy a few weeks before that it was a tradition in the family to exchange one present with each member of the family before breakfast and the rest after dinner.

With Jenny's help they had planned to get up extra early, to be downstairs when Mr Harper came down so, that Timmy could give his father his Christmas Wish.

After her bath, Florrie slipped into the blue velvet dress that she had worn to "Swan Lake". She glanced at her reflection in the mirror and on impulse added a dab of coral pink lipstick.

"Not that he'll notice," she muttered. Then, smoothing down her dress, she hurried across to Timmy's bedroom.

Today Timmy was going to walk across the room without his calliper on. Every day her young patient had grown stronger, the boy's confidence increasing with every extra step he managed.

Of course, it would take many months before the brave boy regained all of his strength again, but very soon he wouldn't need a nurse any more.

He was sitting up on the bed already dressed in his white shirt, a sleeveless blue knitted jumper, grey short trousers, matching socks and black shiny shoes. He looked adorable.

"I knew you wouldn't be late," Timmy said as Florrie crossed to the bed.

"Merry Christmas, poppet," she said, returning his smile.

"Oh, I forgot to say Merry Christmas." Timmy grinned sheepishly.

Jenny entered at that moment and between them they carried Timmy downstairs and settled him on the sofa, near the fire, after which they exchanged presents before Jenny left to spend Christmas Day with her family in Clapham.

Florrie moved to the door leaving it ajar, so that they could hear the doctor approaching the drawing-room. When they heard his footsteps coming down the hall, Florrie helped Timmy to his feet.

When the doctor entered, he stood stock still as he watched his young son walking slowly towards him. The doctor's face was beaming with love and pride. As the brave boy reached him, he gathered him close, hugging him tight.

"I walked on my own, Daddy! I did it!" he cried, wrapping his arms around his father's neck. "It was my Christmas Wish for you."

"Yes, you did," the doctor said, his voice thick with emotion. Then he looked up, eyes filled with tears of happiness. He mouthed a silent thank you.

Florrie thought she couldn't have loved Dale Harper any more than she did, but in that moment her feelings for him overwhelmed her.

The doctor scooped up Timmy and carried him to the sofa, setting him down gently.

"Now, shall we see what Father Christmas has brought you?" Dale asked.

He moved to the Christmas tree and picked up a long package and a smaller one, then he handed Timmy the long package. The excited child removed the Christmassy paper with a little help from his father.

Inside was a model of the "Flying Scotsman" train, perfect in every detail.

"Whoopee, it's just what I wanted!" Timmy exclaimed. "Thank you, Daddy."

The doctor bent and kissed the excited boy who was tugging at his arm and whispering something.

"My son tells me I should kiss you, too, Florence."

Before she could say anything he rose and kissed her cheek lightly. Her heart thumped again. He smelled of winter sunshine and warm skin. Then to her amazement, the doctor handed her the smaller package.

"Happy Christmas, Florence," he said.

Her heart swelled in her chest at his thoughtfulness.

"I never expected . . . thank you, sir," she stuttered.

Florence carefully unwrapped the gift, not wanting to tear the paper, which she would keep safe forever. Beneath was a velvet blue box. She lifted the lid and nestled inside was a little gold angel brooch.

"Thank you," she managed to say over the lump in her throat. "It's perfect."

She would wear it always, she thought. It would be a link with the doctor, Timmy and her time here in their home.

* * * *

When he had entered the drawing-room, to find his son walking towards him from across the room, Dale had known who to thank. Florence Fairchild was an exceptional nurse, a true angel. When he had seen the gold angel brooch in the jeweller's window, he hadn't hesitated.

Dale smiled wryly as he watched her listening patiently to his small son telling her that one day when he was all grown up he was going to be a train driver.

The doctor hid a smile. He could remember when he was a little boy he'd said the same thing to his mother.

Only Florence wasn't Timmy's mother. She was going to marry Edward. His grip on the sofa arm tightened.

She looked pretty in her blue velvet dress and a surge of regret shot through him. He told himself that he was a fool. She was not free, he must remember that.

* * * *

They spent a pleasant hour, talking and laughing together all through breakfast. Florrie couldn't help feeling a little envious of the woman who would be sitting in the seat opposite the doctor next Christmas.

At the end of the meal Mr Harper carried his sleepy son upstairs for a long nap before friends and family arrived for Christmas dinner.

Back on the landing Florrie turned to face her employer.

"I hope you don't mind me going out for a couple of hours, sir. I want to go to the Christmas morning service with a friend."

"You don't need my permission, Sister, today is a holiday," he said, his voice suddenly cool. It was as if all his warmth at breakfast had been for Timmy's benefit.

She nodded, lowering her gaze, so he wouldn't see the hurt in her blue eyes. Once in her room she put on her coat, scarf and hat.

"Well, that will teach you to let your guard down, my girl," she told her reflection.

* * * *

Dale had watched her until she'd reached the stairs. The temptation to follow her upstairs and apologise for his bad behaviour was almost irresistible. She was going to meet Edward, he was sure.

This is ridiculous, he thought. She deserves a happy future – but he couldn't see Edward giving her that. The man had already broken her heart once. Dale was sure he would do it again.

It hadn't passed his notice that Florence had been helping to organise the family Christmas dinner. It had been impossible for his parents to have it at their home this year after his father's accident. She would be a perfect wife for any man. He was in no doubt that she would be a wonderful mother.

He had to stop thinking about her. She would never look at him in the way he needed her to, he finally admitted to himself. Besides, she had never shown any interest in him.

But that didn't explain why she had kissed him back. He headed across the hall to his study, determined to put Florence from his thoughts.

Ten minutes later, he still hadn't succeeded.

Under The Mistletoe

SARAH was waiting for Florrie outside the hospital. The long walk to meet her friend had been helpful in that it gave her time to think clearly. She loved the father as much as the son, but her time with them was growing short, so she was determined enjoy the remainder of her time with both of them, however hard that might be.

"It was so good of you to come with me today," her friend said, as they headed for the church.

"I'm afraid I'll have to leave straight after the service," Florence said, linking her arm through her friend's.

Thankfully Sarah didn't mention Mr Harper. Florrie didn't want to discuss the doctor today. Her feelings were too raw. Even the mention of his name could turn her into a watering pot.

Even worse, it might cause her to confide the truth to her friend how she really felt about the doctor.

The service was beautiful, but Florrie couldn't help wishing that Timmy and her boss were here to share it with her, despite his earlier coolness. The church looked so festive with its boughs of holly and little lighted candles. After the service she said her goodbyes to Sarah before heading back to the house.

She wasn't looking forward to the dinner party. Today she was sure to meet the doctor's intended.

On her return she'd sneaked up the back stairs and removed her coat and hat, before combing her hair, applying a touch of lipstick and a dusting of powder.

"That will have to do," she told her reflection.

She could hear voices in the drawing-room as she approached the open door. She braced herself when she entered the room which was bustling with guests. Florrie felt suddenly shy. Mr Harper senior was sitting on the sofa with Timmy.

The doctor was standing by the fireplace talking to his mother. But there was no sign of the woman she had seen in the car. Florence let out a breath she hadn't known she'd been holding.

"Dale told us you went to the morning service," Mrs Harper said, giving her a warm smile. "Was the service good?"

"Yes, it was lovely," Florrie answered, returning her smile, ignoring the doctor who was frowning at her.

"Now, you must come and meet the family. Timmy has been telling us about his Christmas wish."

An hour later, Florence had been introduced to

two elder sisters and a younger brother who was just starting medical school, as well as a number of uncles, aunts, cousins and a crowd of adorable nephews and nieces whose names she would never remember. But she found them all friendly.

By the time they all went into dinner the doctor's intended still hadn't arrived. Halfway through the Christmas pudding, Mr Dobbs came to tell the doctor there was a phone call for him in his study.

As Florence was seated closest to the door, she couldn't help hearing Mr Dobbs whisper as they went out that it was a young lady caller and she sounded upset.

When he returned the doctor was looking rather solemn. Florrie couldn't help wondering if it was because his intended hadn't been able to make it. Then she reminded herself that it was none of her business.

She looked down the table and as she met his eyes, her heart thumped. Unconsciously she touched her mouth, where his lips had touched. The space between them seemed to shrink, as people and sounds faded. It was as if they were in their own world. She never wanted the moment to end.

Then someone laughed, reality crashed back and the spell was broken.

After dinner everyone moved to the drawing-room where the Christmas tree was lit in all its splendour. Florrie sat beside Timmy, his grandmother and Mr Harper senior on the sofa. All the rest of the family were scattered around on the various chairs, with the children kneeling or sitting on the floor.

Once everyone was seated, Dale Harper handed out the presents. By the time he had finished, everyone had a small mound of presents, including Florrie.

The children opened their presents first, with a little help from the adults. Florrie was pleased when Timmy opened hers first.

He thanked her with a kiss.

After the children had opened their gifts, the adults began unwrapping theirs.

Florence opened her aunt's gift first. Inside was a pretty beaded black evening purse. Then she opened the one from her cousin and family. Inside the layers of tissue paper was a white cashmere knitted jumper, just what she needed. Next she opened Jenny's. Encased in shiny paper was a darling blue woollen scarf. Then Tom and Sarah's – a book of poems.

"Open mine next, I got Daddy to get it," Timmy chirped. "I paid for it with my own pocket money and I wrapped it myself," he added proudly.

Inside were white handkerchiefs, with a delicate lace trim, with the letter "F" embroidered on each corner.

"They are perfect! Thank you," Florrie

whispered, her eyes blurring with tears as she kissed his small cheek.

The doctor's parents had brought her a large bottle of rose scent and the Dobbses had given her a mother-of-pearl comb which she instantly loved.

She still had one parcel to open. She picked up the expensive-looking box tied with yellow ribbons. She untied the ribbons with nervous fingers.

She lifted the lid and inside was a fur hat, the kind she'd seen in fashionable boutiques when she'd been out window-shopping. The kind she'd always admired, but never expected to get. On top was a card with the giver's name.

She couldn't accept it, it was far too expensive. She was about to say so, when she looked up and caught the doctor's expression. He was frowning as if he'd read her thoughts. She decided to tell him later when all his family had left.

"Oh, what a darling hat! How clever of you, Dale," Mrs Harper said, glancing down at the card.

"Wasn't I, Mother. But I wonder if Sister Fairchild thinks so?"

He had put her in an intolerable position. If she refused the hat now, Mrs Harper would think she was ungrateful.

So she swallowed her pride.

"It's wonderful. Thank you, sir," she answered

through stiff lips.

"You must try it on and show me how it looks before I leave, dear," Mrs Harper said.

Much later, when most of the family had gone, Florence went upstairs with the doctor's mother, to try the fur hat in front of the wardrobe mirror.

"It's perfect on you, my dear," Mr Harper's mother declared, smiling. "You mustn't mind Dale buying it for you. Men rarely think about the price when giving gifts." She paused for a moment. "His father was the same at that age – impulsive. Now take off your hat, come downstairs and wave us off."

So Mrs Harper hadn't missed the tension between her and the doctor? The more she got to know her employer's mother, the more she liked her.

While the doctor was helping his father into the car, Mrs Harper had kissed Florrie's cheek and hugged her.

"You are just what both my boys need," the doctor's mother whispered, before hurrying to the car.

Except I'm not the girl your son loves, Florence thought sadly. Soon he will marry and Timmy will have a new mother. The thought was more than she could bear.

She stood on the step waving his parents goodbye until the car was lost from view, tears blurring her vision. Determined not to let Dale see her tears, she blinked them away.

The doctor followed her inside. At the stairs she turned to face him.

"Thank you for my gifts," she said, lowering her gaze.

"Thank you for my notebook, it is just what I wanted."

"Goodnight, sir,"she mumbled as she moved to go upstairs. But something made her turn back to face him and suddenly they were kissing. It was as if his kiss had transported her to another world, a world where everything was possible, where he would love her as much as she loved him.

However much she wanted to stay in that world, she knew she couldn't. He was in love with someone else.

"Don't, please. We shouldn't be kissing; this has to stop now."

"It is customary to kiss under the mistletoe, is it not, Sister?" He smiled. "Look up, there's a bunch hanging right above our heads."

She could no longer hold back the tears that had been waiting to fall. He'd been laughing at her. Except she hadn't heard him laughing.

Long after she had gone to bed, the feel of his kiss still lingered on her lips. Tomorrow while Timmy was taking his nap, she would speak to the doctor about leaving.

Sealed With A Kiss

THE following morning, as promised, Florence walked into Mr Harper's study, not waiting for permission.

The doctor was sitting behind his desk, head bent, studying a report on his desk. Her resolve weakened. She was about to turn and go without speaking to him, but before she could move he looked up.

"Good morning, Sister, can I help you?"

She raised her chin and the words sprang out in a rush.

"As Timmy is well on the road to recovery, with your permission I'd like to return to the hospital as soon as possible, sir."

For a moment, she thought he wasn't going to answer her.

"If that is what you want, I shall arrange it. Though it would be better for Timmy if you left after New Year's Day, which will give him time to adjust to you going."

She stared at the snow falling outside the window. She could hardly see it through her tears. She didn't want to leave, but she couldn't tell him that.

He was getting married. She didn't want to be here in the house when he brought his new bride home. No, it was better she leave, for everyone's sake. It would be a fresh start for all of them.

Of course the doctor's new wife would love the adorable little boy upstairs. Timmy in time would grow to love her, too. It was for the best. So why did it hurt so much?

"Very well, sir, if you think that is best," she said, thankful that her voice didn't wobble.

"I have to go into the hospital for a few hours but I should be back in time for tea," he said. "It is a tradition that we have high tea in the dining-room on Boxing Day. I hope you will join Timmy and me?"

"Of course, sir."

Florence couldn't help wondering why the doctor's future bride wasn't going to join them, though if she was being truthful she was glad. It meant that for today, she would have them to herself and nobody could ever take that away from her.

* * * *

New Year's Eve arrived as if on wings. She would be returning to the hospital the day after tomorrow. Florrie sighed as she headed downstairs to the kitchen to make Timmy a hot drink. She was passing the phone when it rang.

"Miss Fairchild," the doctor said, a hint of surprise in his tone.

"Mrs Dobbs has gone down to the shops. Can I take a message, sir?" Florrie asked, thankful that he couldn't see the blush on her cheeks.

"Thank you. Can you tell her that I'll be bringing a few friends home this evening for a late buffet supper to celebrate the New Year in with – of course you and Jenny are invited."

Florence's heart sank. She knew who one of those friends would be – the woman he was going to marry. She'd told herself that she was being foolish to be jealous, but sometimes the heart rules the head.

"Of course, sir."

When Mrs Dobbs returned, Florence gave her the message.

"It's a bit short notice, but I'm sure I'll manage," the housekeeper said, unruffled as usual, "though I'll have to nip back down to the shops."

"I can do that for you," Florrie offered.

"That's good of you, miss." The housekeeper beamed. "You're a life saver."

Ten minutes later Florrie was heading for the shops, with Mrs Dobbs's list of items.

When she returned to the house, she helped to prepare finger food and later Jenny joined her to give her a hand. Timmy helped by folding some of the napkins.

By the time the doctor arrived home, everything was cooked and ready for his guests.

Afterwards Florrie went off to bathe and

change. She had thought of bowing out of the party, but that would raise questions she didn't want to answer.

* * * *

The doctor looked more distinguished than ever in a white evening suit. He hadn't noticed her join the party as his back was towards her.

Then he turned and their eyes locked. Florrie wished herself back upstairs safe in her room.

Panicked, she turned, bumping into one of the senior surgeons she'd met at the hospital.

"Sorry!" She gasped.

"No problem, Sister, no damage done," he said. "Good party, don't you think?"

"Yes," she agreed, wishing she could make her escape. She saw Tom and Sarah arrive and wished they would join her but they got waylaid by a crowd by the door.

"I heard you were working here, Sister," her companion was saying. "Shame about the boy catching polio, though according to Harper the child is well on the mend because of your great nursing."

Her heart swelled in her chest. Obviously the doctor had spoken well of her.

That was when she glanced across the room. The woman she'd seen in the car with Dale that day was standing near the garden door. She was talking to one of the doctor's relations, who

Florrie had been introduced to at Christmas.

She was standing far too close to the handsome young man and the way she was looking up at him was more than a little flirtatious. Thankfully the doctor was fully occupied in a discussion with Matron.

* * * *

Dale couldn't stop himself glancing across the room at Florence. She looked just as stunning in the blue velvet dress. What was he going to do without her when she left?

He was brought back to the conversation by Matron's hearty laugh.

"I don't blame you, Dale," Matron said, indicating towards Florrie. "Sister Fairchild is very lovely. Shame about her getting jilted like that, practically at the altar. It was supposed to be a secret, but of course the Matron at her last hospital asked me to keep a motherly eye on her."

He knew the man had broken her heart. He hadn't known Edward had practically left her standing at the altar, for another woman! Hope surged through him. He had to make her see sense before Edward broke her heart again.

Dale began to hope. After all, she had responded to his kisses. Maybe in time she could come to love him as well.

"Excuse me, Matron," he said abruptly, "I

need to talk to someone."

"Goodness, was it something I said?" She smiled to herself, waving to Florrie across the room.

Florrie smiled and waved back.

"You didn't tell me Edward jilted you," Dale whispered, leaning in close.

"I didn't think it was a requirement of the job."

Her fingers tightened around her champagne glass, her heart beating in her chest as she strived to think of something more to say. But before she could say anything, he continued.

"You can't trust him, you must know that?"

"You'll have to excuse me, I have a thundering headache," she stammered. If she stayed she'd probably blurt out the truth – that she didn't love Edward. She loved him.

She put her glass down on the nearest table. Pushing past him, she fled upstairs to her room. She knew only one thing, she had to leave now, instead of waiting until the morning. She couldn't stay now.

Florrie buried her face in her hands. There was no alternative. She could slip out though the kitchen.

Dale would be relieved she had gone. Soon he would bring his new bride home to live and Timmy would have a new mother.

There was a tap on the door but before she could say, "Come in", the door opened and the doctor stepped into the room.

"Florence, why did you run away?" he asked, crossing the room in two strides and sitting down beside her. "If I upset you I'm truly sorry. I had no right to quiz you about Edward."

"I should have told you. You're been very kind to me," she said, thankful that her voice didn't tremble.

She bowed her head, not wanting him to read the truth in her eyes, that she never wanted to leave him, ever. If fate had been a little kinder she never would.

He pulled her close then lowered his mouth, covering hers. She responded to his kiss with all her being. His touch sparked the flame of her love for him. She wound her arms around his neck. Immediately the kiss grew in intensity, until they were clinging to each other.

"You are amazing," Dale murmured against her hair.

She gave a gasp as reality punctured her bubble of happiness. What had she been thinking? She had been so carried away by her emotions.

She looked at him face to face.

"You've driven all common sense out of my head," she blurted out, pulling out of his embrace.

He opened and shut his mouth, as if he was going to say something. Then he stood up, walked to the door, then turned around.

"I can see that you are upset. We will talk again in the morning. Goodnight, Florence."

It was only when he'd gone, she realised he'd called her by her Christian name. She moved around her room like a machine, packing her things in her case, not really seeing the jumble she was making of it through her haze of tears.

"It's for the best," she mumbled as she went to collect her toiletries from the bathroom, putting them into her small vanity case. She would ask Mrs Dobbs to send the rest of her things on tomorrow. Lastly she brushed her hair and powdered her nose before going along the hallway to Timmy's room.

He was asleep. She bent and planted a kiss on his cheek, not wishing to wake him.

"Look after your daddy, Timmy," she whispered. "I shall miss you more than you will ever know." Then she left as quietly as she had come in.

Back in her room she collected her case, tiptoed back downstairs, heart hammering, in case anyone came out of the drawing-room. She headed down to the kitchen. Thankfully Mrs Dobbs wasn't there; she must be upstairs serving. Florrie slipped out of the basement door, headed up the back steps to the street and began her long walk towards the hospital.

The desire to return to the house was so strong, she quickened her step.

She decided to ring from the hospital, not

wanting anyone to worry when they found she was gone in the morning.

She would sleep in her flat at the hospital tonight, and catch the six o'clock train early tomorrow to Haslemere for a few days. She didn't have to be on duty until the fourth of January.

The housekeeper answered the phone when she called.

"Will you please tell Mr Harper that I was called away," Florrie said, crossing her fingers at the lie. "So I decided to leave tonight," she added, crossing her fingers again. She liked the friendly housekeeper and didn't like lying to her.

"Off course, Sister, but I can easily fetch him and you can tell him yourself."

"No, don't disturb him now, please," Florrie said, heart pounding now. "I don't want to take him away from his guests."

"All right, if you think so. I'm off to my sister's now so I'll tell him tomorrow morning."

"Thank you," Florrie said, her pulse rate slowing as she replaced the receiver before ringing Aunt Beverly.

"Is everything all right, dear?" her aunt said, concern ringing in her voice.

"Nothing's wrong, darling," Florrie reassured her aunt, amazed at how calm she sounded herself. "I finished the job earlier than expected and thought I'd come down early tomorrow for a short visit, if that's OK."

Florrie had been back on duty for several hours when she heard the office door open but she didn't look round. She didn't want to talk to anyone at the moment.

She heard footsteps cross the room and her heart slumped. She would have to turn round and deal with the situation, whatever it was. She straightened her back, but before she'd moved even an inch she felt firm hands on her shoulders holding her. She sank back against his chest.

"I had to come," he said, his voice deep. "If you send me away, I don't know what I shall do."

She could not believe what she was hearing, yet now he was turning her around to face him, drawing her close against him.

"Why did you pretend you were going to marry Edward? If Sarah hadn't let slip the truth, at the party . . . " he said, hurrying on. "Don't blame her. I practically forced the truth out of her when I found out you'd gone. Why did you leave without even saying goodbye to Timmy?"

"You're getting married soon."

His olive green eyes searched hers.

"Where on earth did you get such an idea?"

She couldn't tell him it was his mother who had broken the news. So not wanting to get that dear lady into trouble, she confessed.

"I heard you making wedding plans on the telephone." She hurried on before she lost her

nerve. "And once I saw you driving past with a beautiful woman sitting beside you in the car. I saw her again at your New Year's party."
Though she didn't add that the lady hadn't been behaving like someone who was about to get engaged.

"So you added one to two and came up with four," he whispered. "Dare I hope you were a little bit jealous, my darling?"

"Yes," she answered honestly, her heart singing. He'd called her his darling!

"Though that doesn't explain why you thought I was getting married. I only talked about you to my father, but I never mentioned you by name. So how could –?" He smiled then, as if he'd just worked out the answer to a riddle.

"Father must have told Mother. I should have realised you were protecting her confidence." He tilted up her chin and smiled down at her. "The girl you saw me with in the car was my cousin Jane, who's been suffering from severe morning sickness. She is happily married to my cousin, an officer in the Queen's guards. Don't you know that I love you, Florence?"

She couldn't believe what she was hearing.

"I . . . I thought you could never love me," she whispered, her blue eyes searching his.

"I thought you must have known how I felt, my darling girl."

"I didn't, but I do now," she replied, pressing her face against his heart, her own heart full

of thankfulness.

"So do you think you could come to love me, as much as I love you?" he said, holding her tighter if that was possible, as if he'd never let her go whatever her answer. Florrie loved him more for that.

"I don't have to think about loving you, Dale. I love you already."

He kissed her then, showing her more than words could ever say.

"I'm not letting you out of my sight, my girl," he said, several kisses later. "You are coming home with me. We'll get a special licence. Mrs Dobbs can be your chaperone again."

"You haven't actually proposed," she said, unable to stop herself from teasing him.

"Oh, heavens, I haven't, have I?"

Then before she realised what he was going to do, he bent down on one knee and took her hand in his.

"Miss Fairchild, will you do me the honour of becoming my wife?"

"Yes, yes, you foolish man, now stand up before one of my nurses comes in and sees you kneeling down and faints."

"I know what will make her faint." He smiled, standing up, before he crushed his mouth over hers.

"Promise that you will never leave me, my love."

"I will never leave you – ever," she promised,

stretching up and pressing her lips against his.

She knew he would never love her the way he had loved Anna. She knew she would have to live with that. Together they had created a beautiful little boy and Florrie was thankful for that.

Many kisses later there was something she had to tell him.

"I thought I loved Edward, but I never knew what love truly was until I fell in love with you. I expect, knowing Edward, he kept his intended in the dark about trying to win me back."

A bark of laughter erupted from Dale, the like of which she had never heard before, but she hoped to hear it again and again all through their life together.

Back at the house in Wimpole Street later that evening in the drawing-room, Dale handed Florrie her sherry before sitting down beside her on the sofa.

They had told Timmy their news first, then rung his parents, after which her aunt who promised to pass on the news to her cousin and his family. After dinner they told Mr and Mrs Dobbs and finally Jenny. Everyone had congratulated them.

"Now it is my turn for confession, my darling," he said, smiling down at her. Florrie hadn't missed the trace of pain in his green eyes.

"I met my wife when I was stationed in a French military hospital." He paused for a moment before continuing. Each word seemed an effort. "She was engaged to a Dutchman. Then the news came that Hans had been killed in the Atlantic.

"I was with Anna when she found out that she was pregnant with Hans's child. I had always loved her from the first moment she came to nurse at the military hospital. I offered to marry her. It took some persuading on my part to get her to agree.

"We never lived as husband and wife, but I hoped after the baby was born she would come to love me. A few days after Timmy's birth she walked out of the hospital. She got knocked down by a speeding driver while crossing the road. I felt my pushing her into marriage so soon caused her to panic and run away. If I hadn't, she might be alive today."

"You don't have to tell me all this."

"I have to, my darling girl. I know now that her death wasn't my fault. Fate has its own plans for all of us."

"I am sure in time Anna would have grown to love you as much as Timmy does."

"Anna left this note in her locker at the hospital for me," he continued, setting his glass down on the table before pulling a paper from his pocket and handing it to her.

She put her own glass down and opened the folded paper.

I need time to think; please take care of my

son, he needs you.

"I thought when I lost Anna I would never love anyone ever again. Then you stumbled into my life and everything changed. I know now that what I felt for my wife was special, but it was nothing compared to what I feel for you, Florence.

"I know, if I should ever lose you, my heart will never recover. You are the other half of me. You were born to be mine," he whispered.

ale moved across to a side-table and pulled out the drawer. He took out a box and flipped open the lid. Inside was the most beautiful blue gem Florrie had ever seen.

"It was my grandmother's," Dale said. "The colour of the stone reminded me of your eyes when I first met you. I hope you like it?" he asked anxiously. "If you don't like blue we can always go out tomorrow and get a new ring."

"It's perfect," she said and meant it, admiring the blue stone ring, surrounded by a circle of diamonds.

She held out her left hand for him to put it on. She looked down at her hand and knew that she would cherish it for always, just as his grandmother had done.

"Till death us do part," he whispered, sealing the promise with a kiss that held such love, passion and the promise of a happy future.

A Place In Their Hearts

HAPPY New Year, wife," Dale said, brushing his lips softly over hers.

"Happy New Year, my love," she returned, gazing up at him with all the love she felt for her wonderful husband.

She still couldn't believe he loved her. Even after nine glorious years of marriage she couldn't believe how blessed she was.

When the twins were born, two years after they married, Florence felt her life with Dale, Timmy, Rose and Mary was complete.

Then, five years later, her family had grown with the birth of their son Andrew, now aged two and seven months, the pet of all the family.

On Christmas Day, after they had all finished opening all the presents, she had told them all that they were going to have another little brother or sister.

"We want a sister!" the girls chorused.

"Brother!" Andrew cried. Which made everyone laugh except Timmy, Florence noticed.

For the rest of that day he'd been unusually quiet. After she'd tucked the smaller ones up in bed and read them stories, she went along to Timmy's room.

He was a handsome young man. The limp was

not noticeable, unless one knew it was there, or if he was tired. He was reading a book when she entered his bedroom.

She moved across the room and sat down on the bed beside him, tousling his hair, though he was almost a young man now.

"Are you pleased about the baby, Timmy?"

"Of course I'm pleased, Mother."

Her heart swelled. From the day she had married his father all those years ago, he had called her "mother".

She loved that he did, for she couldn't have loved him more, even if she hadn't given birth to him. He was her first child and always would be.

"So why so quiet at dinner?" she asked.

"It doesn't matter; I'm just being silly," he replied, scraping his hand through his thick hair, reminding her so much of his father.

"Come on, give me a clue."

"It's just, what with Rose, Mary, Andrew and now a new baby coming, you might not have enough room for me here when I come home from college," he announced.

Florrie had gathered him in her arms.

"Even when you're a grown man and married with a family of your own, there will always be a place here for you and yours. You must know that."

"I guess I do," he said, grinning now. "I was just being a bit sensitive."

"Anyway, how would I control your brother and sisters if I didn't have their big brother to keep them in check? Don't think you're getting out of helping me with this one," she'd told him, patting her tummy.

That was a week ago, it was a few minutes into the New Year, they were toasting it in with champagne. The children were all asleep upstairs and Timmy had been invited to a party with friends.

"Did I tell you how much I love you, Mrs Harper?"

"Yes, every day since we married."

"To all our Christmases and New Years to come, my darling," he whispered, chinking his champagne glass against hers.

"To all our for evers," she whispered back, giggling as she took a sip of her drink, and the bubbles tickled her nose.

Much later, Florence watched her Dale sleeping. She knew she must have done something good to have been given such a wonderful husband. Also to have been blessed with such wonderful children.

She patted her stomach gently.

"That's your daddy, and your brothers and sisters can't wait to meet you."

The End.

A CHRISTMAS CONSPIRACY

by Kate Finnemore

Love-struck

WOW," Grace breathed, as she caught tantalising glimpses between the trees of the Château Beauvallon, their destination for the week ahead.

She didn't like to voice her excitement, in case she distracted her sister Natasha who sat hunched over the steering wheel, driving in second gear along the narrow country lane.

The motorways and main roads had been

cleared of snow, but here it lay on the ground still, compacted and glistening, as treacherous as an ice-rink. The snow-filled ditches on each side were an additional potential hazard.

Natasha darted her sister the briefest of looks.

"Not far now, thank goodness."

So she, too, had glimpsed the château.

"Just in time for mid-morning coffee," Grace said. She saw her sister glance down at the phone that lay between them by the handbrake. The sat nav app was running. "Keep your eyes on the road, Nat," she warned gently.

She looked out again at the winter-white forest that stretched away on both sides. A thick dusting of frost covered the dark trunks and leafless branches that stood motionless in the still air as if frozen.

Beyond the trees on her left, she could see the creamy white walls of the château, a tower with battlements at its top, pointed Gothic windows and gently arching Romanesque ones.

Delight brought a smile to her face. The architecture was haphazard, quirky, a wonderful mish-mash of styles. She was going to enjoy it here, she thought.

And that was when it happened. Natasha's phone pinged. For a split second, they both looked down at it. The car tyres lost traction and the car skidded slowly over the icy surface.

In an instant, Grace reached across to the steering wheel to turn the vehicle into the skid.

It helped, but not enough. The car glided a few metres more before the driver's side rear wheel slid down into the ditch.

For a long moment, the two sisters could only sit there. Grace's heart was beating an uneasy rhythm. Her sister's, too, she guessed, judging by the look of shock in her eyes. The car was at an angle, sloping downwards to the ditch.

"The perfect way," Natasha said with heavy irony, "to start our Christmas break."

"At least we're not hurt." Reaching behind her, Grace took the two hi-viz vests from under the pile of clothes, each garment protected by polythene, laid out on the back seat.

There were more in the boot, Grace knew, carefully wrapped in tissue paper and stored in boxes. She handed one of the vests to her sister.

"Put this on," she said, pulling her own on over her padded jacket.

"Good old Grace," Natasha said with a laugh. "As practical as ever."

Grace laughed, too, relieved that the look of shock had left her sister's face.

"One of us has to be. Stay here a moment. I'll see how close to the edge you are." It was strange pushing up against the weight of the car door to open it and when she did, icy air hit her face.

She scrambled outside, letting the door slam shut behind her, and made her way gingerly round the front of the car, glad she was wearing sensible fleece-lined boots with ridged soles. She reached the driver's side, and the breath stopped in her throat.

Three of the four wheels were safely on the ground. But the fourth hung as if suspended in empty space. Any hope she might have had of stuffing grass and twigs under it to give it purchase before driving off again vanished on the spot. They'd have to call out a breakdown truck. And with their limited French that wouldn't be easy.

At her nod, Natasha opened the driver's side door and eased herself out. She stood on the narrowing wedge of ground between the front of the car and the ditch, puffing out a breath as she looked at the rear wheel.

"Your French is better than mine," she said. "How about you phone a garage and get them to send someone out? I'll call the breakdown insurance guys."

"I'd better put the warning triangle out first," Grace said, edging back round the front of the car.

"Take care, Gracie."

Grace took the light plastic triangle out of the boot and carried it back the way they'd come. She walked on the grass verge between the road and the ditch where the snow was fluffy still, and not at all slippery, counting her paces. The triangle had to be about 30 metres, or 60 steps, away from the car.

Taking her phone out of her jeans pocket as she hurried along, she started to look for the nearest garage. She could hear a car approaching, saw it in the distance coming towards her, and broke into a jog.

The driver had seen her. He slowed, coming to a halt a metre or so from where she'd set the warning triangle down. The car's dove grey paintwork had been dulled by the ice and snow that had splashed up from the road. Even so, it was an impressive vehicle, a low, sleek sports car with smoked glass windows and an engine that growled.

The engine fell silent. Grace watched, a polite smile on her face, as the car door opened and its occupant got out.

But I know that face, she thought. I know this man. A jolt of recognition sped through her; puzzlement, too, for the barest fraction of a second. And then she placed him, and her heart swept into a crazy rhythm. No, not a personal acquaintance, but someone known to countless millions of music fans in the UK. In Europe, too. And in the US, of course.

Her gaze went from his dark hair to those arching eyebrows over beautiful eyes, to the strong line of his jaw, to the long leather coat he wore – and all at once it was as if ten years had been lopped off her age and she was a love-struck, hero-worshipping teenager rather than a mature young woman.

Singer-songwriter sensation Kai Curtis was coming towards her, moving with easy long-legged grace. In moments, she'd be within touching distance. He'd say something to her, he was bound to. And she'd say something back. Just him and her, talking together. She'd be the envy of all her friends.

She smiled, more a smile to herself than a greeting to the new arrival. She was being ridiculous, she had to pull herself together.

"Thank you for stopping, Mr – uh – Curtis," she said, pleased that she sounded her usual sensible self.

His answering smile was brief and meaningless.

"It's the law. I had no choice."

She blinked, taken aback. His words had been curt to the point of rudeness.

"Oh," she said stiffly.

He looked beyond her to her sister's car.

"You skidded?"

"Yes." Natasha had come round the car and was leaning against the passenger-side door, phone to her ear. She was "wearing the product" as she put it, and looked stunning, as always, today in a full-length coat of palest blue with a matching Dr-Zhivago-style hat.

"Who's that? A friend?"

"My sister." She too could be monosyllabic, she thought grimly, aware she was reacting badly to the admiration she'd heard in his voice.

There were purplish smudges beneath his eyes, she saw with some concern, and he hadn't shaved that morning. Had he been driving all night, she wondered, in these difficult conditions?

"Are you both OK?" he asked.

"Yes, thanks, we're fine. But I need to phone for a breakdown truck to get the car out of the ditch."

"No need," he surprised her by saying. He reached into his coat pocket and fetched out a phone. "I'll get one of the neighbours to bring his tractor out."

"One of the neighbours?"

Something like irritation flashed into his eyes.

"Forget I said that." Turning partly away, he opened his phone and was soon speaking into it in fluent French.

Of course he was annoyed, she thought, hugging her arms across her chest and stamping up and down on the spot to stop the cold seeping into her bones. Annoyed with himself. He'd let slip information that he was no doubt usually careful to keep private.

Kai Curtis snapped his phone shut.

"Jérôme will be here in a few minutes. So let's get over to your car. Hop in."

He gestured to his own car and stayed close to her as she made her way round to the passenger side – to catch her if she slipped?

He was an odd mix, she decided. His attitude

was just – only just – the right side of rudeness, a vivid contrast to the thoughtfulness he'd also revealed.

He opened the door for her. As she got in, she glimpsed a guitar in its case on the back seat behind her. Kai Curtis's famous 12-string guitar, she thought, and her pulses leaped as she recalled his latest hit, a powerful haunting lament to a lost love.

Moments later, Kai was sitting in the driver's seat. But he didn't start the car straight away.

"You know who I am," he said, turning to look at her. "But please don't ask me for a selfie. Or an autograph."

Grace frowned, noting the tiredness in that famous voice and the pallor of his face. It was warm in the car, and the scent of leather upholstery and the smoky notes of his aftershave filled the air.

"I wasn't going to. Though my sister might. She's been to quite a few of your concerts."

"My concerts." The look on his face was bleak. "Yeah." Abruptly he turned to face forward, turned the key and brought the engine to growling life.

He drove with confidence, she noted, as he came to a smooth halt a metre or so behind Grace and Natasha's car.

"I got through to the breakdown . . . " Natasha stopped in mid-sentence, eyes widening as she saw who was getting out of the driver's side of the sports car.

"Mr Curtis lives round here. He's arranged for someone to come with their tractor to get us out of the ditch." Quickly Grace filled her sister in on what was happening.

Turning to Kai, Natasha beamed him a smile.

"You live round here? You're a neighbour of Angela's? Wow, she never said."

"You know Angela?"

"Angela Beauvallon de Mottefort. Yes. She owns the château over there," Natasha said, pointing. "She's invited Grace and me to stay for Christmas."

"You're guests of Angela's?"

Only one word could describe the look on his face, Grace thought. Appalled. And it wasn't the cold that sent a shiver of unease down her spine. There was something here she didn't understand.

She heard him swear under his breath, and he turned away, pushing his fingers through his hair in a gesture that spoke of immense weariness.

"That's all I need," he muttered.

Close To You

A ROOK cawed high in the trees, loud in the silence. The occasional snowflake drifted downwards, soundlessly, and Grace looked up at the blanket of white cloud covering the sky. It was going to snow again.

Putting his phone to his ear, Kai Curtis headed a few metres down the road.

Grace looked at her sister.

"I can't believe it," she whispered. "Kai Curtis."

Glancing up from the screen of her phone, Natasha rolled her eyes.

"Thanks for the info, " she whispered back. "I'd never have recognised him."

Grace felt herself flush.

"You're not wearing the hi-vis vest," she retorted.

"Neither is Kai."

Grace looked across at him. He was speaking low into the phone. She couldn't hear what he was saying, but his tone and the movements of his free hand were unmistakably angry.

"No surprise there," she said. "He's built his reputation on breaking every rule in the book."

Standing beside her sister, she watched in

silence as he swung round, flipping his phone shut, and made his way back to them.

A flurry of wind brought a swirl of snowflakes with it, but that didn't explain the shiver that sped down her spine as he came to a halt less than a metre from her. His expression was grim.

"I've just been on the phone to my mother. Since she's invited you to the château for the Christmas . . . "

"Your mother?" Grace cut in. "Angela is your mother?"

A curt nod.

"One of you is a dress designer. You, I imagine," he said to Natasha.

"That's right," she acknowledged with a smile.

"You've come a day ahead of the others," he stated, "to get things ready for a fashion show."

"Right again."

Grace saw him close his eyes for a brief second, and it was another glimpse of the tiredness she'd seen earlier. No, not tiredness – weariness, a bone-weariness that went well beyond mere tiredness.

"Look," she said, "we don't want to be a nuisance. We don't have to stay at the château. We can find a B and B somewhere. We don't have to do a fashion show, even."

Natasha shot her a look.

"Hey . . . "

Kai shook his head.

"It's my mother's house. She's free to invite whoever she wants. Plus it's started snowing again. I couldn't in all conscience send you away."

He drew in a long breath, looking in the direction Grace and Natasha had been travelling as the low rumble of something large and heavy coming towards them made itself heard.

"If anyone goes, it'll be me," he went on, watching the tractor as it stopped a short distance away. "But the place is big enough for all of us. We should be able to keep out of each other's way."

Grace pulled a laughing face at her sister, the antagonism of a few moments before forgotten. For sheer ungraciousness, his last words surely took the prize.

Jérôme, the tractor driver, jumped down from his vehicle. It was clear the two men knew each other well. With much laughter, he pulled Kai into a hug before coming over to shake hands with Grace and Natasha.

Getting back into his tractor, he turned it round and reversed up to Natasha's car. In no time at all, he and Kai had unreeled the cable from the back of the tractor, attached it to fixing points and pulled the car out of the ditch.

"Wow, they've made it look so easy," Natasha said.

"*Merci. Merci beaucoup,*" Grace said, dredging up her schoolgirl French as Jérôme wrapped her hands in both his for another handshake. "Kai, could you thank him for us, please? We're so grateful. Grateful and relieved."

There followed an exchange in rapid French between the two men and more laughter before Jérôme clapped Kai on the back and walked back to his tractor. The snow was falling faster now, settling on the vehicles and on everyone's clothes.

"It's not far to the château, a couple of hundred metres, but will you be all right?" Kai asked, touching his hand to Natasha's sleeve.

There it was, Grace thought, that touch, a fraction longer than was necessary. Emotion tugged inside her.

Natasha smiled.

"We'll be fine."

"I'll be following, if anything happens. Get back in the car now and wait for me. I'm going to fetch your warning triangle."

The two sisters sat in the car in silence. Natasha was looking at the screen of her phone while Grace kept her eyes on the wing mirror, following Kai's progress back up the road.

The direction her thoughts had taken disturbed her. Natasha was stunning to look at. It was only natural that people admired her. Normally, Grace took it in her stride. She didn't mind. So why did she now react with – what? envy? jealousy? – at the way Kai Curtis's hand had lingered on her sister's sleeve?

The small convoy set off, the tractor in front, followed by Natasha driving once again with fierce concentration, with Kai in his sports car bringing up the rear.

Grace sat taut and alert, willing her sister on. They were travelling through a monochrome world, the dark trunks and branches of the trees, all straight lines and sharp angles, veiled by the gently falling snowflakes. So beautiful – but dangerous, too.

The lane grew narrower still as it veered sharply to the left. A short while later, to Grace's relief, they came to the gatehouse that marked the entrance to the Château Beauvallon.

Jérôme and his tractor left them at that point, continuing on while Natasha and Grace, and Kai behind them, turned into the drive, the trees that lined each side marking the way.

Natasha slowed as they reached the turning circle in front of the château. Its façade rose before them, tall and imposing. Two flights of stairs in an elongated S-shape, one the mirror image of the other, curved up to the ornately carved entrance doors. At one corner stood a circular tower that was almost as high as the ridge of the château roof.

"What a fabulous place," Grace breathed.

Kai eased his car past theirs, indicating they should follow him round to the other side of the château, the side they hadn't seen from the road. The high double doors of one of the outbuildings stood open, and Natasha followed Kai inside.

"Well done," Grace said when Natasha finally turned the car engine off.

Natasha puffed out a breath and laughed, visibly relaxing.

"I'm glad that's over."

They were in a vast high space, Grace saw, getting out. It must once have been a barn. Now it housed cars – four, including theirs, with room for two or three more.

At the far end were several curious-looking tractors, perched too high, surely, on their axles. Something to do with wine-making, perhaps. The Château Beauvallon was famous for its wines.

Kai was pushing one of the tall wooden doors shut, and Grace crossed swiftly to do the same to the other one.

"Someone keeps the hinges well-oiled," she said with a smile as the two doors met in the middle. Snowflakes, blown in from outside, had landed on Kai's hair, and she had to resist the urge to brush them away.

"My stepfather," he said. "You can't fault his efficiency."

A strange turn of phrase? Grace wondered, implying as it did that something else could be faulted. Or was it Kai's tiredness speaking? The purplish smudges under his eyes were more pronounced than ever.

"My mother's waiting in the kitchen," he went on. "I'll take you through to her."

"I'm looking forward to it. I've never met her, but Natasha's told me lots about her."

He glanced behind him.

"She and your sister have a lot in common."

Grace too looked across to where Natasha, tall and slender, superbly graceful in the coat and hat she'd designed and made herself, leaned back against the car, head bent as she looked down at the phone in her hand.

Again, Grace felt that twist of emotion – envy? – deep inside her.

"Well, that's good," she murmured, looking away.

They didn't need to go back out into the snow. She and Natasha each took their suitcase out of the boot – they'd come back later for the clothes for the fashion show – and, with all three wheeling their cases behind them, they followed Kai to a door at the rear of the barn which led to an enclosed walkway.

"Purpose-built," he said, and about 30 metres and two 90-degree turns further on, he spoke again. "Here we are. Mind your heads."

It was a low, wide, dark oak door studded with nails. Hanging from it was a bright, welcoming Christmas wreath, sprigs of pine needles, glossy green holly leaves and ruby red berries, tied with a red and green tartan bow.

Standing back to let the two sisters go first, Kai stretched out his arm to push the door open.

Grace stood with Natasha by her side on the threshold of the kitchen. Warmth billowed out, enveloping her, and with it the fragrant scents of coffee percolating and sweet pastries fresh from the oven.

She took in the large room with its high ceiling crossed by smoke-blackened beams, the walls of natural stone, the long table that filled the centre of the room, the bowls of fruit and candles in silver candlesticks.

But what caught and held her attention was the woman who stood by the fireplace on the opposite side of the room. Tall and striking in silk pyjamas that Grace recognised as one of her sister's designs, she had her face in profile as she gazed up at something on her left.

Grace smiled to herself. Angela Beauvallon de Mottefort must have heard the door opening. But she stayed, as immobile as a statue, for just a fraction of a second before turning her head to greet her guests.

"Natasha, darling! How lovely to see you!" She wore some kind of turban on her head, in an orange fabric a few shades darker than her fringed 1920s bob. The long scarf that hung from it swung with the movement of her head, emphasising her cheekbones and sculptured jawline.

She stepped away from the fireplace, and the

purple and orange silk of her pyjamas seemed to flow and swirl as she moved. With a laugh, Natasha came away from the door and into the room, skirting the table to reach her hostess.

Grace felt Kai's hand at the small of her back, and he gave her a gentle push into the room, taking her away from the door which he closed behind him.

"Angela!" Swept into an embrace, Natasha kissed the older woman on both cheeks. "It's great to be here. Thank you so much for inviting us. And you look marvellous. That hat is perfect with the pyjama suit. Where did you find it?"

Angela touched her hand to the back of her head.

"Paris. A simply fabulous little boutique off the Champs Elysées. Jane and Carla won't shop anywhere else. Jane Birkin, Carla Bruni," she explained airily, looking across at Grace who stood near the door.

Kai was behind her, close though not touching, but she imagined she could still feel the imprint of his hand on her back through her padded jacket.

"Hi, I'm Natasha's sister. Grace." She stepped forward, holding out her hand, and found she too was swept into an embrace and kissed on both cheeks.

"Ye-es," Angela said, holding Grace away and looking from her to Natasha and back again. "I think I can see a slight family resemblance.

Though you really are as different as chalk and cheese." She laughed. "Never mind. It's lovely to have you here with us, darling! Oh, and Kai darling!"

Letting go of Grace, she held out her arms and he stepped forward, wrapping his mother in a tight embrace.

"You're looking good," he said when he finally released her. "Everything OK?"

"Yes. You're looking tired, Kai." There was concern in her eyes.

"Where's Vespasien?"

"Angela's husband?" Grace mouthed, looking at her sister. Natasha nodded.

"He'll be in the wine cellars," Angela was saying.

"OK. I'll say bonjour later. I'm going to crash for a couple of hours."

"I'm so sorry, darling. You sounded so angry with me when you phoned when you were rescuing our two damsels in distress here . . . "

He shrugged.

"I'd been hoping for a quiet time over Christmas, that's all."

"I thought you wouldn't mind a few guests. Johnno and Barbs will be arriving this afternoon – weather permitting! Oh – and Cameron, of course."

"Johnno and Barbs? Great," Kai said, his tone devoid of all enthusiasm. "I'll stay to say hello to Cameron. After that, I'm off."

"No, Kai, you . . . "

But his expression was grim, Grace saw, and vying with the weariness that she sensed like a weight across his shoulders. He was clearly in no mood for discussion.

She wanted to murmur something soothing, give his hand a quick, comforting squeeze perhaps, but instead she watched in silence as he crossed to the door the three of them had come in by, grasped the handle of his case and wheeled it over to a door on the other side of the room. There he turned and looked from his mother to Natasha to Grace.

"Goodbye, ladies. I'll see you at lunch."

He left, closing the door behind him, and for a moment there was silence in the kitchen.

"Well," Angela said brightly, beaming a smile. "You two won't need to carry your cases up. I've hired an aged retainer for the Christmas period. He'll do it."

"An aged retainer?" It was such a delightfully quaint expression. Grace found she was laughing – with Angela, not at her, and wondered if that was what Angela had intended.

Angela was narcissistic and snobbish, but she knew it and could laugh at herself for it. It was impossible not to like someone who could do that, Grace realised.

"So, darlings," Angela said, "why don't we sit down and have coffee and croissants, and you and I, Natasha, can run through the arrangements for the fashion show tomorrow."

The aged retainer was called Pierre and had an unlit roll-up stuck to his upper lip. His face, tanned and lined by a life spent outdoors, put him at somewhere between sixty and eighty.

He lifted their cases, one in each of his large countryman's hands, as if they weighed no more than a couple of chickens and took Grace and Natasha through to the entrance hall with its wide, polished stone staircase. A tall Christmas tree, decorated with gold bows and soft-glowing lights, stood at its foot.

The hall was vast and stretched up to the second floor. A stairwell on a grand scale, Grace decided, delighted to see the paintings – portraits of ancestors mainly – that lined the walls.

"No dawdling over the pictures," Natasha said as they followed Pierre up the stairs.

Grace laughed.

"Another time," she warned.

Their rooms were on the second floor, facing west, next to each other with just a bathroom between them which they would share.

"What a view," Grace breathed, crossing to the window of her sister's room and looking out.

The snow was still falling, and everything looked smooth, white, untouched – the park that stretched before them, the forest they'd driven through that Grace could see to her right, the gentle slopes of the hills on her left.

"Just think – Kai Curtis in the same house as us," Natasha said. She'd put her suitcase on the bed and was taking her clothes out and arranging them carefully in the wardrobe. "I can't believe Angela never said he was her son. Clever her, though, for telling us to bring just one present each. I mean, what would you get for someone like Kai Curtis?"

"Hmm, yes," Grace murmured, her mind elsewhere. She'd been given the brief "art collector, early fifties". Johnno or Barbs, she now surmised. She'd found a signed limited-edition print by a contemporary artist that would, she hoped, be just right.

"Hey," Natasha said. "Which room's his, do you reckon? The room next door maybe," she suggested, a hint of mischief in her tone, "or the one next door to yours. What do you think?"

For a long moment, Grace couldn't respond. She stayed where she was by the window, gazing out, seeing nothing. The strong lines of Kai's face, the sheer physical presence of the man and, too, the weariness she'd glimpsed in him – all were so vivid in her mind.

So many things about him drew her to him in a way she'd never been drawn to a man before.

But she recalled the way he'd looked at her sister – her stunning sister – and knew he'd never be interested in her, Grace.

Expelling her breath on a shaky sigh, she found her voice at last.

"Let's not talk about him," she said, turning away from the window. "I'm going to unpack." And she left, before the puzzled look that crossed Natasha's face could turn itself into a question.

As pre-arranged with Angela, at 12.30 they made their way downstairs for lunch. Reaching the first floor, Grace glanced to her left and saw Kai turn a corner and come towards them, and the breath caught in her throat.

He moved with an easy stride and looked wonderful, tall and lean in a dark grey shirt open at the neck and trousers the same colour belted low at the waist. He hadn't shaved, and a day's growth of beard shadowed his jaw. As he drew near, she breathed in the smoky notes of his cologne.

"You're looking good," she said with a smile. "Refreshed."

"I am." He smiled back.

She glanced at her sister, relieved to see Natasha's concentration was fixed on the sketchpad she held.

"There you are, darlings." It was Angela, waiting at the foot of the stairs on the ground floor. "All three of you, good. We're eating in the dining-room. Come and meet Vespasien, my husband."

Natasha fell in with Angela while Grace and Kai followed behind. Although no doubt he'd have preferred to be with Natasha, she thought unhappily.

"Your mother's got some marvellous paintings," she said, her gaze skimming portraits and landscapes as they walked along together.

"Actually, it's my stepfather who's the collector, not my mother."

"Vespasien's family," Angela put in, glancing behind her at the two of them, "have been collecting great works of art for centuries."

"Look, a Monet," Grace said, pointing. "An early Monet. Oh, and a Renoir. I love the Impressionists."

"You certainly know your stuff," Kai said.

"Yes, I . . . Oh." A painting half hidden by a vase of flowers had caught her eye. She stopped and leaned across the small table the vase stood on in order to have a closer look at it. "It's signed 'Sisley 67'. 1867, of course. But there's something about the brushstrokes . . . " She frowned, voice trailing away.

"How clever of you to spot it, darling." Angela had doubled back. Natasha stood just behind her. "I sent it away to be restored, and . . . "

"Restored?" Natasha cut in. "Oh, Grace could have done it for you."

"Grace? I don't understand."

"It's my job," Grace said, conscious of Kai's

unsmiling gaze on her face. "I restore paintings for a living."

  She found herself frowning again as the four of them moved off, heading towards the dining-room. She'd hardly expected a gushing "Oh, how exciting, darling!" But Angela's "Oh. Yes. I wish I'd known" seemed strangely out of character. Far too low-key.

Winter Wonderland

SEATED at the head of the table, Vespasien Beauvallon de Mottefort rose to his feet as Grace and her sister, and Kai and his mother entered the dining-room.

An Irish setter, its fur a rich dark red, lay stretched out on its side in front of the wide hearth where a log fire burned. It too jumped to its feet, long feathery tail swishing a heartfelt greeting.

"Loki, *assis*, sit."

Kai's stepfather was tall, good-looking, and impeccably groomed, his style of dress as unique in its way as his wife's – waistcoat and plus-fours in dark brown corduroy, a soft linen shirt buttoned up to the neck, no tie.

Brown and white two-tone brogues over knee-high socks completed the outfit. His hair was cut short and held no trace of grey though he had to be in his fifties or early sixties.

The total effect was original and, yes, very French, Grace decided.

He shook her hand, then Natasha's, with an *"Enchanté, mademoiselle,"* each time.

"Come and sit down. Make yourselves at home. Do." He spoke English with a charming accent.

He turned to look at his stepson.

"No time to shave, Kai?" he murmured.

His tone was one of mild enquiry, but Grace saw Angela, walking down to the other end of the table, pause for the briefest of moments.

Kai smiled.

"That's right," he replied in an equally mild tone.

Angela continued on to the end of the table. They all took their places, and Grace wondered if she'd been mistaken. Perhaps that moment of tension had never occurred.

A tree, smaller than the one in the hall, stood in one corner. Decorated with pomanders and slices of dried fruit, it filled the room with the scents of pine, oranges, and cloves.

Lunch was a light meal – soup with yeasty homemade bread warm from the oven, followed by a colourful selection of satsumas, kakis and lychees, bright pink in their shell-like skins – all of it washed down with a bottle of Château Beauvallon red.

"Two thousand and five vintage," Vespasien said, raising his glass. "One of the best years ever."

Conversation was lively, and there was much laughter. Sitting opposite Kai, Grace found her gaze drawn to him time after time. She could watch his mobile features for ever, she thought, loving the way his mouth broadened into a grin, eyes crinkling at the corners, when he laughed.

For the time being at least he looked relaxed, the weight of weariness gone from his shoulders, and she was happy for him.

Every now and then his eyes met hers, and her breath would catch. It was as if they were in a world of their own, a special world for just the two of them.

But those moments were short, and Grace knew they didn't mean anything.

"It's not usually like this, darlings," Angela was saying. "I do most of the cooking round here when there's just the two of us. But with a houseful of guests over Christmas . . . " She swept the long trailing scarf of her turban over her shoulder.

"She has hired Pierre's wife, daughter and grandson to cook and serve the meals," Vespasien said. Something in his tone belied his neutral expression.

"Vespasien still hasn't forgiven me for being so extravagant. Have you, darling?"

Her husband shot her a look and didn't reply. Loki growled in his sleep, tail giving the floor one single thump.

"I know," Angela trilled brightly into the awkward silence. "Why don't you show our guests round the wine cellars this afternoon? Later on, when Johnno and Barbs get here."

Kai swore under his breath.

"Count me out," he said, scraping his chair back across the tiled floor and standing up.

"You could do a wine-tasting, Vespi." Angela turned to Grace and Natasha. "What do you say, girls?"

Grace looked at her sister and nodded.

"That would be lovely."

Vespasien too stood up.

"And I'll be delighted to show you how we make our wine here. Shall we say four o'clock?"

* * * *

"Magical." Closing the huge wooden entrance door behind her, Grace stood for a moment at the top of the double flight of steps that led up to it and took several long deep breaths.

It had stopped snowing, and the air was cold but still. The afternoon sun shone low in the sapphire sky, casting long shadows and glinting off ice crystals in the snow.

There was indeed a fairy-tale sense of magic in the scene before her, Grace thought.

She was alone. Angela had announced at the end of lunch that she and Vespasien were going to have their usual short siesta.

Grace and her sister, helped by the aged retainer Pierre and his daughter Séverine, had carried the clothes for the fashion show along to a room off the grand salon. The two of them had then spent some time in Grace's room sending messages to their parents and friends.

"Best not to say anything about Kai Curtis

being here," Grace had cautioned.

"Shame," her sister retorted with a laugh. "We're sitting on the scoop of the century."

Shortly afterwards, tired after the drive in difficult conditions, Natasha had gone to have a lie down in her room.

Grace had thought of asking Kai if he'd like to accompany her on a walk. But, aware she might be motivated by more than a simple wish for his company, she'd shied away from the idea. Besides, she hadn't known where to find him.

Someone had cleared the steps. Grace ran lightly down them before striking out to her right where the snow lay smooth and pristine.

She walked parallel to the front of the château, smiling at the various sets of bird tracks she saw. Once, she caught sight of something larger, the hooves of a deer perhaps, or a boar. She didn't see a single human footprint, though. She could have been the only person in the whole of France.

She rounded the corner of the château – and stopped dead in her tracks.

Kai. Some ten metres away, his tall dark silhouette a sharp contrast to the white of the snow. He had his back to her, the binoculars he was holding to his eyes trained on the forest they'd driven through earlier that day. The trees came close to the château at this point.

He must have heard her or seen her out of the corner of his eye. Abruptly, he lowered the binoculars, twisting round to look at her.

A look of irritation flashed across his face.

"Are you following me?"

"Of course not." Grace bristled at the unfairness of the accusation. Looking beyond him, she saw a trail of footprints in the snow. He must have let himself out through the kitchen and come round the back of the château. "If I'd known you were here," she said icily, "and didn't want company – I'd have gone in the opposite direction."

For a long moment, he didn't react. His eyes stayed on her, his expression hard, unyielding. Then she saw the tension ease from his shoulders. His mouth sketched a bleak smile.

"I'm sorry. There was no call for me to speak to you like that." He drew in a breath. "Come and see what I've been looking at."

"Oh." Intrigued, Grace crossed the few metres between them. His fingers brushed hers as he handed her the binoculars and, even though he, like her, wore leather gloves, she found her heart skittering into a fast, insistent beat.

She could smell his cologne, and the leather of his coat, mingling with the scent of woodsmoke in the air. He was too close, she thought, stepping back a pace.

"Where do I look?"

"Over there, at the base of the treeline. You see the tree that's fallen over? OK, left a bit. Slowly. You'll see a gap. Stop there."

Following Kai's instructions, Grace looked through the binoculars at the gap in the trees. At first she could make nothing out, but when she did, her mouth formed an "Oh" of wonder.

"Oh, wow. I can see deer. Three of them. Their eyes, their faces." She gave a little laugh of delight. "They're looking back at me."

"Keeping a wary eye on you," Kai corrected, and she could hear laughter in his voice. "On you and me both."

Grace lowered the binoculars and turned to look at him. His face had a healthier colour than before, and his stance was relaxed. Yes, relaxed and happy.

"You love it here in France at the château, don't you?" she said.

"It's one of the few places I can be myself."

"Yes. I can understand that," she said, and there was a breathlessness in her voice. Here was a man rather more complex than the bad-boy portrayed in the tabloids, she thought.

"You top the charts time after time. Every song's a number one hit. But fame and success aren't all they're cracked up to be, I guess."

She saw him tense, eyes narrowing as he looked at her face. As though suspecting mockery, perhaps. Then his shoulders eased, and she knew what he'd seen in her expression had reassured him. He'd accepted her words at face value.

"You're right. They're not," he said, his tone

telling her to drop the subject. He gestured towards the trees. "Walk with me."

They moved off, side by side, heading at an angle towards the treeline. That way, Grace supposed, they wouldn't disturb the deer they'd seen. It was several degrees colder here, in the shadow cast by the trees, and her breath – and Kai's – hovered white in the still air. The snow scrunched beneath her boots.

She tried to imagine what it was like to be as famous as Kai Curtis. People must recognise him wherever he went. At the shops, the cinema, if he went out for a meal – all the things she, Grace, and everyone else took for granted would have ceased to hold any pleasure for him.

Screaming fans would come running up to him, clamouring for a selfie. Or he'd have to dodge the paparazzi eager to catch him out at an unguarded moment.

No doubt he'd loved every minute of it when he first became famous – travelling the world, living a life of luxury, pursued by adoring fans. But even adulation, she decided, must become tiresome after a while.

She must have made a sound, some tiny inward pitying sound, for he looked sharply at her.

"What is it?"

"The paparazzi. I've just realised, there aren't any paparazzi here at the château. They don't know where you are, do they?"

"No-one does. Not even my manager."

"You've escaped." It wasn't a question.

"I had to."

How long, Grace wondered, and her heart was full of sadness for him. How long before someone rang the château to see if he was there? How many days of freedom would he manage to grab before then?

They came to the treeline and took a narrow, gently twisting path, barely discernible beneath the snow. A blackbird called in alarm as it swooped low past them. A few metres further on, Kai pointed to the ground.

"Deer."

Grace looked down to see hoof-prints, each one like two long thin parallel ovals, some partly covering others, cutting across from one side of their path to the other.

"Can you tell how many?"

Smiling, Kai shook his head.

About to move off again, he put out his arm, staying her. A tension about him told her to say nothing. She looked where he was looking – and her heart stilled for an instant.

It was a squirrel, no more than five metres away. A red squirrel, she realised, though its coat had a greyish tinge to it. Smaller than the greys she was used to back home, the animal sat on its haunches at the base of a tree, nibbling at the nut it held between its front paws.

Grace stood stock-still, hardly daring to breathe, her whole being caught up in the wonder of the moment. The squirrel's tail was all fluffed up, and its ears were long and tufty, just like those of squirrels in the picture books she'd read as a child. She'd never seen such a beautiful animal.

All at once it stopped eating. Ears perked, it remained motionless for a fraction of a second before dropping the nut, twisting round and darting up the tree, all in one swift, nimble movement.

Grace watched until it was out of sight before turning to Kai. A broad smile, she was sure, lit her whole face.

"That was amazing. He was just so cute!"

"You sound like a two-year-old, not a twenty-something." But he too was smiling, and Grace knew the comment wasn't meant unkindly.

"They don't hibernate?"

He shook his head.

"No, not in this part of France."

As of one accord, they moved off again, following the path as it curved round to the right, heading back to the château.

"So you restore paintings for a living," Kai said.

"That's right. I work for a smallish firm just outside London, and I love it," she said, conscious her face was lighting up as it always did when she spoke about her job.

"Go on."

"I love art – full stop," she said with a laugh. "But I love the variety, too. I could be cleaning years and years of grime off a painting, or re-varnishing it, or repairing and re-gilding a frame. There are never two weeks the same."

"I imagine you have to be well qualified to do the job."

She shrugged.

"I've got a degree in art history and a master's in art conservation."

An eyebrow went up.

"Impressive. Tell me," he went on, "what was it about the Sisley painting that worried you?"

"The Sisley painting?" she echoed, playing for time. It wasn't the abrupt switch that now disconcerted her. No, it was something about his tone. All at once she was seized with the notion that this was why he'd asked her to walk with him.

"Yes," he said. "I saw your face when you first spotted it. Something wasn't quite right."

"Well, yes. It's been restored, but rather unevenly." Grace paused an instant, gathering her thoughts. "In his early work, Sisley tended to favour dark, sombre colours – drab olives, greys and browns. But the restorer seems to have overpainted in places, adding a green that's just a shade too bright."

"Do restorers normally do that? Overpaint? Would you do that?"

"Not unless I had to. And there's another thing . . . the brushstrokes. Nice soft brushstrokes, giving a lovely misty feel to the trees. But the lane – it almost looks as if it was painted a decade or so later."

"The restorer painting over the original again?"

"Must be." She drew in a breath before continuing. "I think very few people would have been able to spot the things that weren't quite right. It takes a trained eye."

"Like yours."

"Yes."

The path had brought them close to the edge of the trees. Grace could see the snow-covered expanse of the château park and, beyond, the creamy-coloured walls of the château itself.

They'd almost reached the open ground when Kai stopped and turned to face her, catching her gloved hand in his.

"I want to thank you," he said, "for not asking too many questions."

Her heart gave a painful thump. How she longed to reach up and touch her fingertips to his beard-shadowed jaw.

"While answering all yours," she said with a smile. The breathlessness was back in her voice.

"Yes." His gaze held hers, and when he drew her closer and bent to touch his lips to hers in the lightest of kisses, it seemed the most natural thing in the world.

Stab Of Envy

ALL pedigree dogs born in 2015," Vespasien Beauvallon de Mottefort was saying in his near-perfect English, "have names beginning with L."

It was just past four, and the three of them – Kai's stepfather, Grace and Natasha – were heading for the wine cellars and the promised wine-tasting. Johnno and Barbs had phoned to say problems with their hire car meant they'd be delayed.

"So a dog born in 2016 . . . " Grace said, "will have a name beginning with M."

"Exactly."

They were in the walkway that led from the kitchen to the barn where the cars were housed. Loki trotted along beside his master, the long silky fur of his tail sweeping happily from side to side.

Vespasien opened the door to the barn and stood back to usher the two sisters through. He gestured across to the far end of the building.

"You see those tractors over there? Narrow, with the operator's cab high up off the ground? Well, they're specially designed so that the wheels go either side of a single row of vines."

"Ah, yes," Natasha said. "Grace thought they were something to do with wine-making."

"*Très bien*." Vespasien beamed at the two sisters. "Follow me, please." He crossed to the huge wooden doors they'd driven in through that morning. The doors she'd helped Kai close, Grace thought, the image of him with snowflakes in his hair uncomfortably vivid in her mind.

A normal-sized door had been built in to the right-hand door. Vespasien unbolted it, and the three of them stepped through and set off in the direction of a large building on the other side of the courtyard.

Loki bounded away, running ahead, circling back, running off again, clearly loving being out in the snow.

The sun had sunk below the treeline and Grace shivered in the cold, glad of the padded jacket she wore over her thick sweater and jeans – glad, too, of her fleece-lined ankle boots which made walking through snow relatively easy.

She saw her sister, stunning as always in her full-length coat, Dr Zhivago-style hat and high-heeled boots place each footstep with care.

"Are you OK?" she asked, concern in her voice.

Natasha shot her a tight smile.

"Fine, thanks."

Like the barn that served as a garage, the wine cellars had tall wooden doors with a smaller door set into the right-hand one. Vespasien took a key out of the pocket of the camel-coloured overcoat he wore, unlocked the door and ushered them inside. A heady mix of alcohol and grape juice assailed Grace's nostrils.

"We're using the back way in," Vespasien said. "That way, you can see the process, how the wine is made, from start to finish, and we'll end up in my office where you can taste some of the wines. How does that sound?"

"Perfect," Natasha said. "It sounds perfect."

"So, the grapes come in here, and first they're sorted in this machine here." He indicated a wide stainless-steel contraption, shiny and gleamingly clean in the harsh electric light, as indeed was everything else Grace could see around her.

Loki had stayed outside, rooting around in the snow. No doubt he was forbidden to come inside the cellars.

"And last year's vintage is maturing in these vats," Vespasien was saying. It was half an hour or so later, and they were nearing the end of their tour and now stood in front of huge stainless-steel containers, each twice as tall as a man.

"All the time the wine is in these vats, it's improving in quality and flavour. We'll bottle it at the end of the winter."

It had been no surprise that Vespasien Beauvallon de Mottefort was a knowledgeable guide, and normally Grace enjoyed and appreciated listening to an expert in any particular field.

But this afternoon was different. It was lucky her sister had asked lots of questions because Grace had remained largely silent, her mind drifting constantly to thoughts of Kai.

What was he doing now, she wondered. After that kiss that was no kiss, he'd held her hand a moment longer as he drew away from her. And there'd been something strange about the way he'd looked at her. As though all at once he was seeing her in a different light.

As they headed towards the château, she'd thrown his question back at him.

"So what is it about the Sisley painting that worries you?"

He didn't answer straight away.

"I wish I knew," he'd said at last. He let her in through a door that opened on to the rear of the entrance hall. "Maybe I'll see you at dinner," he said, and she watched him walk away with that easy stride of his, then take the stairs two by two.

Before going upstairs herself, she'd made for the corridor that led to the dining-room to check that her first impressions of the Sisley were correct. But the painting had gone.

And that was odd, she thought now, coming back to the present with a jolt to see Natasha disappear through a door. Vespasien stood by the doorway, obviously waiting for Grace to follow.

His office was both a workroom and a showcase. A bar counter ran the length of the wall on Grace's left. Bottles of wine, grouped in threes or fives, were displayed at intervals along it.

At the far end, she could see the door by which people who only wanted to taste or buy wine would come in. On her right was the business side of the room – a desk and office chair, a laptop and printer, papers and other documents neatly stacked.

Grace wandered round, captivated by the displays on the walls – photos of a proud, smiling Vespasien being handed a cup or a medal, certificates in frames showing the awards Château Beauvallon wines had received, old black and white photos revealing the clothes and equipment of yesteryear.

"Fascinating," she murmured. Natasha, she saw, had taken out her sketchpad and pencil.

At the desk, a pile of wine bottle labels caught her eye. She picked them up. The name – Château Beauvallon – together with the pen-and-ink drawing of part of the château's façade and the year – 2005 – were self-explanatory. But Grace's schoolgirl French could make little sense of the rest. She looked round.

"Vespasien . . . "

He was standing behind the bar counter, a bottle in one hand, corkscrew in the other, intent on his task. He looked up, and something close to anger darkened his face.

"Put those labels down."

Grace recoiled as if stung. Natasha, startled, glanced up from her sketchpad and looked with wide eyes from Grace to Vespasien.

"I'm sorry," he said, coming round from behind the counter, "I didn't mean to be so abrupt." Swiftly crossing the room, he took the labels from her, opened a drawer in the desk and slipped them inside. "We have to keep the labels as good as new. We try not to handle them too much."

"I'm the one who should apologise," Grace said, her pulse slowing to its usual rhythm, "but I was just wondering if you could explain the wording on a label?"

"Yes, of course. But first I'll teach you how to taste wine."

How? Intrigued, Grace moved with him over to the bar counter and Natasha, and watched as he pulled the cork on a bottle of Château Beauvallon red and poured the wine into three long-stemmed glasses. He handed the sisters a glass each.

"Raise the glass," he said, following his own instructions, "and look at the colour. Is it a good, rich colour? In this case, yes – of course," he added with a smile. "Now, bring the glass to your nose and inhale. What can you smell?"

Silence. She'd never thought about it before, she realised. What could she smell?

"Fruit. I can smell fruit."

"Good. And is your mouth starting to water?"
Both sisters nodded.

"Now take some wine. Don't swallow it. Keep it in your mouth and chew it, as if you're chewing an apple or a peach. Like this."

Natasha giggled. Grace giggled, too. It was crazy – she was rolling a mouthful of wine over her tongue and round her teeth, making the sort of unladylike slurping noises children might make to annoy their parents.

"Swallow just a little at a time," Vespasien instructed, "and breathe as you swallow. Take your time."

And it was working. There was an intensity of flavour in her mouth that she'd never experienced before, Grace thought, pleasantly surprised.

"We'll taste this one next," Vespasien continued in his lightly accented English. "A 2016 white."

In the end, Grace and Natasha ordered a case of red and one of white which they'd share between them when they returned home.

Night had fallen by the time the two of them made their way up the steps to the château's main entrance. Vespasien wasn't with them. He was taking Loki for a walk.

Apart from that odd little hiccup over the labels, Grace reflected, it had all been very enjoyable and they'd learned a lot. For some reason, though, she was uneasy. Something was niggling away at the back of her brain. Something about the missing Sisley?

* * * *

"You look lovely, Grace. You really do." Natasha's tone was reassuring and clearly sincere. She stood behind and a little to one side of her sister, both of them studying Grace's reflection in the full-length mirror in her room.

Grace had put on one of her sister's clever designs. It looked like a dress but was in fact two pieces – a skirt and a long-sleeved boat-necked top – both made from the same soft, free-flowing fabric.

"You're like me," Natasha said. "With your hair and complexion you can wear strong colours. That deep pinky-red, yes, it looks good on you. Don't forget to do lots of swirls," she added, mischief in her tone.

They were dressing for dinner which, they'd been told before they came over to France, was always a formal affair when there were guests.

Natasha looked, as always, beautiful in a knee-length fitted dress in a black and white leopard print.

Grace flipped her phone open, saw the time, and drew in a long breath.

"Let's head on down."

Why was she so nervous, she asked herself as

they made their way along the corridor and down the stairs. Then she recalled the way Kai had joined them earlier as they went down to lunch, and it occurred to her that that was why – she wanted him to notice her, and the sheer stupidity of the notion was frightening. For why would he notice her when her beautiful sister was close by?

"This way, darlings. We're having apéritifs in the petit salon first. Come and meet Johnno and Barbs."

Angela had stayed with her 1920s theme, Grace saw. Tonight she wore feathers in her hair and long strings of pearls over a black and cream mid-calf-length dress. Lipstick and nail varnish matched her hair.

Vespasien, in a nut brown three-piece suit and bright yellow bow-tie, looked understated by comparison.

The petit salon was warm and softly lit. The metre-length logs that burned in the wide fireplace were more for atmosphere than effect, Grace had discovered, glad of the efficient heating system that kept the château snug and dry. Displays of creamy-white mistletoe, glossy holly berries and golden rosehips added to the festive Christmas atmosphere.

"I dabble in antiques. And fine art. Based in Brighton. Wintersley's. You might have heard of me," Johnno Wintersley said airily, no doubt expecting the answer "Ah, yes".

He'd given Grace and her sister a kiss, French-style, on both cheeks even though he'd never met either of them before, and had now somehow managed to corral the two of them into one corner of the room.

His expensive aftershave failed to disguise the odour of cigarettes that clung to his clothes, and Grace couldn't help hoping he'd disappear some time soon to have a smoke. Now she understood why Kai had been so dismayed on hearing Johnno Wintersley would be staying at the château.

"Excuse me," she said, "Angela needs our help."

"Does she? I can't see her," Johnno said, clearly puzzled.

Ignoring him, Grace took Natasha's hand and the two of them slipped away past him.

"Naughty," Natasha chided, laughing.

"I couldn't stand the man a moment longer." Grace sucked in a shaky breath. Kai wasn't there and she was hard put to hide her disappointment. The room seemed empty without him.

Angela came in carrying a tray of tall narrow glasses.

"Kir royale, darlings. Help yourselves. And take one to Barbs over there, will you?"

Grace lifted two of the glasses from the tray. The wine they contained was suffused with a soft pink blush. Streams of tiny bubbles shot to the surface. She brought one of the glasses to her nose.

"I can smell raspberries."

Angela beamed at her.

"Spot on! Sparkling wine and raspberry liqueur. Delicious."

Barbs Wintersley, thankfully, was a complete contrast to her husband.

"Angela and I were at school together. Best friends. So of course we've known each other for years. She says you're a brilliant dress designer, Natasha. . . "

With that, the two women fell into a happy discussion of the dress Natasha was wearing, the outfit Grace was wearing and the colours that would suit Barbs.

Grace sipped her kir, smiled a lot, did a twirl when asked, but her mind was elsewhere. What was Kai doing? Was he happy – or deeply unhappy, pacing up and down or pounding the walls with frustration because guests had invaded the place where he found sanctuary?

Something, some sixth sense perhaps, made her glance across the room – and there he was, standing in the doorway, and her breath caught in her throat.

He'd dressed for the occasion and looked magnificent in black jacket and trousers, bright white shirt and black bow-tie. The shadow of beard had gone, accentuating the sculptured quality of the strong lines of his face.

He was looking at her, the hint of a smile curving his lips. But his gaze flicked to Natasha and on to Barbs, and Grace realised with a pang that it was pure coincidence. He'd happened to have been looking at her at the same instant she'd glanced over at the door.

With an inaudible sigh, she turned her attention back to Natasha and Barbs, watching from the corner of her eye as Kai crossed the room to join Vespasien and Loki by the fireplace.

Shortly afterwards, the party moved through double doors into the dining-room. Loki lay down and stretched out in front of the fire while his master took his usual seat at the head of the long rectangular table. Grace was placed on his left, with Barbs opposite her.

Kai sat diagonally opposite – with Natasha talking in a low voice to him on his right, Grace saw, not liking the stab of envy that twisted inside her.

Séverine and another woman brought in the starter – a tangy cream cheese and smoked salmon concoction on a bed of salad leaves – and Vespasien opened a bottle of white wine.

"So where's Cameron, Angie?" Johnno, on Grace's left, said. "I thought he'd be here for Christmas."

"Angela. Call me Angela, please." Kai's mother sat on the other side of Johnno, which meant Grace couldn't see her face. But she heard the sharpness in her tone.

"Kai's brother," Barbs supplied.

"He's in Paris," Vespasien said, pouring himself a glass of wine. "He's got a lady friend there."

There was something odd about the way Kai looked across the table at Angela, and Grace wished she could see the older woman's face. She only heard her words.

"But he'll be here tomorrow. Tomorrow morning, darlings."

"So what have you got planned for us all, Angela?" Barbs asked.

"We-ell, tomorrow afternoon's the fashion show, of course. We'll be doing the final preparations in the morning. Séverine's daughter and two of her friends will be here at ten, Natasha darling. Lovely girls, tall and willowy. No experience of the catwalk but full of enthusiasm."

Vespasien rolled his eyes.

"Sounds horrendous. If you need me tomorrow, I'll be in the wine cellars. All day."

"Think I'll join you, Vesp," Johnno said.

"What can I do to help?" Kai asked in his deep growl of a voice.

"The sound system, Kai darling. The music, the amplifiers . . . things like that."

"Grace can help with that," Natasha put in. "She's the practical one out of us two."

Thanks a bunch, Grace thought, conscious of the colour that swept over her face when Kai turned his head to send her a long look.

"We'll have an early-ish lunch," Angela continued. "Our guests will start arriving about one, and the show will start at two. Pierre's cousin operates the snow plough for the commune. He'll make sure the road's clear."

"Wonderful," Barbs enthused.

Kai and Natasha were deep in conversation, Grace saw, biting her lip.

"Costing me a fortune," Vespasien grumbled, so low Grace suspected she wasn't meant to hear.

Angela went on to detail the programme for the rest of their stay – a murder mystery evening the day after the fashion show, the traditional big meal – the Réveillon – the evening of Christmas Eve, and church followed by a quiet winding-down on Christmas Day itself.

The evening progressed. Grace listened and laughed, she ate the delicious food, drank the delicious wine, joined in all the talk. Time after time, though, she found her gaze drawn across the table to Kai and her sister. Heads close, they were clearly engrossed in each other.

So he found her beautiful, talented sister attractive. What was so surprising about that? Natasha worked hard and had had little time to devote to relationships. But a romance with Kai, even a short-lived fling, might be just what her sister needed.

Think positive thoughts, Grace told herself. But the notion did little to ease her unhappiness.

What's Not To Like?

I'M so nervous," Natasha said, crossing Grace's bedroom and sitting on the edge of her bed. She'd left open the door to the bathroom that separated their two rooms, and light from it spilled into the bedroom.

"Oh Nat, love." Blinking, Grace pushed herself into an upright position. She'd been in that warm, drowsy halfway state, somewhere between being asleep and being awake, and in her sleeping daydream she'd been in Kai's arms. "It'll be fine. You've done fashion shows before."

Natasha's eyes flashed in the yellow light.

"You're always so sensible. So down-to-earth. Yes, I've done fashion shows before. At college. That doesn't stop me being nervous now."

"Hey," Grace said gently, taking both her sister's hands in hers. "Your clothes are fabulous. You're fabulous. The setting for the show is amazing – and you've got a whole load of wealthy women coming here, just itching to spend their money."

Natasha laughed and pulled a rueful face.

"I'm sorry. You're right, and I shouldn't have snapped at you."

Grace was proud of her sister. Natasha worked

hard and deserved every bit of success that came her way. She had a small niche boutique in the Lanes in Brighton that she'd built up from scratch, designing and making gorgeous clothes, especially wedding and evening dresses. Her list of moneyed clients never stopped growing, and her website was flourishing.

Natasha sucked in a breath, then expelled it slowly.

"This could send my career in a whole new direction. If I get lots of orders, I'll need to take on more staff."

"More staff?"

Another laugh, lighter this time.

"OK, staff, full stop." Up till now in her career, she'd had people she could call on at busy times but no-one permanently on her payroll. She grew serious. "And it's not just me. Angela has a lifestyle to keep up. She needs the commission."

"Vespasien muttered something about her extravagance at lunch yesterday, didn't he?" Grace murmured.

"A place like this must cost a fortune to keep going. Maintaining the grounds, keeping the buildings in a good state of repair, redecorating, not to mention the day-to-day bills."

"Yes, but the Château Beauvallon vineyards are the best in the region. They must earn quite a lot from the wine side of things."

Natasha shrugged.

"Maybe. I think Kai's put quite a lot of money into the place," she added after a moment.

"What?" Grace shook her head. "Even if he has, he'd never tell you something like that, surely."

"No. He didn't. But I reckon he helps his mother out financially. On the quiet, though. He probably wouldn't want Vespasien to know." She smiled. "I'm just reading between the lines. Something he said last night."

Last night.

"You and Kai were getting on like a house on fire," Grace said, hard put to hide the envy that swelled her throat. In her dreams, she'd been the one sitting next to him, looking into his eyes, smiling, happy simply because she was with him.

"Grace!" Natasha was staring at her sister, eyes wide with concern. "You twerp," she said, giving Grace's hands a squeeze. "It's not what you're thinking. Why do you think I said you'd help Kai with the music?"

"To point out the contrast between plodding, practical me and wonderful, creative you?" Grace suggested, hating, but unable to prevent, the resentment and cattiness she heard in her voice.

"Idiot. You don't plod." Another squeeze of the hands. "He doesn't fancy me, if that's what you're thinking."

"No?"

"No. Well, maybe he does." Another light laugh. "But last night he talked about his brother, about the music I wanted for the show – and he talked about you," she added, dropping the words in lightly, one by one, a smile on her face.

"Me? What did he say about me?"

Natasha jumped to her feet, letting go Grace's hands. The smile on her face was broader, full of mischief.

"Ask him yourself." She pulled back the duvet. "Come on, get up. It's my big day. We need to shower, get dressed, go downstairs and get busy."

As Natasha disappeared into the bathroom, Grace looked at her phone. Seven thirty. And she found she was humming as she got out of bed, drew back the curtains and opened the shutters, quickly closing the windows when icy air fell into the room, chilling her skin and filling her lungs. It was one of Kai's hits she was humming. Not the latest. The one before that.

Day hadn't yet broken, and the sky was a slate grey starless mass that might or might not presage snow.

Humming still, she looked out over the grounds. Had it snowed again overnight? The trees didn't move. Nothing moved. The scene before her was so smooth and untroubled she could have been looking at a painting.

Yes, she thought, still humming when she and

Natasha ran down the stairs, following the scent of coffee and fresh bread baking as they made for the kitchen and breakfast, Kai had got well and truly under her skin. She was looking forward to the time she'd spend with him, helping him with the sound system. And she might just ask him what he'd said to Natasha about her.

* * * *

The two sisters had just started breakfast when Kai's brother Cameron arrived. From the enclosed walkway outside came the sound of footsteps approaching rapidly, then the low iron-studded door swung open and he ducked his head as he came into the kitchen.

"Brr, it's cold out there," he said, beaming a smile at Grace and Natasha. "Just the two of you here?"

Two or three years younger and not quite so tall, with his dark hair and strong-boned face he was unmistakably Kai's brother. He was dressed as impeccably as his stepfather Vespasien always was, although his style was far more casual – a thick jacket, its wide collar pulled up around his ears, narrow-legged jeans and ankle-high trainers.

"I'm Cameron," he said, pulling off his jacket and throwing it over the back of one of the chairs. "And you're . . . ?"

"Natasha," Grace's sister said, holding out her hand.

"Ah, so you must be Grace."

The way his gaze lingered over her face, as if studying her features, for just a fraction of a second longer than was comfortable, was puzzling – and unnerving.

"I hear you went all woozy over a squirrel," he said.

Woozy? All at once she understood. Hot colour washed over her cheeks. Kai must have phoned or texted his brother about her. What had he said? And why? To poke fun at her?

With an effort she brought a smile to her lips.

"He was very cute."

"The squirrel or my brother?" Cameron laughed. "Hey, don't answer that. So what have we got for breakfast?" he said, sitting down next to Natasha, opposite Grace. "I'm starving."

They passed round flaky, butter-rich croissants, still warm from the oven, homemade apricot jam and creamy unsalted butter while Cameron poured coffee into cups as big as soup bowls.

"No-one else down yet?" he asked, dropping sugar cubes into his coffee.

Grace shook her head.

"We haven't seen anyone."

"Though two people have already had their breakfast," Natasha said, gesturing towards two crumb-covered plates at the far end of the table.

"Hey, great detective work, Natasha,"

Cameron said with a light laugh that robbed the remark of all possible offence. "Let's hope Vespasien's been and gone," he went on. "I spend a lot of time in my studio when I'm here. Avoiding him. Keeping a low profile."

"Studio?" Grace asked. Cameron was fun and made her smile, and she found she was intrigued and wanted to learn more about his relationship with his stepfather. But it seemed safer to stick with the more neutral topic.

"Has no-one told you I'm an artist?" His eyebrows shot up. "I'm amazed. Maybe it's because I'm not much good!"

"Oh, I'm sure . . . ." Natasha began.

"My work's been shown in a couple of galleries in Paris, though," he said, "so it can't be that bad." He paused, eyes narrowing as he looked at Grace. "You've got such a good face, you know. Not classically beautiful. But interesting. With that flawless skin and your striking hair, I can see you in a Rossetti painting."

"Why, thank you."

"Hey, I might have to paint you myself."

Grace laughed.

"I think I might enjoy . . . "

She broke off as the internal door opened. Kai walked in – and her heart skittered into a faster beat. He wore a grey and white striped shirt and dark grey trousers, and looked magnificent. But then did he ever look anything other than magnificent, she asked herself.

"Cameron. Thought I could hear you chattering away. Grace, Natasha," he murmured with a quick nod of greeting as he came away from the door. His brother stood up and moved round the table, and they met in a warm hug. There was clearly a great deal of affection between the two of them.

They drew apart and looked each other up and down.

"You're looking good, Cam."

"Not sure I can say the same about you, mate. You're looking a bit ragged round the edges."

Kai's smile was brief, meaningless.

"It's been tough. My heart's not in it any more."

"But things might be about to change?"

Kai shrugged.

"We'll see. Long journey?" he went on.

"It was OK. All the roads have been cleared."

"Vespasien said you'd been visiting a lady friend in Paris."

A slow grin spread over Cameron's face.

"Did he now?"

There was amusement in Kai's eyes too, Grace saw, and all at once she understood: not a lady friend in Paris. A boyfriend.

She didn't know whether to be pleased or dismayed when Kai sat down beside her, opposite his brother. Passing him the basket of croissants, she breathed in the smoky notes of his cologne and the scent of freshly laundered clothes and watched his fine-boned hands as he poured himself coffee and refilled her cup.

In many respects she was the luckiest woman alive. Millions of fans would give their eye-teeth to be sitting where she was now. But what Cameron had said about the squirrel incident was casting its shadow over her. The notion that Kai might have been laughing about her was almost impossible to bear.

Hearing Natasha ask Cameron a question about Paris, she swallowed.

"I guess I behaved like an idiot yesterday, going all gaga over a squirrel," she said.

"Going all . . . ?" He turned his head and looked at her, and Grace could see the flecks of gold in his brown eyes. "On the contrary," he said. "It was lovely to see your face."

She saw him hesitate, as though deciding whether to continue or not.

"It's something we share," he said, "that sense of wonder at the natural world. Don't ever lose it."

His gaze held hers, Cameron and Natasha's voices faded to a murmur, and for the space of a heartbeat it was as if only he and she existed. The breath caught in her throat, and she wished the moment could go on for ever.

"I won't," she promised.

Less than an hour later, and everyone was gathering in the grand salon, a magnificent room, the size of a small parish hall, and perfect for the fashion show.

The ceiling was high and decorated with intricate plasterwork and paintings of nymphs and goddesses from Greek mythology.

The walls were panelled in eau-de-nil silk that gleamed softly in the light from two huge chandeliers, while the floor was a warm polished oak parquet.

Tall arched windows on two sides let in a pale wintry light, and Grace imagined the curtains, abundant folds of fabric a shade darker than the walls, would be drawn closed for the afternoon's event.

A tall tree, decorated in glowing reds and golds, stood in one corner while long, trailing sprays of pine, holly and rosehips hung from the other three.

Natasha was talking earnestly to Marie-Laure who taught English in the local collège, Grace had learned.

Angela, resplendent in a full-length purple gown and matching turban, together with Vespasien in a Prince-of-Wales-checked three-piece suit, were sitting in armchairs upholstered in pale green silk, placed alongside what would become the catwalk.

Kai and Cameron were deep in conversation by one of the windows. Séverine and three other middle-aged French women stood in a group chatting while their menfolk stood in another group close by. They were all waiting for Pierre and his cousin to arrive.

Barbs would be a guest at the show that afternoon – Johnno, too, in the unlikely event he wanted to be present – so they weren't expected to help with the morning's preparations.

Grace moved across to the wall on her right and tried to study the paintings there. Portraits of ancestors, and well preserved.

Normally she never failed to enjoy studying the details of a painting, the details often brought back to light by the work of restorers such as herself. But today – today it was what Kai had said at the breakfast table that dominated her thoughts: so different in so many ways, yet the two of them had something in common, a passion they shared.

Pierre, unlit roll-up as usual stuck to his upper lip, came in with his cousin, carrying a gilded Louis XIV sofa between them which they deposited next to Angela. The meeting was complete.

Everyone gathered round Natasha. She cleared her throat.

"I'd like to thank you all for coming along to help with the preparations this morning." She paused to allow Marie-Laure to translate. "May I take this opportunity," she continued, "to thank Angela for coming up with the idea of a fashion show here, in this beautiful part of France, and

Vespasien for so kindly agreeing to let us hold it in these splendid surroundings."

A smattering of applause greeted her words. Grace could detect only the barest hint of nerves in Natasha's voice.

"You're doing great, Nat," she muttered to herself, willing her sister on.

"The models will be arriving at ten," Natasha said, "so I'm just going to tell you what's happening because it's important you all know who's doing what."

Grace only half-listened. She already knew her sister's plans for hairstyling, make-up, and the rehearsal scheduled for 11.30. She wasn't sure how it had happened, but Kai was standing next to her, and she was acutely aware of his closeness. She had only to move an inch or so and her arm would brush against his.

"Natasha darling . . . " Angela's imperious tone brought Grace's attention back to the meeting. "My son must sing this afternoon. Just a couple of songs at the start and finish. It would be a total waste to do otherwise." She turned to Kai. "What do you say, darling?"

Grace had heard him swear under his breath, but he nodded.

"Of course. If Natasha would like me to." No doubt he'd seen how Natasha, startled at first, was now beaming a smile of absolute delight.

"Need you ask! But, uh, the music for the show? Grace?"

Grace brought a smile to her face.

"No probs," she said, biting back her disappointment as her dream of spending several hours in Kai's company vanished into the ether. "I can handle the music."

"Maybe Cameron can help you."

"That layabout?" Vespasien, behind her, muttered scornfully, and she recalled Cameron's wish to avoid his stepfather. For good reason, it would seem.

She brought another bright smile to her face.

"It's all right, Nat. I can manage by myself, thanks."

* * * *

Shaking her head, Grace watched Vespasien disappear from view before she turned to Kai. It was some time later, the two of them were in a screened-off section of the grand salon and she couldn't stop the feeling bubbling up inside her that all was right in her world after all.

She stood by a small table on which she'd placed her sister's laptop, and was running through the music Natasha had chosen for the show. To her surprise – and delight – Kai had brought in a chair and his guitar.

"Mind if I join you?"

He now sat less than a metre away, the ankle of one leg resting on the knee of the other as he tuned his guitar.

Beyond the silk-covered screens she could hear the excited chatter of many voices, the scrape of furniture being moved. And Vespasien had just threaded his way between the two screens, carrying the amplifier which he set down on the floor near the socket. She and Kai weren't alone by any means but it didn't matter. She was close to him – that was what mattered.

"Your stepfather doesn't seem to have a very high opinion of Cameron," she said.

Kai glanced up.

"One, he hasn't got a proper job," he said drily. "Two, he doesn't pay anything towards his keep. Three, he's twenty-six but shows no sign of settling down. In short, he ticks all the wrong boxes. Vespasien's opinion of me isn't much higher."

"Oh?"

"Painting and music – for him, they're not proper jobs." Kai strummed a chord, turned one of the tuning pegs, his attention as much on his guitar as on what he was saying. "He's an old-style deeply conservative rural Frenchman. Conservative with a small C. There's nothing political about it. For him, it's the land – working the land, conserving it – that's what counts."

"He's certainly passionate about his wines."

"And he'd do anything for my mother. That's a big plus." His fingers fell across the guitar strings in a sudden discord. "But if he ever finds out about Cameron's . . . " He stopped.

"Lady friend in Paris?" Grace supplied.

He shot her a sharp look.

"How did you know?"

"The way you looked at your mother when he said it. Oddly."

He smiled.

"As simple as that. You're a perceptive woman, you know."

His eyes didn't leave hers, and she felt herself colour. She could hardly explain that if she'd happened to notice the look he'd sent Angela it was simply because he constantly drew her gaze.

"You're starting to thaw," she said, speaking to fill the silence. "You're not so grumpy now."

He shrugged.

"This place is working its magic. I've turned my phone off. No-one from the outside world knows I'm here. Peace and quiet – for the time being." His voice took on a harder edge. "It won't last, though."

A shadow seemed to cross his face, a reminder of the weariness that had been so much in evidence the day before, and her heart twisted with compassion for him.

"Do you want to talk about it?" she offered quietly, closing the programme on the laptop.

He didn't answer straight away.

"Yes. I'd like that," he finally said. He paused, clearly gathering his thoughts. "You know, it was brilliant when I started – and for a long time afterwards. It was eleven years ago. I was seventeen when I won that TV talent show . . . "

"I voted for you," Grace said with a laugh. Leaning back against the small table, she was conscious of the smile that hovered over her face, and knew she was happy simply to be listening and watching him.

He laughed.

"Why, thank you for being one of my earliest fans. Yes, it was great at the beginning. I received a big cheque and signed a deal with a record label, my debut album was an immediate hit, and it's been the same with all the albums that followed, one a year on average.

"I'm writing and recording my own songs, I'm touring all over the world, my fans adore me. What's not to like?"

"It sounds wonderful," Grace murmured, "but I can imagine some of the downsides. Gruelling schedules, a growing tiredness, adulation that goes to your head . . . "

"That's it. It all becomes unreal. Your plane lands and your manager tells you you're in Tokyo or Sydney. But you could be anywhere. And the tiredness builds and builds. After a while my mind goes numb, I can't write my music any more." His eyes looked inward, his smile was bleak. "I become nothing more than a money-making machine."

He fell silent, and Grace didn't speak.

"So the question is, where do I go from here?"

he continued some moments later, looking down at his guitar, idly strumming a few chords.

"My manager and I don't see eye to eye about the direction I should take next. Music is my life. I can't stop writing songs and singing them. But touring? That's a different matter. I've been touring for eleven years. More than a decade. Do I really want to be doing it for ten years more?"

He looked up, his eyes meeting hers.

"My manager and I have had our disagreements over recent months. Things came to a head on Thursday, at the concert in Amsterdam. We had a big row, I walked out – and here I am." He came to a halt, gaze moving over her features, and smiled, a disarming smile that would melt the iciest heart.

"Thank you, Grace, for listening," he said softly, "and for understanding."

"Thank you for trusting me," she said, flustered. "But now, I'd, uh, better check the amplifier's working." She turned to pick up the long, trailing flex. The plug was a French one, two pin, no earth, and it wasn't in good condition.

Even as she pushed the plug into the socket, a warning bell was ringing in her head. Too late.

She yelped as goodness knew how many volts of electricity thudded through her. The shock threw her backwards. The back of her head hit the floor with a crack.

Underneath The Stars

PERHAPS Grace lost consciousness for a second or two. She didn't know. One moment Kai was sitting in the chair strumming his guitar. The next, the guitar dropped to the floor with a clatter and he was up and over to where she lay.

He knelt on one knee beside her, like a sprinter preparing to run.

"Don't move. Don't try to get up." There was urgency in his voice, fear in his eyes.

"But I . . . "

She heard the noise of feet as people came running, the scrape as both screens were pushed aside. Voices, frightened, distraught, came at her in a rush of questions.

"What's wrong? What's happening?"

"Grace!" Her sister's voice, harsh with concern. "Tell me you're all right."

Kai looked up, beyond her.

"Cam, call one-five. Get an ambulance here. Emergency. Quick. Séverine . . . " And he broke into rapid French.

"I can get up, Kai," Grace protested, and tried to lift herself on to one elbow. "I'm fine."

"Grace, please, just do as I say." His tone was gentle, as were the hands that pushed her back down to the floor. "You've had an electric shock. Let's get you to hospital, double-check you're OK."

How she ached. As if a runaway train had thundered across every bone in her body. When Kai draped her in the blanket Sévérine handed him, tucking it in snugly round her neck and shoulders, she couldn't help but surrender to its soft warmth, secure in the knowledge she was safe in his hands. Perfectly safe.

* * * *

"Where am I?" Grace said to no-one in particular when she opened her eyes. Plain painted walls, lime green alternating with beige. No pictures, no paintings.

"In one of the rooms in the emergency department of the hospital."

Kai! His gravelly voice brought her to full alert.

"What are you doing here?" Never in her wildest dreams could she have imagined herself lying in a hospital bed with singer-songwriter legend Kai Curtis at her side.

She was propped up by pillows and wearing a sleeveless hospital gown over, yes, all her clothes apart from her sweater. Had Kai seen her when they took it off, she wondered, cheeks growing warm at the thought. The blood pressure cuff round her upper arm tightened, and a machine somewhere behind her beeped.

"I came in with you," Kai said. His hair was

mussed up, as if he'd been constantly pushing his fingers through it. "I followed the ambulance. Your sister wanted to come, too, but I said no."

Grace smiled.

"The show must go on."

The concern in his eyes eased.

"Exactly."

She saw him hesitate before he spoke.

"Grace." He took her hands in both his, and she didn't question it, loving the warmth and strength they imparted. "For one horrible moment back there, I thought you were dead. You weren't, thank God, but I still feel responsible."

"Don't be ridiculous, Kai. How . . . ?"

"It was my amplifier. You can't imagine how I feel about that."

"Look, if we're shouldering responsibilities, I should shoulder my fair share. The plug was moving – just a little – at the end of the flex. The wires must have been loose, and the plug looked a bit battered. I should never have plugged it in."

"That's what I don't get. My equipment is always in good condition. My manager sees to that."

Grace shrugged.

"Well, who knows? But I'd already sensed something wasn't quite right. I'd half taken my fingers off the plug."

From the corridor outside came the sound of footsteps approaching. Kai gave her hands a gentle squeeze before letting them slide from his grip, slowly, as if reluctantly.

"I'll take you back to the château when the doctors give you the all-clear," he said, standing up. "Is that OK with you?"

She could only nod. It occurred to her that he'd said he would say hello and goodbye to his brother, then leave, and she now wondered why he hadn't. All of a sudden her heart was full to bursting. She watched his broad back as he walked out the door and found herself wishing she could call him back.

But how could she?

His concern for her was genuine, she didn't doubt it. Of course he'd been worried. Everyone had. There'd been nothing special about the way he'd accompanied her to the hospital and stayed with her, though. Anyone else would have done the same, wouldn't they? She mustn't read too much into his actions.

Even so, she was in danger of falling in love with him. She recognised it now. While he, of course, would never feel the same way about her.

* * * *

"Even if I were a world-famous artist . . . " Cameron began. Hand cupping Grace's elbow as he steered her across the grand salon, he leaned close, his words for her ears only.

"Which I'm not – yet," he added with a laugh. "I still wouldn't have to spend my time dodging photographers. Not like Kai."

There was envy, and a hint of petulance, in his tone. But Grace heard relief too. Though jealous of his brother's fame, he almost certainly welcomed his own anonymity.

"Let's sit here, shall we?" Grace said, stopping at a two-seater sofa midway along the catwalk. It was two o'clock. Music played in the background, people chatted and greeted old friends, the fashion show was due to start and there was a definite buzz of excitement in the air.

"Perfect," Cameron said.

The doctors had given Grace the all-clear. Her heart rhythm was normal, the shock hadn't caused any burns, she'd broken no bones when she was thrown back on to the floor. Kai had brought her back to the château, driving past the cars that were already lining up in the front and straight into the barn where the family's vehicles were housed.

"I'd like to stay with you for the fashion show," he'd said, and her heart had leaped at his words, "but if I do," he went on, "before the week is out your picture will be on the front page of all the tabloids. And you won't want that, believe me."

So he'd asked his brother to sit with her, and part of her – a very small part – was happy about the arrangement. Cameron knew everyone, it seemed, and delighted in bringing her up to speed on all the gossip.

"See the woman with my mother? The ex-president's wife," he now said. "A real coup for my mama, getting her here."

Moments later he leaned forward conspiratorially.

"See that man over there? The one with the camera? He's with 'La Mode de Demain', the fashion mag. Looks like your sister's going to get good coverage."

Then he nudged her again.

"Uh-oh. That woman with my brother?" Grace watched Kai come into the grand salon, accompanied – or perhaps pursued – by a young woman half-turned towards him, matching his every step. "She works for 'Bonjour!', the gossip mag. So now they'll all know where he is. He made the right call, keeping you away from him."

Grace bit her lip, heart heavy as she caught this glimpse of the lack of privacy, the hounding he must endure on a daily basis. He made his way across the room, stopping frequently to say a few words here, clasp a hand or shoulder there, and his smile reminded her of a politician meeting and greeting out of duty, not pleasure.

He glanced across at her, and she thought

there was genuine warmth in the smile he sent her before taking a seat at the far end, next to Barbs.

Natasha was nowhere in sight. Doubtless she was in the side room, checking the models' clothes before they came out on to the catwalk. One of Pierre's grandchildren, Cameron had told her, was a DJ at weekends, and had been put in charge of the music. There was no sign of Vespasien or Johnno.

"They're in the wine cellars," Cameron said. "Where else?"

News of Grace's accident with the plug had clearly done the rounds, and she was moved when people she knew, and others she didn't, came up to her to wish her well, glad to see she was fully recovered, that no harm had been done.

Angela was in her element. She'd changed into a floaty dress with a handkerchief hem, its vibrant cherry red both clashing with and complementing her orange hair and nails and the long shocking pink scarf she'd tied bandana-style across her forehead.

She thanked everyone for attending, making sure to include a famous star of stage and screen, the ex-president's wife, and a highly regarded poet in her thanks. Grace couldn't help smiling at her snobbery. Deliberate or unconscious, it was harmless and rather endearing.

The music swelled, the models walked out on to the catwalk – simply a long narrow space between the chairs – and the show was underway.

Angela gave a brief commentary of each outfit while Marie-Laure translated into French. The models strode up and down the catwalk, tossing back their hair, putting hands to hips, striking a pose like true professionals.

The clothes were fabulous, and the audience oohed and clapped their enthusiasm. Grace could see almost immediately that the show was going to be a huge success, and she was filled with pride for her talented sister.

At last the music came to an end, the three models stayed on the catwalk, the audience clapped and clapped and Angela darted into the side room. When she reappeared seconds later pulling a broadly smiling Natasha out behind her, the clapping rose to a crescendo.

"Thank you, thank you," Natasha said over and over again. "Thank you so much for your support and enthusiasm." She spoke in breathless gulps as if she'd just run a marathon. "It's greatly appreciated, believe me. If any of you would like to come backstage . . . " she gestured towards the side room " . . . to look at the clothes in greater detail, please don't hesitate. But first . . . " She paused with the dramatic pause of someone about to make a big announcement. "First, Kai Curtis is going to sing for us."

A buzz of voices, quick movements of heads as people turned to speak to their neighbours. The excitement was tangible, the hush instant when Kai got to his feet, guitar in hand.

Grace's heart jolted into a fast, insistent beat. She'd seen him sing in videos on the internet, of course. She'd never seen him perform live.

The grand salon was a large room, but there was something very intimate about performing there, she thought as she listened to his first song. Something close-up and personal that you wouldn't get in a vast stadium, or by watching a video.

He stood leaning close to the microphone, and she watched his fingers move over the strings and frets of the guitar, watched his lips as he sang the words of his song, and she recalled with a pang the way those fingers, warm and strong, had held hers, and how those lips – just once – had touched hers in the lightest of kisses.

He sang a selection of his hits, all-time favourites with a fast, rhythmic beat that had his audience tapping their feet or clapping in time or singing along, while others were slow, lyrical numbers whose raw emotion brought a painful lump to Grace's throat.

"Wow, that was something special," she breathed when Kai took his final bow. It almost hurt to speak, so moved was she by the sheer power of his performance.

"He's good, isn't he?" Cameron said, hand at her elbow as she stood up. "Come on. Let's circulate."

Grace looked along to the far end of the catwalk. The star of stage and screen had draped herself around Kai. Congratulating him on a brilliant performance, no doubt. The woman from "Bonjour!" hovered close behind. She and Kai lived in different worlds, Grace thought, conscious of a bitter realisation. His was a world of fame, success and beautiful people. How could she compete with that?

She brought a smile to her face.

"Let's go and congratulate my sister, Cam."

"I'm just so relieved," Natasha said when first Grace then Cameron wrapped her in a heartfelt hug. "People are ordering my clothes in their droves."

Natasha's cheeks were pink, her eyes held tears, a huge smile filled her face, and Grace squeezed her hands, sharing her happiness.

"You were fantastic, Nat. Well done!"

Sévérine and her group of helpers brought round dishes of nibbles and glasses of Château Beauvallon red and white. Angela, as flushed with the success of the event as Natasha, moved from one small group to another, clearly loving every moment of the afternoon.

Barbs was chatting to Marie-Laure and the models. Johnno, looking rather unsteady on his feet, together with Vespasien, had finally put in an appearance. They stood in one corner, nursing a glass of red each. Loki lay stretched out between them.

Grace stayed with Cameron. Like Angela, they moved from group to group, talking about Natasha and her clothes – and, inevitably, about Kai's performance.

It was a special kind of torture, she thought, to be reminded so often about the man. Every time someone spoke about him, she couldn't help looking his way, and every single time, she found, he was surrounded by women, deep in conversation with them.

As the afternoon progressed and night fell, people took their leave, driving off in their twos and threes, until only the family and their house guests were left. Pierre brought in a tray holding two bottles and eight long-stemmed glasses which he placed on a table by the wall.

"A glass of pétillant each, I think," Vespasien said, taking one of the bottles and twisting undone the metal wire round its top.

Grace, along with the others, crossed towards the table and their host. Where was Kai, she was wondering, when her hand was clasped by someone behind her. She turned, and pleasure whispered across her skin. Kai.

"Do you want some bubbly?"

She shook her head.

"Then come with me." Already, he was drawing her with him, across and out of the room. His hand round hers was warm, assured.

"Where are we going?" she asked, breathless, caught up in the adventure of it.

"Up to the second floor. You'll need your jacket. We can access the tower from there."

"The tower? Oh!" She recalled the circular tower as high as the roof ridge that stood at one corner of the château.

Kai snatched up his coat from a chair, hooked it over his shoulder, and they ran side by side up the stairs, past the first floor and on to the second. He waited while she ran along to her room to fetch her jacket.

Seconds later, she was back, zipping it up as she went. Kai, she saw, had put his long leather coat on, pulling the collar up around his ears.

"This way," he said, taking her hand again.

He led her along the corridor. No time to stop to look at the paintings that lined the walls. Grace's pulse was racing. She knew where he was taking her, didn't know what he had in mind. But she trusted him totally, she realised. Despite his reputation with women, she somehow knew he meant her no harm.

They came to a low door dark with age and studded with nail heads. Kai pressed down on the latch and pushed it open, reaching inside to click on a light switch. Cold air and the earthy smell of stone met Grace's nostrils. In the yellow light of an unshaded bulb, she could see wide steps twisting both upwards and down.

"Go up," Kai said. "And hold on to the rope."

Grace seized the thick, rough rope secured at intervals to the curving wall and climbed. She could hear Kai coming up behind her. Over the centuries, the stairs, carved from the soft creamy-white local stone, had been hollowed out in the middle by the passage of many feet. There were only ten of them and they ended in another door. Kai reached past her to push it open, and freezing outside air hit her face.

"Go on," he said.

Grace looked around her as she stepped through the doorway – and gasped. What a beautiful surprise. She stood on a circular platform open to the elements, the tower's flat roof, she supposed. A chest-high wall ran all the way round.

The moon hadn't yet risen, but there were stars in their millions, sparkling, twinkling against the velvet blackness of the cloud-free sky.

"Oh, Kai," she said, breath catching. Standing beside her, he too was looking out. "Living where I do, I've never seen so many stars. Look," she said, "there's Orion, the hunter."

"And look – there – the Plough."

"Where?"

He put his arm round her shoulder, drawing her close so she could look along the line of his other arm into the night sky.

"Can you see it? Like a scoop with a long

handle. Follow the front edge and you'll come to the pole star. True north."

And somehow she wasn't looking at the stars any more. Breathlessness of a different kind had her in its grip, and she was twisting round within the circle of his arms, looking at Kai instead.

His face was a paler shadow against the dark of his hair and coat. She breathed in the scents of him – leather and cologne – and the woodsmoke that drifted through the still air.

For a long moment neither moved. Then, with a swiftly murmured "Grace", he placed his hands at her waist, pulling her against the length of his body, and she'd brought her hands up to his face, running her fingertips across his beard-roughened jaw, pushing them up into his hair.

And she closed her eyes when his lips came down on hers in a kiss that sent waves of sensation pulsing through her body.

Fire In His Kiss

WHEN at last they drew apart, it was as if she'd lost some part of herself, Grace thought, and a tiny chill of warning shivered down her spine.

She made no protest, though, when he pressed her head against his shoulder, and wrapped his arms around her, holding her tightly to him. There'd be no harm if he held her a little longer, would there? It seemed so right.

"I've been wanting to do that all day," he said, brushing the pad of his thumb up across her cheek, "ever since that dreadful accident."

"Kissing it better?" she murmured.

She sensed him smile.

"And have I? No headaches? Pain? No after-effects?"

Hmm, she thought, body still a-tremble from his kiss. Definite after-effects, but not from the electric shock.

"I'm fine, Kai. Really. I got off lightly."

"Good. I'm glad." His arms tightened round her in a brief hug.

"And I understand totally why you couldn't kiss me before," she said, reaching up, fingers of one hand twisting in the hair at the back of his head.

"I have to be so careful what I do in public.

That sounds self-pitying. It's not meant to be."

"I know." With sadness in her heart, she recalled how insistent he'd been that she shouldn't be seen in his company during the fashion show. At the hospital too he'd been distant, for fear perhaps that one of the staff would take photos and sell them to the tabloids. "You have to behave with decorum at all times. Like a politician."

"Or the royals."

Grace laughed.

"Now you're sounding smug."

Kai laughed, too, and they fell silent, at ease, Grace sensed, in each other's company. From below, far off, came the bark of a fox, and nearer the château the unearthly hoo-hoo of a tawny owl. Snow-covered hills rose to the south, ghostly white against the black of the sky.

"It's wonderful out here," Grace said into his shoulder. "Timeless. Beautiful. Thank you so much for showing it me."

"We're above the world. Away from it all."

"We'll have to re-join it soon." Regret was heavy in her voice. "It must be almost time for dinner."

"You're right. But before we go . . . "

Grace lifted her head, frowning at the sudden switch in his tone, now grave yet oddly hesitant.

"What is it?"

He cupped her face in both hands, tilting it up towards him.

"I want you to take care, Grace. There's something going on here at the château. Something's not quite right." His words, quiet, earnestly spoken, carried the weight of conviction.

"I don't understand."

"My equipment's always good quality stuff, and well looked after. You should never have got an electric shock. You could have been killed."

"It could have been you. You could have been the one to put the plug in the socket."

"True. But it was you who flagged up the problem with the painting."

"The painting?" she echoed. "The Sisley? It's gone. It's not hanging on the wall any more."

"I know. I went back, saw it wasn't there."

"So did I." And as she spoke, she felt a coldness in her veins that had nothing to do with the freezing night air. Her first instinct was denial. Kai was being melodramatic, overly protective. She was surely in no danger. But perhaps he was right. There had been two incidents, two occurrences that were hard to explain.

"You think the two things are connected?"

"I don't know. But I aim to find out." There was no disguising the steel of determination in his voice.

"There has to be a simple, rational explanation. For starters, we can ask Angela about the painting – she was the one who sent it off to be restored. She should know where it is now."

"And I've left a message with my manager, asking him what he can tell me about the amplifier. No reply as yet. But I meant what I said – I can't always be with you, Grace. You must be watchful, alert." And he pulled her towards him, gently, and pressed a kiss to her mouth, a soft tender kiss that left her aching for more.

* * * *

"Wasn't it just brilliant, darlings?"

Grace couldn't help smiling as Angela returned yet again to her theme. She glanced across at Kai who sat opposite her, and felt warmth steal over her when he smiled back.

He'd left her at the door to her room on the second floor before heading for the main staircase and the floor below. In her room she'd had a quick shower and changed into a simply styled zinging yellow dress, another of Natasha's creations. Her sister was nowhere to be seen. She'd already gone down to dinner, Grace supposed.

And so it turned out. Grace had run down the stairs and along to the dining-room to find Kai waiting for her by the door. The others were already seated or in the process of sitting down.

"You look wonderful," Kai murmured as he escorted her to her seat, earning an archly raised eyebrow from Cameron, in the chair next to hers, that brought stinging colour to her cheeks.

"The ex-president's wife was a darling, wasn't she?" Angela was saying to the table at large. "A positive darling."

"She's ordered three dresses and a skirt," Natasha said. Her sister was almost bubbling over with happiness, Grace thought, and was immensely pleased for her.

"You've worked very hard, Natasha dear," Barbs said. "You deserve every bit of your success."

The starter, scallops in a delicate sauce, was brought in. The room was warm, and filled with the scents of pine, orange zest and cloves from the tree in the corner.

Vespasien, seated as usual at the head of the table, peeled the foil off the top of a bottle of wine.

Cameron leaned in close to Grace.

"So what kept you and Kai away from the dinner table? You missed apéritifs."

Vespasien pulled the cork out of the bottle with a pop.

"I think you'll all enjoy this one."

Cameron's glance flicked from Grace to Kai and back to her. She felt herself colour again, and turned away, towards Vespasien.

"The 2005 vintage?"

A moment's hesitation, swiftly followed by a gracious smile.

"As good in its way," he said. "Two thousand and thirteen. An interesting year. Here, try some," and he took her glass and half-filled it. "Remember – inhale – and chew."

Grace laughed and did as she was told.

"Hmm, that's lovely," she said a short while later. "Smooth summer fruit – tangy and delicious."

"Got some for me?" Johnno said, holding out his glass.

"Angela . . . " Kai said. His mother sat at the foot of the long rectangular table, at the opposite end to her husband. "That painting Grace was a bit puzzled by – I couldn't help noticing it wasn't there any more."

Vespasien, in the middle of pouring Johnno his wine, looked up sharply.

"Which painting?"

Angela paused before replying, and when she spoke there was reluctance in her voice.

"The Sisley, darling. Chestnut trees along a country lane."

"So where is it?" He looked at Grace. "Puzzled? How can anyone be puzzled by a Sisley?"

"It's been restored," she said, "but rather clumsily in places." Vespasien made an impatient circling movement with his hand, indicating she should go on. She drew in a breath and told him what she'd told Kai.

He heard her out.

"This is your job?" he then said. "You know about these things. Correct?"

She nodded. He looked down the length of the table at his wife.

"It's a valuable painting. I don't recall being asked if I wanted it restored."

Loki, alerted perhaps by the coldness in his master's voice, looked up from the floor and gave a low growl. Cameron shifted in his chair. Grace bit her lip and looked at Kai. The conversation, already uncomfortable, risked turning into a full-scale domestic row.

"That's something," Kai said, "that should be discussed later perhaps."

Vespasien held his stance a moment longer before sinking back into his chair, one hand dropping to the floor to tangle in Loki's fur.

"D'accord," he said at last to his stepson. "But let me get this straight," he continued, eyes on his wife again. "You sent the painting away to be restored. It's been restored – badly. It's come back. And now it's disappeared. Have I got that right?"

"Uh, maybe I can help with that," Cameron said, to Grace's surprise. "I took it up to my studio. I wanted to study it, and the light's much better there."

Vespasien turned his cold gaze on his younger stepson.

"Put it back where it belongs. Although it's always useful, I suppose, to study a talented artist."

The slight emphasis on the word "talented" brought a flush to Cameron's face, and Grace knew to her dismay that Vespasien's barb had found its mark.

"Hey," she said faux-brightly, "you promised to show me your studio, Cameron. I'd love to see your paintings."

"Yes, me too," Natasha added.

"And me," Barbs chimed in.

And all of a sudden, everyone was talking, tucking into their starter, relieved that the awkward moment was over.

Everyone except Kai. Scraping back his chair, he stood up and moved down the table to his mother, bending low to squeeze her shoulders and murmur in her ear.

An apology, perhaps, for raising the subject, Grace thought, touched by this private moment between mother and son, and reassured when Angela squeezed her son's hand in return and he went back to his seat.

They talked about all sorts, reliving – yet again – the success of the fashion show, discussing wines, firming up plans for the next day.

"Our murder mystery dinner tomorrow evening, darlings. Possibly the start of a brand-new business venture for me so it's important it goes well. Nineteen-twenties costumes, remember," Angela cautioned. "It'll be great fun. Won't it, Vespi darling?" she said, beaming a smile at her husband.

He raised his glass to her.

"I'm looking forward to it." Sitting back in his chair, with his Irish setter stretched out on the floor beside him, he looked relaxed and content. Marital harmony had been restored, Grace sensed.

After a long, rambling but surprisingly funny story about a disaster at an auction, Johnno stood up.

"I'm off outside for a ciggie. Anyone care to join me?"

No-one did, but Angela stood up.

"I need to check on the main course. I'll come with you."

"He's giving up on the first of January," Barbs said. "He says the same thing every year," she added drily.

And that, of course, led to a discussion of New Year's resolutions.

"I intend going to Florence, to the Uffizi Gallery, for a week at least," Grace said, "so I can spend as much time as I want studying the paintings."

"That's a wish list, not a resolution," Natasha protested.

"You've never been to Florence?" Kai asked, a smile in his eyes.

"Just one day. It was terribly rushed."

"I'm going to lose a few kilos," Barbs said.

"And I'm going to make big changes in my life," Cameron announced.

"About time too," Vespasien muttered.

It occurred to Grace that Kai had remained silent about any plans or resolutions he might have made for the future. Knowing he'd come to the château to get away from his ordinary life – extraordinary life, rather – she didn't bring the matter up. Neither did anyone else, she noticed.

Johnno returned, and Angela, Séverine and another woman carried the main course in – a gigot of lamb that filled the room with its aroma, together with a selection of winter vegetables.

"And we have some very British mint sauce to go with the lamb." Angela laughed.

The main course was a great success, as was the next, tangy cheeses served with dressed salad leaves and crusty, yeasty home-baked bread. The wine Vespasien poured for each course was excellent, and the conversation lively and wide-ranging, all awkwardness over the Sisley just a memory.

Grace talked and smiled and laughed, and more often than she could count, her eyes met Kai's across the table in long moments of shared warmth.

The last course was a café gourmand, coffee served with a selection of mini-desserts.

Vespasien dropped a sugar cube into his cup

and looked down along the table at his wife.

"Where did you send it? The Sisley. Who did you get to restore it?"

Grace tensed as the table fell silent. She sensed Cameron, beside her, stiffen. Kai looked grim. Vespasien was worrying at the subject like a dog at a bone, refusing to let it go. But was that so surprising? He'd had to be single-minded to run his thriving wine business and keep the château and grounds in good order.

"Ah." To Grace's surprise, it was Johnno who spoke. He cleared his throat. "Confession time, Vesp. It was a friend of mine."

He stopped, and Vespasien frowned.

"So what's his name?"

"That's just it." Johnno's tone was apologetic. "I've been racking my brains ever since you asked about the painting. I can't remember."

"Not a good friend, then?"

"More of an acquaintance really."

Vespasien stirred his coffee thoughtfully, put his spoon down, and all the time his eyes never left Johnno.

"Why that painting? Why not one of the others?"

Kai moved restlessly.

"Let's drop it for now, shall we?" His voice was a growl.

Vespasien turned his gaze on his stepson. For the space of several seconds he seemed to be debating whether to pursue the matter.

"Very well," he said at last, and it was as if everyone else expelled a collective breath.

It had been a good question, though, Grace thought. One she'd love to know the answer to.

* * * *

"Kai kissed me. Did he kiss you? Yesterday, I mean," Grace said, sitting down on her sister's bed, tucking her legs beneath her.

"Ah, now, that'd be telling."

"For goodness' sake. Don't be so irritating, Natasha. Tell me. Did he?"

It was a couple of hours later, and Natasha was already in bed. Grace, not sure she could fall asleep straight away, had come to join her.

"No. He didn't," her sister admitted, and Grace felt the tension ease from her shoulders. She didn't know why her sister's answer should matter so much, but it did.

"Oh Grace . . . " Natasha was pushing herself upright, concern on her face. "You've fallen for him, haven't you?"

She nodded.

"I rather think I have."

"Grace, love . . . " Her sister took both hands in hers. "You've got to take care. I don't want to see you hurt."

"I had a look online. He's had two long-term relationships. Some short-lived ones too, of course. So you never know . . . " Her chin tilted, and she braved a smile. "I could be the third long-term one."

"Grace . . . " Natasha's arms went round her, pulling her into a hug. She stroked her hair. "Let's hope you are. But . . . "

"I know, I know. Pie in the sky." Grace was glad her sister couldn't see her face and the tears that filled her eyes. "At best, Kai and I will be together for the few days we're both here at the château. And then – and then we'll go our separate ways."

It didn't bear thinking about. But she had to face reality. Kai could have his pick of beautiful, interesting women. Why would he choose her? She drew away from her sister and cuffed the tears from her cheeks.

Natasha took hold of her hands again. Her eyes were bright with curiosity.

"So what was it like, his kiss?"

Grace's mind flashed back to those long moments at the top of the tower, high above the world. She recalled the warmth and strength of his arms around her, the intensity of his lips on hers, and her whole being was suffused with a warm glow. She smiled.

"It set me on fire," she said simply.

Special Someone

THE following morning, Grace waited until Natasha had finished getting ready. That way, they could go downstairs to breakfast together. Safety in numbers, she reasoned.

She'd been inclined to dismiss Kai's conviction that something was not quite right at the château, his warning to her to take care and be on the alert. Imagining she was in some kind of danger had all seemed just too far-fetched. But now, after a restless night, she was more ready to give him credence.

She'd slept badly, reliving the events of the day before. The thud as electricity jolted through her body, throwing her backwards, had occurred and recurred in her dreams, over and over, in an endless loop.

Over and over, too, were a terse exchange between Cameron and his stepfather and a face-off between Kai and Vespasien, taut and tense, two stags prepared to lock antlers in the crash of battle.

And most pervasive of all, still achingly vivid in her mind even now she was awake, the dream of herself in Kai's arms, as the two of them shared a passionate embrace.

She couldn't stop thinking about him. She

slowed as she and Natasha reached the first-floor landing. Maybe she could be looking – casually – at one of the paintings just as Kai came along, heading down for breakfast.

"Grace!" Her sister's voice held a warning. "It won't work, Grace."

Grace laughed.

"I didn't realise I was so transparent." Anyway, she thought, as delicious aromas of baking and coffee drifted up towards her, maybe he was already in the kitchen having his breakfast, and she hastened her pace down the stairs.

Arriving first at the kitchen, a few metres in front of her sister, she pushed open the door. He wasn't there, and she felt a twist of disappointment.

Séverine was at the oven. Wearing oven gloves, she'd pulled a tray of croissants out and was lifting one up to check its underside.

Angela and Cameron stood over by the door that led to the barn.

They stopped talking, abruptly, heads turning to the door to see who had come in, and it seemed to Grace they both had to make a deliberate effort to shake themselves out of the conversation they'd been having. A serious one, clearly, judging by the expression she'd glimpsed on their faces.

"I'm sorry. I should have knocked."

"Grace, darling – no need to apologise." Angela beamed a bright smile. "And Natasha.

Did you sleep well? Hungry? Come on in, darlings."

With a bustle of movement and a scraping of chairs across tiles, the four of them sat down – and Grace gasped in shock as two hands, warm and strong, hands she'd dreamed about, gripped her upper arms. Kai. She had her back to the door, hadn't heard him come in. Twisting round to look at him, she couldn't prevent the shy smile that spread over her face.

"Hi."

He smiled back, and his hands stroked down her arms and up again, just once. She could feel their warmth through the thickness of her sweater, and her heart did a crazy flip-flop.

"All right?" he asked.

She nodded, and he sat down beside her, shifting his chair so close that his shoulder brushed against hers.

"Vespi's already had his breakfast," Angela was saying. "Barbs and Johnno will be down shortly, I expect." She was looking with interest at the two of them. Cameron had a knowing smile on his face. There was concern in Natasha's eyes, though.

Yes, Grace thought. There was danger here. Her sister was right to be concerned. Grace was in danger of losing her heart – to a man who was way out of her league.

"Hey, Grace," Cameron said, breaking into her thoughts. "What do you say to coming up to the studio this morning, having a look at my work?"

Was that what he'd been discussing so earnestly, so anxiously, with his mother as she came into the kitchen? Grace gave herself a mental shake. Surely not.

"Thanks. That'd be great. I'd love to."

"What's everyone else planning for this morning?" Kai asked, and Grace felt herself tense, sensing he wasn't simply making small talk.

"It would be really fabulous, darlings," Angela said, "if all four of you could spend the morning in the studio. Till eleven? Twelve? How does that sound?"

"Fine by me," Kai said.

"Me too," Natasha agreed. "After yesterday I just want to chill. I don't mind where."

"Perfect," Angela said with a laugh. "Vespi and I are going to be planting the clues for the murder mystery dinner and, of course, we don't want you to see where we've hidden them. Barbs and Johnno are being absolute darlings, too. They've promised to stay in their suite until lunchtime at least."

The studio was on the second floor. Cameron pushed open the door, holding it back to let Grace and Natasha go on in before him.

Kai stood beside his brother, guitar and sheets of music in his hands. Grace looked back at him as she entered the studio, and their eyes met.

He had a small smile on his face. A smile for her, Grace wondered, pulse fluttering.

The room was large and airy, and cluttered with easels, two sofas arranged at right angles to each other, small tables covered in loose-leaf papers, sketchpads, half-finished drawings, and a huge old-fashioned dresser so tall it almost touched the room's high ceiling.

Pots and jam jars, filled with brushes and charcoals, and trays of paints in tubes covered every available horizontal surface. The familiar smells of oil paint, linseed oil and mineral spirit were strong in Grace's nostrils.

She smiled with delight, her gaze drawn to the windows set high into one wall of the room, and the soft, even light that came through them.

"We're north-facing here, aren't we?" she said, turning to Cameron and adding with a laugh, "I hope you realise just how lucky you are."

"Oh, I do. Believe me, I do."

Kai came to stand beside her, and awareness of his closeness whispered down her spine.

Natasha was sitting on one of the sofas. Legs curled beneath her, pencil in hand, she was flicking through the pages of her sketchpad.

"A nineteenth-century Beauvallon de Mottefort," Kai said, "one of Vespasien's distant ancestors, had this room converted into a studio. He was quite a famous artist in his day."

He cast a swift glance round. "The Sisley isn't here?"

"Uh, no," Cameron said, clearly flustered by the sudden change of subject. "I took it back downstairs."

"That was quick."

"Yes," Cameron said with a laugh that sounded just a little forced. "My stepfather's wish is my command."

Grace moved away. Canvasses on the floor were propped against the walls. Others, lots of them, hung on the walls, crammed together in a higgledy-piggledy display. Grace went from one to the next, stooping close to examine them.

Vespasien had been wrong to dismiss his stepson's ability, she decided. And cruel to do so in company. Cameron did have talent. His work was precise and painstaking though still immature, perhaps. He hadn't yet found a style, a vision, he could call his own.

She stopped by a group of just under a dozen sketches, all framed in the same blond wood. The first showed the dome of Montmartre, with the head of a priest in the foreground. Another portrayed a souvenir seller, the Eiffel Tower in the background.

"These are good," she said, impressed.

Cameron's face broke into a wide smile.

"My Paris places and faces series. I'm glad you like them."

"They remind me of Naymar-Ferris's work. The

subject matter. The style, too."

She spoke absently, her attention not fully fixed on what she was looking at. Kai had sat down at one end of the second sofa. Leaning back, the ankle of one leg resting on the knee of the other, he was playing his guitar and singing, quietly, for himself alone. It was a song she'd heard so many times before. A haunting love song, the bittersweet words and melody bringing an ache to her throat.

She saw Cameron hesitate.

"Kai says you know – why I go to Paris so often, I mean."

"There's someone there," she said softly. "Someone special."

Kai was singing another love song, slow and lilting, one she hadn't heard before, and the ache in her throat swelled with emotion.

"That's right . . . " He stopped, and she had the impression he'd come to a decision. Twisting away, he crouched down beside the tall, ornately carved dresser, pulled open one of its two lower doors and drew something out. He stood up and handed it to her without speaking, and Grace could sense he was holding his breath, waiting for her reaction.

She saw Kai glance up at her and Cameron, then down again at his fingers as they played across the strings of the guitar. Whatever Cameron wanted to show her, it was plain Kai had seen it before.

It was a sketch the same size as the others, and housed in the same blond wood frame. The sketch that completed the series, Grace thought, the one that meant the most, hidden away for obvious reasons.

It showed a man in his thirties, standing in a space whose walls were hung with paintings, a space too large and impersonal to be someone's house. He was almost certainly, Grace surmised, the owner or manager of one of the galleries in Paris where Cameron had shown his work. With the classical perfection of his features and his carefully crafted hair, he reminded her of a statue from antiquity.

"I can see why you fell for him," she said, and saw the tension go from Cameron's shoulders.

"He means the world to me."

A heartfelt statement, simply spoken, and the ache in her throat was an ache of longing. How wonderful if she ever meant as much to Kai!

With a sigh she looked away. Cameron had left the door to the dresser ajar, and she caught sight of canvasses propped inside, some wrapped in cloth. She smiled.

"What else have you got in there? Have you done some paintings of him?"

All at once bright colour stained Cameron's cheeks, and he pushed the door closed with his foot.

"No, they're nothing. Just some old rubbish of mine."

Grace frowned as the noise of a motor, growing steadily louder, drew her attention. The others had heard it too. Kai's fingers had stilled on the strings of his guitar.

It was a rumbling roar, low overhead, very loud now, a sound Grace had heard before but couldn't place. And then she did, and looked at Kai in horror.

A helicopter, circling above the château.

"They've found you," she said, and her voice shook. No need to say who "they" were. She could have wept for him.

His expression was grim.

"It had to happen sooner or later. I'm surprised they took so long."

Natasha looked stricken.

"It's my fault. If I hadn't had the fashion show here . . . I'm so sorry."

"Don't cut yourself up about it," Kai said. "I've had two days of freedom. I've done well."

Two days. Grace's heart was heavy.

"If it's any consolation," she said, "they can't land. With all this snow, they won't be able to see where they're landing."

Natasha rolled her eyes.

"Good old Grace. Practical as ever."

"There's a calmness about you," Kai said, "an inner calm that helps me see things more clearly."

They'd reached the treeline, and he put his arm round her shoulders, drawing her to him with that easy familiarity she found so beguiling. He'd waited deliberately, she knew, until they entered the forest. Surrounded by trees, there was less risk of being seen.

"You must have been like that right from the start," he went on. "That's why your parents gave you the name they did."

She laughed, her breath forming a cloud in the cold air.

"'Fraid not. By all accounts I came kicking and screaming into this world."

He laughed. She leaned her head against his shoulder, and they walked on along the woodland path, their feet crunching into the snow.

It was late afternoon and the light was beginning to fade. Grace breathed in the scents of peat and mushrooms, from time to time picking up the rustle as a small hidden creature – her squirrel, perhaps? – moved through the undergrowth.

She was happy, and hoped Kai was, too. The moments when his privacy was guaranteed, when he could be himself, had to be rare indeed, she thought sadly.

The helicopter had circled the château and gone away again. Shortly afterwards, the landline had begun ringing, over and over, prompting Kai to issue a statement via his manager saying he was spending a quiet Christmas with his family and asking for his privacy to be respected.

Almost all newspapers and magazines would comply, he explained. But it wouldn't stop the paparazzi, for ever on the hunt for the exclusive photo.

Pierre, the aged retainer, had come in during lunch to report that there was indeed a group of photographers standing outside the gatehouse, and that his son had caught two of them trying to climb over the high stone wall that ran all round the château park.

"They'll have cameras with telephoto lenses," Angela said. "Do be careful, Kai darling."

Another reason to stay inside, and that had been fine. After a snack lunch – a tasty croque-monsieur each – the four of them had helped with preparations for the evening's murder mystery dinner.

"There'll be twenty-four of us altogether," Angela said. "It'll be fabulous."

Vespasien had said nothing, but his mouth tightened into a thin line, and Grace had the uncomfortable impression he'd been totting up the cost.

But he'd smiled and nodded his approval later in the afternoon when he saw Cameron and Natasha shoulder to shoulder in the dining-room, one straightening the cutlery and the other the glasses.

"Hmm," he murmured, "the lady in Paris had better watch out. She might just be about to lose him."

Grace smiled at the memory. Vespasien couldn't have been more wrong, though it was up to Cameron to put him right, of course. All in all, the afternoon had been great fun. They'd worked hard and laughed a lot.

Kai, out of concern for her safety, she supposed, had stayed with her the whole time. And who could complain about that?

"You don't need to stay with me all the time," she now said, wondering even as she spoke how she could be so foolish, wishing him away from her when he was like a fever in her blood, a drug she could hardly bear to do without.

"I'm really not convinced there's anything going on at the château. And the thing with the plug – it was an accident, Kai, surely. Faulty wiring."

He shook his head.

"I'm playing it safe. Until I find out what's going on I want you to be with me or your sister or in your room with the door locked. No wandering off alone. Just in case." He paused.

"Maybe I stay with you because I want to," he added quietly, and her heart stood still for an instant.

They walked on in an easy silence broken only by the crunch of their feet on the snow and the cawing of rooks high in the trees. Kai's arm was a warm, welcome weight across her shoulders.

"Hey." There was a smile in his voice as he

slowed to a halt and pointed down at the ground. "Do you see that?"

They'd stopped where another path cut across the one they were on, and it looked as if someone had been digging, randomly, turning over large clods of earth here and there, the dark soil and mulching leaves a vivid contrast to the white of the snow.

"Wild boar," he said. "Rooting around for food."

"Let's hope they found some. It can't be easy, in the middle of winter."

He laughed.

"Your sister's right, you know. There's a very practical side to you." He drew her round to face him, and Grace was conscious of his hands at her waist and, when he spoke, of a subtle change in tone and expression. "I like that. Very much," he said softly.

"Oh." All at once, she felt breathless. Her gaze took in the warmth of his eyes, the smile that curved his mouth, the strong lines of the face she knew so well, and her heart lurched into a fast, insistent beat.

His hands came up to smooth a strand of hair from her face.

"My brother showed you his sketch of the special person in his life." The pad of his thumb trailed tantalisingly across her lower lip. "I rather think I've found my special person in you."

Grace was lost for words. She reached up,

fingertips brushing along the rasp of his jaw before moving round to his nape, almost imperceptibly urging him closer.

"Oh, Grace." With something like a groan, he pulled her against the length of his body. His arms went round her, holding her tight, and his lips claimed hers in a kiss whose intensity made her senses sing.

Horror In The Darkness

WOW!" Natasha said. "You look amazing! Do a twirl, go on."

Grace laughed, and the scalloped hem of the sleeveless emerald chiffon dress she wore flared out as she spun round. Another of her sister's designs, of course, and it was exquisite. The crystal beadwork round the scoop neckline must have taken hours of hand-sewing.

Following Natasha's advice, she'd put her hair up into a high bun, leaving curling tendrils loose around her face. A velvet headband across her forehead, complete with a sparkling diamanté ornament and ivory-coloured feathers, finished the outfit.

"You're brilliant, Nat," she said with another laugh. "We look so nineteen-twenties. Both of us."

Her sister's dress was rose pink, and made, like Grace's, of soft, floaty chiffon over a cotton voile base the same colour. She, too, wore a headband – a wide band of pink satin with a large oval jewel placed at the centre of her forehead.

From downstairs came the clang of the brass bell that hung outside the château's main entrance, announcing the arrival of more guests to the murder mystery dinner.

Natasha tilted her head, the hint of a frown on her face.

"You look different, Grace. Bubbly. Is there something I should know about?"

Well yes, Grace thought, smiling. She was in love with Kai and he with her, it seemed, and it was the most wonderful thing that had ever happened to her. But she wouldn't share it, not yet, not even with her sister. She wasn't sure she believed it herself yet.

"Maybe." She felt colour warm her cheeks. "We'll talk later, OK? Right now, we ought to be making our way downstairs."

She turned towards the door of her room, but Natasha caught hold of her arm, staying her.

"OK," she said, and Grace was touched by the concern she could see in her eyes. "You can tell me everything later. But take care. Please. Promise?"

Grace didn't hesitate.

"Promise."

The two of them moved out into the corridor, and Grace locked her bedroom door behind her.

"Have you locked yours?"

Natasha nodded. Angela had asked them to do so. The evening's guests would have a more or less free run of the château, so it made sense to take the precaution of locking their doors. On the first floor, she'd explained, one of Pierre's grandsons would be making sure none of the guests strayed into the family's rooms or Barbs and Johnno's suite.

"Angela's got it all planned out, hasn't she?" Grace said as they headed along the corridor and down the stairs. She could hear music coming up the stairwell from the ground floor, and the buzz of excited chatter. The brass bell rang again as more new arrivals announced their presence.

"Oh, yes," Natasha replied. "She's nobody's fool."

Rounding the bend in the stairs, Grace caught sight of Kai at the very moment he saw her. He smiled up at her – and her heart swooped into a faster beat.

He stood on the first-floor landing. He'd been waiting for her, she thought, filled with happiness at the idea. Cameron was at his side, but her eyes were for Kai alone.

He wore a black dinner jacket with black satin lapels, black trousers turned up at the ankles, a white shirt and waistcoat, and a black bow-tie. His thick hair had been slicked back, giving extra emphasis to the strong lines of his face.

Grace was smiling broadly as she ran the rest of the way down the stairs, coming to a halt so close she was almost touching him.

"You've certainly dressed the part." It wasn't the run downstairs that made her so breathless. "You look wonderful."

He caught her hands in both his.

"So do you." His eyes didn't leave her face. "I want to kiss you," he said softly, for her ears alone, stepping backwards, taking her with him.

"Kai, what . . . " she protested, stumbling, laughing.

But his arms were around her, his mouth on hers, and she gave herself over to the beauty of his kiss.

As if from a great distance came the sound of the double doors opening and closing, Angela's excited greetings, Vespasien's more measured tones.

It was real, she thought, breathing in the smoky notes of Kai's cologne. This amazing feeling was real. She'd imagined herself in love before, but it had never been like this. Natasha was right. She was bubbly. Bubbling over with happiness, and it was the most marvellous feeling ever.

As of one accord, they drew apart. It was time, Grace knew. The noise level from down below was much diminished now. Most of the guests had no doubt moved along to the grand salon.

Kai cupped her face in his hands, kissing the tip of her nose before stepping back.

"I've got to put on my public persona. I'm going to keep my distance, stay away from you. I don't want anyone guessing about us, taking a photo on their phone, selling it to the papers. It's too soon." Another kiss on her nose. "Can you understand that?"

With an effort, Grace brought a smile to her face.

"Yes, Kai, I understand."

She looked around her. They were in a narrow bay about a metre deep, set back from the corridor. A bust of a Roman emperor on a plinth took up about half the space. A curtain, partly shielding them from view, gave a glimpse of the stairs.

A gangling teenager, almost certainly Pierre's grandson, was leaping up them two at a time, followed by Loki, long feather-like tail wagging furiously.

Grace frowned.

"What's Loki doing here? Is Vespasien all right?" Master and dog were never normally away from each other.

Kai asked the newcomer, receiving a reply in rapid French. He turned to Grace.

"Vespasien's fine. One of the guests doesn't like dogs, that's all. So Loki's going to help keep an eye on the family's rooms." He caught her hand in his and smiled. "Shall we join the party?"

She smiled back.

"Yes."

But he didn't keep her hand in his for long. He didn't want her to be seen with him, with all the attendant publicity and speculation that would provoke, she knew that and understood it. When his hand slid from hers, though, and he moved ahead of her, several stairs below her, she felt bereft.

Expelling her breath on a long sigh, she squared her shoulders and continued on down. The hall was empty now. She saw Kai's back as he disappeared past the Christmas tree and through a door, second to last into the grand salon.

Nineteen-twenties jazz was playing. People of all ages were chatting, laughing, joking, waving the glass of kir they held to emphasise their point.

As she threaded her way through the crowd, Grace heard both English and French voices, though she suspected the French guests all spoke good English.

She saw long ropes of pearls, mouths lipsticked into a cupid's bow, cigarette holders brandished airily. Some of the men wore fedoras, brims pulled low. One had a deerstalker. All wore formal suits and starched white shirts. It was clear that everyone had caught the spirit of the event, and Grace felt a thrill of excitement for Angela. Her murder mystery evening was going to be a huge success.

Angela's orange hair had been sculpted into tight waves lying close against the scalp.

"Marcel waves, darling," she explained. "All the rage in the Twenties. I'm getting into character."

"You've certainly done that," Grace said with a happy smile. "You look wonderful."

Kai's mother was resplendent in gold. The fabric of her sleeveless, low-necked gown had a metallic sheen to it and fell in soft flattering folds to her ankles. A gold headband in the form of a snake crossed her forehead while thick snake bangles, also in gold, circled her upper arms.

"It's the Egyptian look," she said. "Very fashionable at the time. They'd just discovered Tutankhamun's tomb."

"Is the dress another of my sister's creations?"

"Of course. Isn't she a marvel? The whole outfit, jewellery as well, cost a fortune though," she added, voice sinking to a whisper. "Don't tell Vespi."

Vespasien stood with his back to the fireplace, a long-stemmed glass in one hand. Like his stepson, he wore black dinner jacket and trousers, white shirt and waistcoat, but with the addition of shiny black patent leather shoes – and a monocle. Grace gave a little laugh of delight.

"Angela insisted," he said in a tone that was half grumble, half laughter, and Grace was reminded how Kai had said he'd do anything for his wife.

"Looks like an English lord, doesn't he?"

Johnno, joining the two of them, positioned himself just a shade too close to her. She stepped back a pace. Wearing a black fedora and a wide-lapelled suit, brown with white chalk stripes, he looked – very appropriately, Grace couldn't help thinking – the epitome of a 1920s gangster.

"See you're serving the 2005 vintage tonight," Johnno said to Vespasien, raising the glass he was holding, a third full of red wine. "Opened a bottle. Tried some of it. Hope you don't mind. Good stuff." He swallowed a mouthful. "Not as spectacular as you'd led me to believe, but . . . "

With that, the two men fell into a discussion of vintages, and Grace moved away. Kai, she saw, had put his arm across the shoulder of one of the women he was talking to. But it didn't mean a thing, she told herself, not a thing.

She found Natasha with Cameron and several others at the far end of the grand salon. Earlier in the day, a space had been cleared, and the carpet rolled up and taken away. There'd be dancing here later on in the evening, Grace knew.

Amid much laughter Cameron was teaching Natasha how to do the Charleston. He was a good dancer, Grace saw, and wasn't overly surprised. From the clothes he wore to the paintings and sketches he produced, he was careful and precise at all times.

He'd pencilled in a thin, dark brown moustache above his upper lip.

"Hey, I'm Rudolph Valentino," he said with a

laugh. "The nineteen-twenties' sexiest heart-throb."

And all of a sudden Kai was there at her side, the soft wool of his jacket brushing against the bare skin of her arm. He handed her a glass of kir, his fingers touching hers a moment longer than was necessary, and her breath caught in her throat.

"Enjoy," he said, warm eyes smiling, and then he was gone, pounced on by a woman with kohl-smudged eyes and a beauty spot at the corner of her mouth.

Grace sipped her kir and moved around the room, chatting, joining in. It occurred to her that she was smiling at everyone and everything. But of course she was. She was in love. Kai's touch was fresh in her mind, his scent was on her clothes and on her skin. It was as if he was with her wherever she went.

A gong sounded, the music was turned down low, and an expectant hush fell. All eyes turned toward Angela who now stood by the fireplace next to her husband.

"How lovely to see you all. But I'm not sure you realise what you've let yourselves in for," she said, good humour in her voice. "You're going to have a busy evening, darlings. So let's go into the dining-room and when you're all sitting comfortably . . . " a murmur of laughter from some of the older guests ". . . we will begin."

"She's so good at this sort of thing," Barbs said into Grace's ear as they moved with everyone else from the grand salon to the dining room. "Always has been."

Pierre had extended the table that afternoon and spread a snow-white damask cloth over it. Settings were laid for 11 people either side with one each end, for Vespasien and Angela.

The starter, a selection of seafood on a bed of edible seaweed together with the necessary tools, had already been set out, and by each plate a small envelope.

"Don't open it yet, darlings. Let me explain first."

Grace found her place and sat down. Kai was diagonally opposite her, she was immensely pleased to see, Cameron was next to her and Natasha a few places further down.

"You've all found the envelope with your name on it," Angela said when everyone was seated. "Inside, there's a riddle, a different one for each of you. Your task is to solve it – either before, during or after your starter. It will lead you to a second envelope containing important information about the character you are to play tonight, plus . . . " her voice took on a dramatic note " . . . secret knowledge you have about one or several other people in this room."

There was a buzz of excited chat. With a smiling glance across the table to Kai, Grace picked up her envelope, opened it and drew out a slip of paper. It read:

"Up and up
And round and round
You do that
And I'll be found"

"Too easy," Grace said, showing the paper to Cameron at her side. "It's got to be the tower. The top of the tower." Warmth crept up over her cheeks as she recalled going there with Kai, the beauty of the view from the top – and the sweet intensity of his kiss.

She looked around at the other guests. Some had clearly decided to have their starter first, attacking oysters and prawns with relish, while others were getting to their feet. Johnno was pouring himself a glass of wine.

She scraped back her chair and stood up. Kai was doing the same. But when she reached the door and glanced back she saw that Barbs had caught his attention and he'd stopped to speak to her.

She hesitated. Should she wait? Together, they could find her second envelope, then his. The thought of stolen moments alone in the tower with Kai was more than tempting. But he was still talking to Barbs, and the decision was made. She wouldn't wait.

They'd accessed the tower via a low door on the second floor, she remembered. The stone steps had gone down as well as up, so logically there had to be an entrance to it on the ground floor, or if not then the first floor, she decided. Taking an instant to orientate herself, she headed along the wide gallery on her left.

And there it was, hidden behind a floor-length velvet curtain, a low door as dark with age as the one on the second floor.

Grace pushed down on the latch and pulled the door open. Recoiling as the cold air and the musty, earthy smell of centuries-old stone hit her, she had a moment's misgiving. Perhaps she should have waited for Kai.

Reaching inside, she found the light switch, turned it on, and saw grey-white steps winding upwards. As with the second floor, a thick rope was attached at intervals to the curving outside wall. Closing the door behind her and taking a steadying breath, she grasped the rope in her left hand, placed the palm of her right hand against the central pillar, and started up.

She must have climbed a dozen steps when the light went out. She stilled, instantly, frozen by shock, by sudden fear. Her heart jolted in a single sickening thump.

It was pitch black. There were no windows, no arrow slits that starlight could filter through. She was effectively blind. The rough rope in one hand, the cold stone against the palm of the other, the solid step beneath her feet – they were her only points of reference.

Continue on up? Or go back down? She had to be nearer the first floor than the ground, she reasoned. There'd be a door, wouldn't there? Or a light switch.

Her heart was pounding an uneasy rhythm. She lifted one foot on to the step above, slid her hand along the rope, the other up the central pillar, then brought the second foot up on to the same step.

Her tension eased a fraction. So far, so good. Do it again. And again. Step by slow step she made her way up the tower. She had to be almost at the first floor by now. And that was when it happened, in a tangled confusion of thoughts and events.

The sound of breathing. Hers? No. Someone else. Kai! It had to be, and her pulses leaped. An arm reaching out. The soft wool of his jacket against her arm. Kai had come for her. He'd get her out of here. A faint whiff of his cologne – from her skin? Or from his?

No. How could it be? He was grabbing her. Pushing her. She heard a grunt of effort. And with a cry she was going down. The air whooshed from her lungs as her body came down hard, and she slithered, crashing from side to side like a dodgem car gone mad, elbows cracking against the stone steps and walls, spine jarring against the sharp edge of each and every step.

Kai had pushed her, she thought as she came to a juddering halt, and her disbelief was total. The man she loved had pushed her.

Sinister Discovery

GRACE groaned. She knew she had to stay still. She could hear footsteps running, coming her way. Then Kai appeared in the open doorway – and she flinched. She couldn't help it. It was an instinctive reaction.

He frowned. Reaching inside, he flicked the switch. The light came on. One look at his face when he saw her lying there and she knew she'd been wrong to doubt him.

"Grace, sweetheart." Pulling off his jacket, he knelt down beside her, spreading it over her, tucking it in round her shoulders. "Tell me you're OK." There was desperation in his voice. His face had lost all colour.

His brother appeared at his side.

"Cam, call one-five. Get an ambulance here."

"No," Grace murmured. "I'm fine." It was an effort to speak. "No bones broken."

"You can't know that, sweetheart." Kai's tone was soothing as he brushed strands of hair back from her face. "Let's get you checked over at the hospital."

"Don't tell Angela. This dinner's important to her. I don't want to spoil it for her."

He frowned.

"All right. If that's what you want."

"I didn't fall, Kai. I was pushed." She saw his expression harden and he started to get to his feet. She touched her hand to his sleeve. "There's something else."

"What?"

She swallowed.

"I thought it was you who'd pushed me." She paused, plunged on, mouth dry. "Swear to me it wasn't."

His head jerked back as if she'd landed a punch to the jaw.

"You really need to ask?" His voice was a growl.

She could see the hurt in his eyes. She wished she hadn't spoken. Shock, perhaps, had put the words into her mouth.

"I'm sorry."

"Why on earth would you think I was the one who pushed you?"

"I . . . " She was close to tears. "It was so dark. Pitch black. Your jacket, the sleeve of your jacket, I felt it." She hesitated, shaken still. "And I could smell your cologne."

He sat back on his heels, shaking his head.

"You could have been killed."

"I was lucky. I fell feet first. On my back." She shivered, remembering.

"Head first and you might not be here to tell the tale." His tone was grim. Anger had replaced the hurt. "Someone did this to you, someone wanted to kill you, and we need to find out who."

Abruptly, he stood up, taking the phone out of his pocket. He tapped a two-figure number into his phone and was soon speaking in fluent French to the person at the other end of the line. At last he snapped the phone shut and took her hands in his.

"The gendarmes will take a statement from you at the hospital. Two of them. They both speak English. Security there is excellent, they say. You'll be perfectly safe."

Grace absorbed the words, saw the concern in Kai's eyes, and a shudder coursed through her body. For, of course, she was still in danger – just so long as her assailant remained uncaught.

* * * *

"How are you feeling this morning?"

"Nat!" Grace winced as she pushed herself into a sitting position, smiling with pleasure as her sister came into the hospital room carrying a bag and a bunch of flowers.

Natasha put the bag down on the bed.

"Clothes. Skinny jeans, brown boots, underwear, and the sweater with the penguin on it – because it's Christmas Eve," she added with a laugh. "And these are from guess-who," she said, handing the flowers to her sister. The cellophane they were wrapped in rustled and crackled. "Lucky you."

Roses, a beautiful deep pinky-orange colour. Grace held them to her nose, inhaling the sweet scent and, inexplicably, she felt tears well in her eyes as her thoughts went back to the previous evening.

He'd knelt beside her on the cold floor at the foot of the tower, stroking her hands, murmuring soft words. Natasha had arrived at the same time as the ambulance. Maybe he'd texted her or sent Cameron to fetch her, Grace didn't know.

"Stay with her until the gendarmes have been and gone," he'd said to Natasha, getting to his feet. "Keep her safe for me," he had added.

"Why? Aren't you coming with me?" Grace had asked.

He shook his head. The look he turned on her and his voice when he spoke were steely with determination.

"I've got things to do here."

At the hospital Grace had been x-rayed and scanned, and had been given the all-clear. The doctor who'd examined her had asked some very searching questions, no doubt worried she was in an abusive relationship.

Grace suspected she would have called the gendarmes if they hadn't in fact turned up 15 minutes later. She'd told them everything she could remember, and Kai had been right, they spoke very good English.

"You didn't answer my question." Her sister's

voice broke into her thoughts, bringing her back to the present. "How are you feeling?"

"Battered and bruised, a bit shaken still, but otherwise OK. They wanted to keep me in overnight just to double-check, but I'm fine. Really I am."

"Your dress isn't. I took it back with me last night. I'm not sure I'm going to be able to repair it. You know," she continued, "I don't think we should wait till the twenty-sixth. I think we should go back to the UK today."

"No." Grace was shaking her head.

"We can leave here then collect our stuff from the château. You stay in the car while I sort it with everyone, then we head off up to . . . "

"No. No, Natasha." She stopped for an instant, thinking, putting some of the pieces of the jigsaw together in her mind. "I originally thought getting that electric shock was an accident. But now I'm not so sure. Being pushed down the stairs of the tower was definitely not an accident. It was a deliberate act."

"All the more reason to leave."

"No," Grace repeated with a determined shake of her head. "I need to find out why. Why me? Why have I been targeted? I must go back to the château."

She couldn't prevent the shiver that chilled her skin despite the warmth of the hospital room. She was scared, and wasn't afraid to admit it to herself. It was the only way, though. She had to do it.

"Listen, Nat," she went on. "I don't want you to stay with me. The roads are clear. Go on up to the port, get the ferry home."

"No, Grace." Natasha's turn to shake her head. "You're my little sister. I'm not leaving you here alone."

Grace was moved beyond words. She reached for her sister just as Natasha's arms came round her, wrapping her in a tight hug, and the tears that had been threatening all night spilled at last down her cheeks.

* * * *

Kai didn't speak until he'd closed the door to the barn that housed the family's cars behind the two of them. Natasha had stayed with Angela and Vespasien, bringing them up to date.

"Nothing but negatives so far," he said as they set off across the snow, heading for the forest's edge. They walked side by side, not touching, and Grace was uneasy, missing the way he'd always thrown his arm across her shoulders, drawing her to him.

He was the other reason she'd had to come back to the château, of course. She wanted her time with him to last for as long as possible. She couldn't bear to cut it short.

He could have his pick of any woman in the

world. He'd soon tire of ordinary, unremarkable her. But until then she had to make the most of every moment she had with him. While it lasted.

Perhaps the relationship – brief as it was – was waning already, she thought, and her heart was heavy at the prospect.

Heavy grey-white clouds hung low in the sky, threatening snow. A cold little breeze played over the exposed skin of her face. The cawing of rooks as they flew from one treetop to the next pierced the silence of the land around them.

"I found the piece of paper with the riddle you were given," he said. "It was about halfway up the tower, between the ground and first floors."

"I must have dropped it," she murmured, "when he made a grab at me."

"Grace, my sweet." She heard the pain in his voice, then his arms went round her, pulling her against him, and he was rocking her from side to side. The bruises down her back protested but she didn't mind. She didn't mind at all. He pressed kisses to her face, her hair, and all at once her spirits were soaring. She barely registered his words.

"What you must have gone through – I blame myself. I should have been there."

"Kai, no. It was my fault. I should have waited for you."

Keeping her within the circle of his arms, he lifted his head from hers, and brushed the tears from her cheeks with the pad of his thumb.

"Don't cry, sweetheart. You're safe now."

They walked on as snowflakes began to fall. Both his arms were round her, clasping her to his side. She leaned her head against his shoulder. The aches in her body were forgotten, and she found she was smiling – from the sheer pleasure of being held by the man she loved.

"The door that leads to the first floor," he said a while later, "is set back from the staircase. That's where he or she must have been hiding. They turned the lights off, then lay in wait."

"He. It was a man. I heard him grunt."

"Did you tell the police that?"

She thought back.

"Yes."

"Good." He paused, clearly gathering his thoughts then spoke again. "I went on up to the top of the tower, looked all over but there wasn't a second envelope anywhere. The riddle sent you on a wild goose chase, its sole aim to get you into the tower."

Grace shuddered as the memory of that wild, slithering fall came flashing back into her mind, and Kai's hands closed even more tightly round her upper arm.

"I had a word with Vespasien and my mother. A quiet word because the murder mystery dinner was still going on and you were right, it meant a lot to my mother. It was going very well. I didn't want to ruin it for her."

"You did the right thing, Kai." The snow was

falling more thickly now, settling on their heads and shoulders.

"I told them what had happened, and they were shocked. Horrified. My mother went white. They confirmed what I already knew – they weren't the ones who'd written the 'up and up' riddle."

"So someone substituted their own riddle for the one Angela and Vespasien had put in the envelope?"

He nodded.

"They'd prepared a different one for you – one that wouldn't have taken you to the tower at all, but to the second-floor landing. I went up there and found the second envelope where they'd said it would be, taped to the back of the painting of Napoleon winning the battle of Austerlitz."

"I know the one you mean. You know," she went on, speaking slowly, thinking as she spoke, "it all comes back to paintings, doesn't it? Or rather, a painting. The badly restored Sisley." She twisted in his arms so that she could see his face. "I think we need to have another look at the Sisley."

He took her hand in his as they retraced their steps across the snow, through the barn and covered walkway and into the kitchen. There, they pulled off hats, coats and gloves, leaving them draped over chairs.

Urgency gave Grace speed. Kai, too – no

doubt for the same reason. Were they at last about to find the explanation for – what? The accidents that had befallen her? The attempts on her life? Grace's mind shied away.

The two of them met no-one on their way to the corridor that led to the dining-room.

The first time Grace had noticed the painting, she'd given voice to little more than fleeting impressions. When Cameron returned it to its position on the wall, almost completely hidden by a vase of holly, she'd barely glanced at it on her way in to or out of dinner.

But now, as she and Kai came to a halt in front of it, she took several long, steadying breaths, forcing herself to slow down, to give herself the time to examine the painting properly.

She wondered at the holly, all glossy, spiky leaves and fat red berries, that had replaced the flowers. Could it be there to discourage people from peering too closely at the painting, she couldn't help thinking as she lifted the vase. Kai took it from her and set it down on the ground further along.

The light was poor here, and Grace unhooked the Sisley, turning it over to see a couple of old auction labels on the back. Carrying it over to the window, she angled the painting as she studied it. Though muted by the falling snow, the even, northern light was an improvement.

The painting showed a country lane running diagonally across the canvas, bordered on both sides by leafy chestnut trees. A woman leaning back against the trunk of one of the trees gave human scale to the landscape while two other figures, made tiny by distance, could be seen at the far end of the lane.

Grace saw again the inconsistencies that had caught her eye that first time, the green that was just a shade too bright, and the little curls of white paint on the lane which had struck her as more consistent with Sisley's later style.

But it was something else she saw now, something that drained the colour from her face.

"This isn't a badly restored painting, Kai."

He stood behind her, hands on her upper arms.

"That should be good news." His tone told her he knew it wasn't. Tears filled her eyes. She blinked them back.

"It's a copy," she said. "And I know who made it."

Holding the painting so the lower edge of the frame rested against her stomach, she pointed with her free hand.

"The two men there, in the distance. They're holding hands." She sucked in a breath. She couldn't even begin to work out all the implications. Not yet.

"Sisley would never have painted that," she said, as a tear slid down her cheek. "But Cameron did."

Accusations And Denials

LET me take that." Without waiting for an
answer, Kai took the Sisley from her and tucked
it under one arm.

"Kai. Where are we going?" He'd grasped her
hand, was drawing her at speed towards the
château's main staircase. The bruises on her
arms and legs protested furiously.

"To his studio. It's mid-morning. That's where
he'll be." His hand was like a manacle round
hers. Every inch of his body spoke of steel
determination.

"Kai, please. Maybe it's not what we think."

"You mean, my brother didn't set out to kill
you?"

She could hear the anguish in his words, saw it
in his eyes when they reached the stairs and he
looked quickly back at her.

"That's quite a leap," she said. She was
breathless and her voice shook. "From knowing
the painting's a copy to . . . " A leap she too
had made, she knew, and a sick feeling swirled
again in her stomach.

He started up the stairs, taking her with him,
and she dragged at his hand, slowing the pace.

"Don't hurt him, Kai. Please."

Another quick look back at her.

"I mean to find out the truth. Come on." He tugged at her hand, and she found she had to run, taking the stairs two at a time to keep up.

"I've come to no harm." Her words came in gasps as they rounded the bend in the stairs and headed up the second flight. "I'm all right, Kai. Promise me you won't hurt him."

He didn't answer, and Grace's heart was thumping a fast uneven beat when they arrived outside the door to the studio.

He didn't knock, simply twisted the knob and pushed the door open.

Cameron stood at an easel, his back to them, palette in one hand, brush in the other. He jumped, turning his head to the door, clearly startled.

In one swift movement Kai had put the painting down on the floor, let go Grace's hand and was crossing the room to his brother.

"Hey . . . " Cam got no further.

"Tell me the truth." Kai had caught hold of the neck of his brother's shirt in one hand, and was forcing him backwards against the dresser. His other hand was bunched in a fist at his side. Grace's pulse raced, shocked by the sudden violence and by his anger, thrumming through the air. "Tell me you didn't push her down the stairs."

"Are you crazy? No! Of course I didn't." His gaze flicked wildly from Kai to Grace and back to Kai. All colour had left his face. The palette and brush had dropped, bouncing, to the floor. "What's all this about?"

"The Sisley's a copy."

"OK, yes. I admit it. But that doesn't mean I'm going to go round pushing people down stairs."

He spoke fast, as though desperate to convince, and darted pleading looks at Grace who'd remained by the door. Relief washed over her. She needed no more convincing.

"Let go of him, Kai. He's telling the truth." She had no doubt of it.

For long moments Kai didn't move. His stance as he held his brother pinned against the dresser remained as rigid as before. His eyes stayed fixed on Cameron's face, as if searching his features for clues.

Then, at last, Grace saw the tension ease from his shoulders, and the hand that held the neck of Cameron's shirt slid away, letting go.

"Very well," he said, flexing the fingers of both hands as he stepped back a pace. "You've said you had nothing to do with it, and I accept what you say."

There was a touch of theatricality in the way his brother rubbed his throat, brushed down his paint-spattered shirt and bent to pick up his brush and palette. Luckily it had landed paint side up.

"Thanks a million," he said. Unusually for him, he hadn't shaved that morning and looked rather the worse for wear, Grace thought.

"You had no reason to push me down the tower," she said, speaking slowly, working it out as she spoke. Whoever had tried to kill her, it wasn't Kai's brother, and the relief of knowing that was like a heady rush of alcohol to her bloodstream.

"This business with the Sisley, it's not a secret you've got to protect at all costs. After all, you put your signature . . . " she sketched quote marks in the air " . . . in plain sight."

"The two men holding hands. Yes."

Grace saw the small, complacent smile that curved Cameron's mouth, and more pieces of the jigsaw fell into place.

"You almost want to be found out, don't you? You want the world – and Vespasien especially – to know how clever you are. How talented you are," she said, using the word that had caused those awkward moments at dinner – how many evenings ago?

Cameron flushed.

"He never looks at his paintings."

"He doesn't appreciate them. They're investments," he finished, giving bitter emphasis to the last word, and darting a quick glance at his brother who stood, tall and unyielding, less than a metre from him.

Kai had his hands in his pockets, thumbs hooked through the belt loops of his trousers. He was listening intently, Grace sensed, and watching the play of emotions across his brother's face.

"In fact," she said, "I bet you used the wrong green and those short curling brushstrokes deliberately – little anachronistic details that would make a fool of him when they were found out, as of course they surely would be if he ever tried to sell the painting."

"Is Grace right?" Kai spoke quietly. A deceptive calm, Grace thought. "Is that why you did it? Copied the Sisley?"

Cameron nodded, chin tilting up in a small show of defiance.

"Have you done any more?"

Grace saw Cameron hesitate before he spoke, reluctantly.

"I'm working on one at the moment."

"Show me."

Another hesitation. Then, twisting round, he crouched down, opened one of the doors of the lower part of the dresser and drew out two rectangular shapes covered in cloth.

Curious, Grace crossed the room to join the two brothers. He'd accidentally left the door ajar, she recalled, that morning she, Kai and Natasha had spent in his studio, had coloured and pushed it closed with his foot. She'd supposed, she remembered thinking, that the canvases covered in cloth had something to do with his lover. Obviously not, she now decided, watching as he removed one of the cloths.

It was another early Sisley, still in its frame,

showing a footpath along a river or stream, with trees and a tumbledown cottage in the middle ground.

"He hasn't even noticed it's gone," Cameron said. Handing the Sisley to Grace, he removed the second cloth. "Here's my version. It's almost finished."

Kai put his arm across Grace's shoulders, drawing her to him. She glanced up, saw his gaze flick from one painting to the other, comparing the original and the copy Cameron was holding out.

"I must admit," Kai said, "it's good."

"I've studied his technique."

"Ah, so now we know," Grace said, "why only Sisleys get – quote – restored. Oh!" All at once she stopped. A chill of unease sped down her spine.

Kai pointed to two tiny figures, both men, standing hand in hand by the door of the tumbledown cottage.

"You say Vespasien never looks at his paintings, but you're chancing your arm with this."

"I don't care any more," Cameron said.

"You're making the announcement." It was a statement, not a question.

"Yes. It's my New Year's resolution. I'm moving in with . . . him."

Grace was only half-listening to what the two brothers were saying, only half-registered the defensiveness that had entered Cameron's voice. A growing dread of what was to come was seeping into her bones, and she twisted away from Kai. His arm fell to his side, leaving a chill across her shoulders where the warmth and weight of it had been.

"In the meantime," he was saying, "you're going to put the Sisley originals back where they belong. Today."

"I can't do that. I can't put chestnut trees back."

Grace hugged her arms across her chest. If only she'd never drawn attention to the Sisley. Or, having done so, why couldn't she have said moments later with a laugh that she'd been wrong? If only!

She heard Kai swear.

"Why on earth not?" She held her breath.

"Because our dear mama has sold it."

The words dropped like a rock into still water. Cameron fell silent. Kai stared at him, frowning, shaking his head. And Grace wished she could vanish in a puff of smoke. She'd never wanted to cause such hurt to the man she loved.

"Sold it to a private collector," Cameron was saying. "Someone Johnno knows."

Kai turned pained eyes on Grace, and she knew the implications were sinking in. She'd dismissed the notion that a woman had pushed her down the tower steps. Only Kai had entertained that possibility – and perhaps he'd been right to do so.

She swallowed against the painful ache in her throat.

"I'm sorry, Kai."

"Hey, no. She'd never do that."

How Grace hoped he was right. But of course Angela had to be involved. She was the one who'd spoken of the painting being sent away to be restored, had tried to make light of the whole subject.

Grace thought, too, of the old auction labels on the back of the painting she'd examined, and was in no doubt Angela and Cameron had set out deliberately to deceive Vespasien into thinking the copy – the fake – was a genuine Sisley.

She looked at Kai's grim face, and a sick dread swirled uneasily through her. This was not going to end well.

There was contempt in the look he directed at his brother.

"Let's get this straight." His voice was cold as steel. "You painted a copy, and it was kept here on the walls of the château. Angela sold the original. Correct?"

Cameron nodded.

"You intend doing the same with this second one?"

Another nod.

"Well, it's not going to happen." Kai took his phone out of his pocket, flipped it open. "At least she didn't sell the copy. Small mercies."

The phone call to his mother was brief and curt.

"She'll be here shortly," he said, putting the phone back in his pocket. With the heel of his boot, he hooked a chair out from under a table covered in tubes of paint and pots of brushes, turned it round and sat, legs apart, forearms resting on his thighs.

His head was bowed, and Grace couldn't begin to guess what he was going through.

Suspicion had been thrown first at his brother, now at his mother. She put her arms across his shoulders and pressed a kiss to the back of his neck.

"What a mess," he murmured, giving her arm a brief squeeze before letting his hand drop back down between his knees. There was a finality in the way he spoke, she thought, and the ache in her throat grew more painful still as she realised he didn't want her close.

They waited.

With a heavy heart, Grace moved round the studio. Glancing up at the high window, she saw the sky was white with snowflakes, carried this way and that like a flock of starlings by the gusting wind.

Leaning back against the dresser, Cameron was muttering, not so much to be heard, more to fill the silence, Grace guessed. Perhaps to break the tension that gripped the room.

"This hasn't improved my hangover . . . supposed to be something special . . . rough old stuff . . . "

"Shut it, Cam." Kai's voice was a growl.

Grace looked round at Cameron's paintings, the two Sisley copies, his clever Paris places and faces sketches, his current work in progress, a moody abstract.

He was a talented, versatile artist, she thought, and hoped he'd soon find his way – a way that didn't involve deception and petty revenge on a disliked stepfather.

Angela arrived at last, sweeping in through the door with a swish of satin and a flurry of movement. She wasn't beaming her usual smile. Kai's tone over the phone must have warned her.

She looked round, gaze fixing for a fraction of a second on each person in the room before dropping to the three paintings – Cameron's two copies and the Sisley original – now on the floor propped against the dresser. She turned to Kai.

"I had to do it, darling. Vespi's cut my monthly allowance. Drastically. I . . . "

"It's the last time you sell any of his paintings," Kai cut in, sitting back in his chair. He spoke quickly, like a man wanting to get the nuts and bolts business over with as soon as possible. "Or any of the treasures round here. That's a given. Understood? If you want money, ask me."

"But I . . . "

"I need to know how far you were prepared to go to protect your secret."

"I . . . what?" Angela frowned, looking with worried eyes from one brother to the other. "What do you mean? What are you getting at?"

"Did you push Grace down the stairs in the tower?"

There was an instant's disbelieving hush before Angela spoke.

"No!" Angela stepped back, shaking her head, over and over. "No, of course not!" Her gaze darted from Kai to Grace and back to Kai. "No, I could never do that! Kai." There was desperation in her voice. "Kai, say you believe me."

He briefly closed his eyes, tilting his head back, and his relief was almost tangible.

"Of course I believe you," he said gruffly, as he got to his feet and crossed to his mother, wrapping her in a hug, burying his face in her hair.

Tears filled Grace's eyes. The ache in her throat made it almost impossible to swallow. With a quick glance at Cameron, she turned to the door. There was no place for her here.

The Awful Truth Dawns

GRACE drew in a shuddering breath before continuing her story. Her voice was thick. Tears weren't far from the surface.

"Kai asked Angela how far she'd go to protect her secret, and it was obvious she didn't have the faintest idea what he was going on about."

"But that's good, Grace. Isn't it?" There was concern in Natasha's voice, and she reached across, taking her sister's hands in hers and giving them a strength-imparting squeeze.

They were sitting side by side in armchairs – small upholstered chairs with padded arms – by the window of Grace's bedroom, looking out over the château's park. Snow, smooth and untouched, covered everything, reminding Grace of the day they'd arrived. How much had happened since!

She looked now at Natasha.

"Of course it's good. I could see she was sincere, and I was so, so happy she wasn't the one that had pushed me." A single tear spilled and she brushed it away. "She sold the Sisley to a private collector Johnno helped her find. For less than market value, I imagine. If she'd tried to sell at auction, there'd have been publicity, and Vespasien might have heard about it."

She paused, sniffed, cuffed away another tear.

"Then Kai wrapped his arms round her, and Cameron was about to hug the two of them, and it was so moving to see, I was close to tears. And that's when I had to leave." She looked again at Natasha, glad of the warmth of her sister's hands round hers.

"I wasn't part of it, Nat. And I don't think I'll ever be a part of his life. I don't belong here. I keep telling myself to make the most of the time I have with him, but it's no use. I want to mean more to him than just a quick fling. And of course I never will."

"You can't know that," Natasha protested.

"I've brought nothing but disruption and upset to his life . . . "

"That's not your fault. He's hardly likely to blame you, is he?"

Grace shook her head.

"I don't know. I just don't know."

She fell silent, conscious of the thoughts and doubts and emotions crowding her mind, and she couldn't rid herself of the notion that the happiest chapter of her life was drawing to an unwanted close.

Outside, the snow had almost stopped. Snowflakes zigzagged lazily down to the ground. Grace looked over to her right where the dark trees of the forest stood motionless, spattered by lines of white along their branches.

She and Kai had walked the pathways there,

hand in hand, or wrapped in each other's arms. They'd talked and laughed, breathing in the crisp country air, and it had been a wonderful, magical time.

She looked in the other direction, at the vineyard-covered hills on her left. They had yet to explore those gentle slopes. But with a small sound of annoyance, she caught herself up. That would never happen. She and Kai would never walk there together.

"I want us to go home, Nat," she now said. "As soon as we can."

"I'm fine with that – we still don't know who tried to kill you. We're best out of here. It won't be today, though."

Grace bit her lip.

"As soon as the roads are cleared." The fact that her assailant remained at large seemed of little consequence. What did matter was that she was trapped, here at the château – with her memories, and with the man to whom she'd brought nothing but unhappiness.

"Grace . . . " Natasha's voice had taken on an added seriousness. "I think you're wrong about Kai. Will you promise me one thing?"

"What?"

"That you'll hear what he has to say before we leave?"

True to her word, Grace sought Kai out after lunch, a ham and cheese sandwich each that Natasha popped down to the kitchen to make, and that they ate in her sister's room. Conscious that her unhappiness was written in every feature of her face, Grace hadn't wanted to risk meeting anyone, and least of all Kai.

After lunch, a shower and a change of clothes, though, she felt stronger, more able to face him. Together with Natasha, she followed the sounds of his guitar as they made their way downstairs.

The music came in short bursts. He'd play the same few bars several times, then with a subtle variation. He was clearly working on a new song, one whose haunting, evocative notes threatened to bring fresh tears to her eyes.

The two sisters stopped outside the petit salon.

"I'll be in the kitchen," Natasha whispered just as the air was filled with the discordant clash of all twelve strings being strummed at once.

Grace's heart was beating fast as, with a single knock, she pushed the door open.

He was alone, sitting – as she'd seen so often – with the ankle of one leg resting on the knee of the other, his guitar across his lap. He looked up as she came in, putting his guitar aside and getting to his feet in one fluid movement.

Grace faltered, confused, not understanding. He'd seen who'd come in and his face had lit up, she was certain. She glanced down at his guitar, giving herself a mental shake, and when she looked at him again, she knew she'd been mistaken. He wore the polite smile of an acquaintance. No more.

"Natasha and I will be leaving as soon as the roads are clear. Tomorrow, I hope."

Kai's eyebrow went up.

"Do the ferries run on Christmas Day?"

"I don't know. Easy enough to go online and find out," Grace said, horribly aware that there was an awkwardness between them that hadn't been there before.

They stood facing each other, less than a metre apart, and the smoky notes of his cologne mingled with the scents of the oak logs burning in the fireplace.

"It's for the best," he said. "We're no closer to knowing who it was that pushed you down the stairs."

"At least we know it had nothing to do with the Sisley."

"True." He was then silent, and Grace knew he, too, was thinking back to the awful scenes that had taken place in his brother's studio.

A log shifted in the grate.

"So it must have been something else I saw. Something I heard, maybe." After all the hours they'd shared, how could she sound so stilted with him?

Her heart was aching. She longed to reach out, to take his hand in hers, or run her fingertips along the line of his jaw and up into his hair, to try to recapture that sense of closeness she'd felt so often with him.

With a sound low in his throat, he part-turned away, pushing fingers like claws through his hair.

"I don't want to go through anything like that ever again." He turned back, his gaze holding hers. "I wish . . . " His hand came up, and Grace's pulse leaped.

"I wish," he said, "that we could put the clock back to the start of the morning, rerun this whole business with my brother and mother. Better still, if none of it had ever happened."

His hand dropped back to his side, and Grace felt the loss as acutely as if he'd been holding her tight in his arms, then let her go.

"But it did happen, Kai," she said quietly. "We can't undo it."

He said nothing. His eyes still held hers. His smile was bleak. From outside came a flurry of footsteps, and the door to the petit salon was flung open. Cameron.

"Hey, sorry," he said, glancing from his brother to Grace. "I'm not interrupting anything, am I?"

"No," Grace said, and the weight of sorrowmade every word an effort. "Nothing at all."

* * * *

"We're stuck here," Natasha said, "and we'll just have to make the best of it. All of us," she went on. "If I know Angela, she'll be playing it as if nothing's happened. She'll be bright and gushing, and every other word will be 'darling'."

Grace smiled at the mental picture her sister was painting, and was amazed that, somehow, she too could act as if nothing had happened.

The two of them were in Natasha's room, getting ready for the Réveillon, the big Christmas celebration meal for family and friends that would go on till midnight and beyond.

"After all," Natasha continued, "she won't want Vespasien to know anything's up. Cameron will be – Cameron," she said with a laugh, "and Kai . . . " The laughter left her voice. "Well, he'll be back to being Mr Moody, I imagine."

Kai. Throughout the afternoon, the sound of his guitar had drifted up the central staircase, filling the château with the haunting notes of the melody he'd been working on earlier. From time to time she thought she heard his deep growl of a voice as he sang. And, too, the discordant clash of all twelve strings played at once that spoke of anger vented.

Kai. How was she going to survive – what? Four hours? Five? – in the same room as him when her heart was breaking? When all she longed for was to be in his arms again.

At eight, dressed in the deep pinky-red two-piece she'd worn the first evening at the château, she went downstairs and along to the petit salon with Natasha. To her dismay, her eyes went directly to Kai, tall and lean, and devastatingly attractive in his black dinner jacket and trousers, white shirt and waistcoat, and black bow-tie.

Their eyes met across the room, her breath caught in her throat, and it was an effort to look away.

Natasha had been right about Angela. Splendidly flamboyant in sapphire blue silk that rustled and fluttered with every movement, she was the perfect hostess, ensuring that everyone mingled and no-one felt left out.

So Grace made small talk, though she was certain she would never be able to recall a word she'd said or heard, not even five minutes later. She even welcomed it when Johnno corralled her into a corner.

"Itching to propose a toast," he said, raising his glass of kir. "Vesp doesn't want any fuss made, though." He nodded towards his host who stood with his back to the fireplace, Loki asleep at his feet, talking to Barbs.

"Ah." She could hear Kai's deep tones from the other side of the room. He had his back to her, was talking to his brother.

"Got the e-mail this afternoon. Three hundred cases of the 2005 red. Vesp's best ever vintage. Business acquaintance of mine. Pleased as Punch. Got it for what the French call an interesting price." Chuckling, he leaned closer,

and placed his hand high on the wall beside her.
To bar her escape? Grace wondered. She could
smell the cigarette smoke on his clothes.

Sensing movement, she looked past him – and
couldn't help smiling. She didn't need it but Kai,
her knight in shining armour, had come to the
rescue.

"Hmm." Johnno was looking behind him.
"Time for another ciggie, maybe."

Kai followed with his eyes as Johnno threaded
his way through the salon. Grace thought he
was about to say something to her. But, with a
brief, neutral smile, he turned and walked away.

"Was Johnno propositioning you?" her sister
asked moments later as they all left the petit
salon, heading for the dining-room.

Grace shook her head.

"Boasting about some deal he's helped
make."

Natasha laughed.

"Another dodgy deal?"

The dining table glittered and glowed. Slender
white candles in gold candelabra threw a softly-
flickering light over fine gold-rimmed china and
long-stemmed glasses. The warm, spicy scents
of pine, cloves and orange filled the air.
Christmas music played low in the background.

Grace took her place at the table. Kai sat down
opposite her, the last thing she wanted. The
play of candlelight over his features took her
breath away. Her throat was aching, and she

lowered her head.

She ate mechanically, barely registering the food or the conversations going on around her or the clack of knives and forks on china, and forced herself not to think about Kai.

Her mind went back to her sister's throwaway remark. Yes, Johnno had helped Angela sell a painting that wasn't hers to sell, thus proving he wasn't above a little dishonesty. And he'd said Vespasien didn't want a fuss made over his wine sale. So, was there something dodgy about this deal, too?

Three hundred cases of the 2005 red. Vespasien's best ever vintage, Johnno had said. Were there six bottles or 12 in a case? Either way, it meant an awful lot of wine, and all sold at a price cheaper than the going rate for an exceptional vintage.

She watched Kai stand up and leave the room, heading upstairs, at Angela's request, to fetch a stole for his mother. The longing for what might have been was constantly on her mind.

Cameron, sitting on Grace's right, nudged her and handed her a bottle of wine, indicating with a nod that she should pass it on down to Johnno. Grace looked at the label as she did so, and an image came to her.

The afternoon of their arrival at the château, when Vespasien had shown them round the wine cellars, she'd happened to see a pile of labels on the desk, and he'd snapped at her and taken them from her. She could picture them clearly, even now, several days later – the familiar pen-and-ink drawing of the château's façade, the words Château Beauvallon, and the year. 2005.

She frowned, unease prickling across the back of her neck. Something was wrong there. A 2005 vintage would have been bottled and labelled in 2006, wouldn't it? Why would anyone be labelling a 2005 vintage now, 12 years later?

And all at once she understood. A shiver ran down her spine despite the warmth of the room. She looked along the table, at the man who sat at its head, the man who was cheating his customers.

Vespasien Beauvallon de Mottefort. The man who had tried to kill her.

An Impossible Romance

HIS eyes met hers in an instant that lasted an age. She saw the jolt of recognition in them. He'd seen that eureka moment, knew she'd found him out, and there was anger in the hardening of his expression.

She looked away, down at her plate. What was she to do? What should she do for the best? Accuse him there and then? In front of his family and guests?

No. She couldn't do it. Couldn't bring yet more upset, disruption and, yes, ugliness to Kai's family. Ignore it? Of course not.

That left only one option.

She drew in a long breath, gathering her courage. Her eyes never left his as she dropped her serviette on to her plate, pushed back her chair and got to her feet.

She hesitated for the barest fraction of a second. Should she wait for Kai to come back? Or gesture to Natasha to come with her? No. This was something she had to deal with alone.

Her heartbeat was loud in her ears as she made for the door and the corridor outside, knowing Vespasien would follow. She heard the dining-room door close behind him and spun round to face him.

"I should have guessed way before now, shouldn't I?" She spoke with quiet vehemence, angry as much with herself as with him. "When I first saw the labels over there in the wine cellars. You overreacted and snatched them from me. That should have told me there was something wrong."

"My mistake," Vespasien murmured, looking her full in the face, not at all contrite. From the other side of the dining-room door came the muted sounds of people talking, the odd burst of laughter, and Loki's plaintive high-pitched whine.

She'd been thinking of Kai, Grace recalled, moving further down the wide corridor, in the opposite direction from the central hall.

"So you've been relabelling other bottles. Or you've bought wine in from somewhere else and put your own labels on. Which is it?"

They had come to a halt several metres from the dining-room door and stood facing each other. Vespasien didn't answer straight away. Pulling at his shirt cuffs, he inspected the sleeves of his jacket.

"Relabelling the 2013, mademoiselle" he admitted at last. "It wasn't a good year."

"Passing inferior wine off as an exceptional vintage. Selling cheaper stuff at an inflated price."

"And about to make a tidy profit. Thanks to Johnno, I have a buyer all lined up."

There was an arrogance, a total lack of remorse about him that threatened to break Grace's self-control. Her hands clenched at her sides.

"And for that you were prepared to kill me."

He flinched, and ugly colour stained his cheeks. Grace could hear Loki scrabble at the dining-room door, desperate to join his master.

"No. Not kill you," Vespasien said. "Just drive you away." Another pause. "It was an impulse. A moment of madness that I've regretted ever since."

Grace's eyebrows shot up.

"An impulse that took some planning, surely."

"No." Looking down, he pushed the fingertips of one hand hard across his forehead. All at once his arrogance was gone, and Grace felt the tension ease from her shoulders.

"Angela wanted to change into her outfit," he said. "She asked me to print out the riddles and put them in the envelopes. Easy enough to make up a new – very simple – riddle and put it in your envelope.

"Pierre's grandson was looking after Loki so I was free to go up to the first floor of the tower and wait. However, I was already regretting the idea."

"Not enough to stop you pushing me down the stairs."

He looked looked away.

"No."

"What about the amplifier?"

"Amplifier?"

"The one that gave me an electric shock. Just before the fashion show. You carried it into the grand salon. Did you tamper with it first?"

He shook his head.

"No. No, I . . . No!"

He appeared genuinely perplexed. But Grace recalled the amplifier's loose plug and Kai's insistence that he kept his equipment in excellent condition. Could Vespasien's protestations be nothing more than a clever act?

She sucked in a shaky breath.

"The deal with this business acquaintance of Johnno's – you realise it can't go ahead now. You'll have to cancel it."

His head jerked back. He was looking at her as if she were mad.

"Why on earth should I do that, mademoiselle?" he asked with a full return to arrogance, and Grace was seized by the conviction that he might now regret his ill-judged attempt on her life, but certainly didn't regret selling his wine as something it was not.

"Have you any idea," he went on, "how much it costs to maintain and run this place? A small fortune, I assure you. Not to mention my dear wife who has great difficulty reining in her extravagances."

Grace thought of Angela's beautiful but very expensive clothes and her lavish entertainments.

"What you're doing is fraud," she persisted. "Dishonest. There are other ways to make money."

"Unfortunately, mademoiselle, the dishonest ways are often the most lucrative."

The sound of footsteps on tiles broke the silence that fell. Kai came round the corner, two trailing cashmere scarves, one orange, one purple, draped over his arm. He'd plainly had trouble deciding.

"What's going on?" Frowning, he looked from Grace to his stepfather. He stopped by the dining-room door, heard Loki scrabbling at the wood, and opened it.

The dog bounded up to his master in a flurry of legs and wagging tail. Vespasien crouched to fondle the setter's long silky ears.

"I'm a proud man," he said with a glance at Kai who was heading towards the two of them. He spoke so quietly Grace knew only she was supposed to hear.

"I've always refused to allow my stepson to help me financially. I've never wanted, or asked for, his charity." He straightened, pulling himself to full height. His eyes held hers. "I'm in your hands, mademoiselle. Do your worst."

With that he turned, passing Kai without a word before re-entering the dining room.

"Are you all right?" Grace could hear the concern in Kai's voice, saw it in his eyes.

She turned away, hugging her arms across her

chest. Her confrontation with Vespasien had shaken her. Conflicting emotions – anger, but pity too – swirled in her brain.

"I'm fine," she said, eyes filling with tears.

"What were the two of you talking about?"

"Not now, Kai. Please." She needed time to think, time to make sense of it all.

She jumped when his hands closed round her upper arms. He was behind her, and his lips brushed like a caress against her hair as he spoke.

"Are you sure you're all right?"

A single tear spilled over. She could feel it sliding down her cheek. She brought her hand up to cover his, but let it drop back to her side.

"I'll tell you tomorrow," she said. She paused. "Before I leave."

A moment of stillness. Then Kai was turning her round, enfolding her in the warm strength of his arms, pressing her head against his shoulder.

"No. Tell me now."

There was no avoiding it. Briefly, Grace closed her eyes and sucked in a long breath.

"Your stepfather's been relabelling rubbish wine and selling it as 2005 vintage."

Kai stiffened.

"And for that he was all set to kill you?" She heard disbelief in the question, vying with anger.

"There's a lot of money involved." Grace's

voice was thick, reluctant. She'd never felt so wretched.

"Tell me. Tell me everything," he urged. "Start at the beginning."

With a shaky intake of breath she did so, starting with the guided tour of the wine cellars and finishing with her confrontation with Vespasien. And all the while she spoke, Kai held her in his arms, stroking her hair, murmuring soft words of comfort and reassurance, and she wished her time with him didn't have to end.

At last she fell silent.

"I'm going to have to phone the gendarmes," Kai said.

"I know." First his brother, then his mother, now his stepfather – she was tearing Kai's family apart. The sooner she left the better.

She lifted her head from his shoulder and he drew away, hand going to his pocket for his phone.

"Kai, wait. Phone them later. Vespasien's secret is out." She spoke quickly, anxious to convince. "It's not just between him and me any more. He knows I'll have told you, which means he's no longer a threat to me. So phone the gendarmes later, after the meal. Let's all eat together, family and friends, one last time."

"You think I can sit at the same table and calmly eat, knowing what my stepfather tried to do to you?"

"Maybe not." Grace's voice was husky with

emotion. She could see the pain and anger in his eyes, and the sight brought her own tears closer to the surface. "But try – for your mother's sake."

Was she doing the right thing? She didn't know. She only knew she couldn't face the thought of bringing yet more disruption to Kai's family.

And so they re-entered the dining-room and took their places, and she watched Kai smile and chat, eat something from every dish and taste every wine. Only the set line of his jaw and the narrowing of his eyes each time he looked at his stepfather told her the effort it cost him.

* * * *

The following morning before breakfast, Grace let herself through the low door and on to the circular platform that formed the roof of the tower. She stood looking out, forearms resting on the chest-high wall.

It was very still, with not a breath of movement in the freezing cold air. Dawn was breaking, a pearly grey glow in the east while further to the west, where the sky shaded to indigo, one of the planets – Venus, she thought – shone brightly close to the horizon.

Snow-covered hills, crossed by lines of trees and stone walls, stretched out in front and to her left, while to her right stood the dark snow-capped trees of the forest she and Natasha had driven through on their arrival.

How much had happened since then. And now it was over. One of Pierre's cousins would soon be clearing the road of snow, the gendarmes were coming at nine to take statements – and to take Vespasien away? – then she and Natasha would leave, heading for the ferry port and the UK.

It was Christmas Day but she couldn't rejoice. She felt empty, drained of all emotion.

Perhaps the soft click of the door latch had alerted her, she didn't know, but she wasn't surprised when Kai joined her.

In so many ways they were on the same wavelength. In other circumstances . . .

She bit her lip and tried to banish the thought. A lasting relationship between the two of them was unthinkable, impossible – even more so after all that had happened.

Knowing it, though, didn't make it any easier to face the truth of it.

Kai stood behind her, his arms criss-crossing round her neck, a welcome weight on her shoulders. His chin rested lightly on the top of her head.

"I don't want you to go," he said.

"I have to." Tears had filled her eyes, and she was glad he couldn't see her face. "I've caused enough damage round here already. And . . . "

"And what?" he prompted.

"There's no future for the two of us, Kai."

"Don't say that." And all at once he was twisting her round to face him. One hand was at her waist, pulling her against him, the other at her nape, tangling in her hair, and she gasped as his lips claimed hers in a kiss that sent fierce desire shooting through her. "I love you, Grace. Together, we can make a future – our future. We can make it happen."

How tempting it would be! How tempting to yield to the beauty of his kiss, his sweet words. But she mustn't do it. Too much had come between them. It would never work.

"No, Kai," she said softly, pulling away.

The sky was much lighter now. From afar came the rumble of a heavy vehicle moving slowly. The snow plough was doing its job. The day was getting underway.

But for Grace it felt as if the day was already over.

New Beginning

FOUR days.

Grace moved restlessly between the lounge and kitchen of the house on the coast she rented with three friends. She had the place to herself. It was late on New Year's Eve, and the others were out partying.

They'd been the happiest four days of her life. The danger she'd faced had faded to a distant, unreal memory – while the love she'd shared with Kai remained frighteningly vivid.

A week had gone by and she couldn't stop thinking about him, couldn't rid her mind of the memories – the warmth of his hand round hers, the strength of his arms as they enfolded her, the fierce intensity of his kisses and, too, that ease in each other's company, that precious sense of togetherness.

Fighting back the tears, she touched her fingers to the sketch in its gilded frame that sat on the mantelpiece propped against the wall. It was one of Cameron's clever pen-and-ink drawings, and her thoughts flashed back to the day he'd given it to her.

Christmas Day, the fifth day of their stay at the Château Beauvallon, and definitely not a happy one. The memory of it numbed her still.

The faces stood out above all. Angela's, brittle and weighed down by guilt. Barbs's, sad and soft with concern.

Even Johnno had looked subdued.

And all of them had been trying to keep up a pretence of normality even though everyone now knew Vespasien had pushed Grace down the tower steps and why he'd done it.

The gendarmes had taken her statement in the dining-room. Kai had sat on the other side of the table – as far away from her as possible? – ready to translate if necessary. His expression was set in grim, taut lines.

She longed to reach across the table, take his hand in hers, give it a comforting squeeze. But the distance between them had seemed unbridgeable and her hands had stayed in her lap.

Another face, Vespasien's, an aristocratic mask revealing nothing as he left his home, a gendarme on either side.

"Natasha and I will be leaving very shortly," Grace had said to Kai. They stood in the vast entrance hall watching his stepfather's departure.

Angela was a few metres away, crying quietly into a handkerchief.

Barbs had put her arms round her and was patting her back and making soothing noises.

Cameron and Natasha were standing close together. He'd taken her hands in his, while

Johnno, looking uncomfortable, was pulling his cigarettes and lighter out of his pocket.

"There's no need to see us off," Grace had continued.

Though neither of them had moved, the distance between them seemed to have grown greater still.

"As you wish." Kai's eyes met hers.

The expression on his face was unreadable, his tone was devoid of emotion, but she thought she could see pain in his eyes, and it tore at her heart.

She'd felt her face crumpling.

"I must finish packing," she'd managed, blinking furiously to hold back the tears as she twisted away, heading for the stairs.

She could hear the sound of her own breathing loud in her ears, and the clack of Natasha's high heels on marble as she followed her.

But it was Angela's quiet sobs that echoed over and over in her mind.

It was all Grace's fault. She was the one who had ripped this family apart.

She alone was responsible. How could she ever forgive herself?

When the two sisters came downstairs a quarter of an hour later, they'd found Cameron waiting for them by the Christmas tree.

"This is for you, Natasha."

With the side of his boot, he slid a heavy

package wrapped in shiny gold paper a few inches forward.

"I'll carry it to your car for you. It's your present from all of us. My stepfather chose it. A case of Château Beauvallon bubbly.

"Don't worry, it's genuine. Hey, sorry, bad taste," he added with a laugh.

He bent to pick up a smaller package from the foot of the tree.

"And this is for you, Grace. My choice for you. Happy Christmas."

Bringing herself back to the present, Grace now ran her fingers round the frame. The sketch showed her face in semi-profile. She was smiling.

There was a radiance about her in the portrait. Cameron had captured it perfectly. And it was a bittersweet sorrow to see it, for it was the radiance of a woman in love.

* * * *

The doorbell rang. Grace looked at her phone and frowned. It had gone 11. She wasn't expecting anyone.

She'd arranged to have lunch with her parents and Natasha the next day, so it was unlikely to be them.

Friends, maybe, wondering why she'd been avoiding them all since returning from France, insisting she see the New Year in? Or friends of one of her housemates?

It was Kai on the doorstep, a tall shadowy figure in the light that spilled out from the hall, and her heart did a crazy somersault. Her face, her whole being, lit up.

She couldn't help it. Pleasure at seeing him was like a warm glow speeding through her like wildfire.

For the space of a heartbeat, his face too lit up, she was sure of it. Then cold air gusted in through the open door.

She took in the set of his face, now stark and unsmiling, and shivered.

She'd been mistaken. Nothing had changed, and it was as if something inside her froze. Her smile faltered before sliding from her face.

"Kai. Do you want to come in? How did you know where I lived?" The words came in a rush.

"Angela gave me your sister's e-mail address," he said, stepping into the hallway. "She told me."

And Natasha had said nothing! Grace thought. She could at least have warned her.

"Come on in. Let me take your coat. Sit down." Conscious she was babbling, Grace forced herself to take a long, steadying breath. "What can I get you to drink?"

"Nothing, thanks. I won't keep you long. I want to bring you up to speed with what's been happening, that's all."

Both his expression and tone were neutral. He

was a polite stranger. Nothing more. He unbuttoned his long wool coat but kept it on, and remained standing in the centre of the lounge, looking round.

"I share with three others," she said, feeling the need to explain the marvellous mix of colours and styles in the objects displayed on the walls and shelves.

She, too, stayed standing, and couldn't help inhaling the smoky notes of his cologne.

"I remember. You told me." He paused, and Grace had the impression his thoughts had slipped back to the previous week. "Barbs and Johnno left the same day you did."

He sighed.

"There won't be any more business deals – of any kind – with Johnno in the future."

An edge of steel had entered his voice, and Grace was in no doubt Kai had been the one who'd laid down the new ground rules.

"Cameron has promised me," he went on, "that he'll never copy a Sisley or any other painting ever again.

"He'll concentrate on his own work from now on. He's going to Paris tomorrow to join his lover. A fresh start for him."

"His New Year's resolution," Grace said, and a smile came unbidden to her face as she remembered.

Cameron had spoken about making big changes in his life.

"I hope he'll be very happy."

"Yes, so do I."

Their eyes met in a brief instant of fellow-feeling before he looked elsewhere.

"My mother has also made a promise." There was pain as well as steel in Kai's voice now. "If she decides to sell something that doesn't belong to her, she will at least ask the owner's permission first."

He fell silent, and Grace was all too wretchedly aware of the pain and disruption she'd caused. Kai's family would never be the same again – and it was all her fault.

"And Vespasien?" Her voice had dropped to little more than a whisper.

"He's been allowed back home for the time being. He'll be charged with attempted murder and fraud.

"There's a possibility he'll be acquitted on the attempted murder charge because you weren't sure he actually intended to kill you – and he denies it. If found guilty, he could get anything up to five years in jail."

Grace sucked in a shaky breath.

"I hope he is acquitted, Kai. He's not a bad man at heart."

Another silence, broken when Kai crossed to the mantelpiece and picked up Cameron's sketch of Grace.

For a fraction of a second he simply looked at the drawing. Grace couldn't tell from his expression what he was thinking.

"We have to talk," he said, replacing the sketch. "Put your coat on. We'll walk down to the beach."

"We've said all that needs to be said." What on earth could they have to talk about? It was over between them.

"I disagree."

And Grace gave in, the thought of a short time more in Kai's company bringing an ache that was both pleasure and pain to her heart.

The wind off the sea was cold and moist with the tang of salt. She pulled the collar of her padded jacket up round her ears and recalled with a pang the still air of Kai's part of France.

They walked side by side, not touching, along the 100 or so metres to the end of Grace's road. It wasn't until they crossed the main road and were on the beach that Kai started to speak.

"You said, that last morning, on the roof of the tower, you said you blamed yourself for tearing my family apart."

"That's right." Grace's feet crunched across the pebbles that shifted and slid beneath her. She was glad the light from the streetlamps high above the main road barely reached the shingle. She didn't want Kai to see her face. The crash of wind-driven waves was loud in her ears.

"But you're wrong," he said. "It's hardly your fault. You didn't make my brother forge a major artwork. You didn't force my mother to make money by selling one of her husband's paintings. And it was entirely my stepfather's choice to pass a mediocre vintage off as an excellent one."

"I was the catalyst," Grace said unhappily. "If I hadn't been there . . . "

"No." Abruptly he stopped and turned, facing her. He closed his hands round her upper arms so that she lifted troubled eyes to his. "In their various ways they were doing wrong. They'd have been found out sooner or later. You being there made it happen sooner, maybe – and that's a good thing, surely."

Grace looked away, beyond him to the wide sweep of the bay. Lights glittered and sparkled all along its length. Overhead, a crowd of gulls screamed and shrieked as they flew inland.

What he was saying made sense, she thought, and the notion ignited a tiny spark of hope deep inside her.

"I thought you blamed me. You were so cold and angry."

"Angry with them. I love my mother and brother dearly. Up till now I've always respected Vespasien. But there were times when I was ashamed of the three of them, and that made me angry – with myself. Can you understand that? My family had shown themselves to be a bunch of crooks. My stepfather had tried to kill you. How could I possibly ask you to . . . "

"Ask me what, Kai?" The breath had caught

in her throat.

"You love me, Grace. I know you do. Cameron saw it, too. It shines out of that sketch he did."

His tone had softened, grown huskier, and he drew her closer. Though the light was poor, she sensed something very loving about the look he gave her as he smoothed strands of her hair back from her face.

"We haven't known each other long, Grace. But sometimes you know, straight away, that you've met the person you can't bear to live without. That's how I feel about you."

He gathered her closer still, hands going to her back, pulling her to him.

"I'm asking you to marry me, Grace. Will you be my wife?"

She didn't hesitate.

"Yes, Kai, I will."

And all along the coast, fireworks cracked and popped into life, signalling midnight, the new year, and a wonderful new beginning.

The End